2/4
4-12

DATE DUE

GAYLORD   #3523PI   Printed in USA

HOMEBOUND

Coming Up for Air

**Center Point
Large Print**

Also by Patti Callahan Henry and available from Center Point Large Print:

Driftwood Summer
The Art of Keeping Secrets

**This Large Print Book carries the
Seal of Approval of N.A.V.H.**

Coming Up for Air

PATTI CALLAHAN HENRY

CENTER POINT LARGE PRINT
THORNDIKE, MAINE

This Center Point Large Print edition is published
in the year 2011 by arrangement with
St. Martin's Press.

This is a work of fiction. All of the characters,
organizations, and events portrayed in this novel are
either products of the author's imagination
or are used fictitiously.
"With That Moon Language" from the Penguin anthology
Love Poems from God. Copyright © 2002 by Daniel
Ladinsky. Used with his permission.
Artwork on page 98 by Daniel H. Wallace,
author of *Big Fish*

ISBN: 978-1-61173-217-7

Library of Congress Cataloging-in-Publication Data

Henry, Patti Callahan.
Coming up for air / Patti Callahan Henry.
p. cm.
ISBN 978-1-61173-217-7 (library binding : alk. paper)
1. Self-realization in women—Fiction. 2. Family secrets—Fiction.
    3. Alabama—Fiction. 4. Large type books. I. Title.
PS3608.E578C66 2011b
813′.6—dc22
                                                         2011023039

b19797485

This book is dedicated to my children,
Meagan Steele Henry,
Patrick Thomas Henry, Jr., and
George Rusk Henry.
They are the most open piece of my heart;
the most creative part of my soul.

Acknowledgments

I am surrounded by love and for this I am the most grateful. Although I write alone, I create from the love given and received. There are many people I want to thank for helping me craft this story.

My agent, Kimberly Whalen, labored with me on this novel, pushing through every version and every word until we found the story that wanted to be told. Thank you, Kim. I am blessed to have you in my corner.

Much gratitude to the following:

To my editor, Jennifer Weis, who would not give up on this story, pushing me to get it "just right." I am thankful for your keen eye and intuition.

To the team at St. Martin's Press: I feel extremely blessed to be part of your "family." What an honor. A special shout-out of thankfulness to Sally Richardson, Matthew Shear, and Mollie Traver, for their immense support of this very particular story at this very particular time.

To my loving and understanding friends who support me, my work, and my irregular life. What, oh what, would I do without you? During this year of change, you were my rocks. Special hugs to Susan Clark, Sandee O., Beth Fidler, and

Cate Sommer, for always, always listening.

To my writing community. It is a blessed thing to find souls who care about words and story and books as much as I do. Special jewels of gratitude to those who encouraged me to dig deeper, go further. Many thanks to Mary Alice Monroe, for reading the manuscript and encouraging me. Bless those authors who read early versions and sent words of praise: Emily Giffin, Robyn Carr, Diane Chamberlain, Sherryl Woods, Susan Wiggs, and Donna Ball. To my writing friends who find me on book tours and shelter me in their kindness; who listen with empathy, and encourage me and speak the truth; who laugh and speak on stages with me; who love writing and reading with the same passion: Ad Hudler, Kerry Madden, Michael Morris, Marjory Wentworth, Ellie Davis, Dorothea Benton Frank, Mary Kay Andrews, Shellie Rushing Tomlinson, River Jordan, Karen Spears Zacharias, Jackie K. Cooper, Thomas Bell, Carol Fitzgerald, Stephanie Bond, Annabelle Robertson, Kathy Patrick, and many, many more (too many to list!). You remind me to keep on keeping on, and to find those words.

To my bookstore community, libraries, and SIBA: You are the steel backbone of why I do what I do. I am eternally thankful for your support.

I am consistently surprised and touched by the support and love I receive from my readers. I so wish I could thank every single one of you. This year you have touched my life in ways you can't imagine.

Special thanks to you, Daniel Wallace, not only for your encouraging friendship and wise writing advice, but also for contributing your drawing skills to my written words (page 140).

And to the bookstore that inspired the store in this novel: Page and Palette in Fairhope, Alabama. I love you all!

Much love is sent to my college friend Lee Rogers Milstead, who introduced me to *The Jublilee* and opened my heart to its mystery.

And in the miracle that is life: I want to thank Catherine Barbee, for opening her heart and her family to mine.

Of course, I could not and would not have written this book without the love and support of my family: Pat Henry, Meagan, Thomas, and Rusk Henry. My parents, George and Bonnie Callahan. My sisters and their families: Dan and Barbi Burris and Mike and Jeannie Cunnion. I am grateful, also, to my "chosen" family: The Henry Clan: Chuck and Gwen Henry, Kirk and Anna Henry, and Mike and Serena Henry. And those children—all of them—who make me laugh and value life more every day: Colin, Gavin, Cal, Brennan, Owen, Kirk, Sofia, Stella, and Sadie. These families' support is more than I deserve. This writing life, this wonderful life, is more than I deserve.

To love at all is to be vulnerable. Love anything, and your heart will certainly be wrung and possibly broken. If you want to make sure of keeping it intact, you must give your heart to no one, not even to an animal. Wrap it carefully round with hobbies and little luxuries; avoid all entanglements; lock it up safe in the casket or coffin of your selfishness. But in that casket—safe, dark, motionless, airless—it will change. It will not be broken; it will become unbreakable, impenetrable, irredeemable.

—C. S. Lewis

One

There are both wonderful and awful moments in a woman's life. Many of them, really. Standing in a white dress in front of family and friends, vowing to forever love the handsome man in front of me, is on top of my wonderful list. Then years later, standing in the receiving line at my mother's funeral and pulling away from that same man's touch because I knew I didn't—couldn't—love him anymore is more than awful. It's tragic.

In these pages, I will try to wrap words around all of the tumultuous, confusing emotions, attempt to make sense out of what at the moment feels senseless.

MOTHER'S FUNERAL

On the day of my mother's funeral there was only one type of flower: lilies. Everywhere. There were too many to count. With all the flowers in the world, the millions of blossoms and buds, you'd have thought that someone would have brought another sort.

I know what the lily means in the language of flowers: innocence, purity, and beauty. But this is not why the church overflowed with lilies. For twelve generations, or maybe longer, the firstborn daughters of firstborn daughters in our family are named Lillian. I understood why mourners brought these blooms, but God, the aroma was overwhelming, drowning me in cloying sweetness.

Sadie, my best friend, stood next to me in the funeral receiving line. "Ellie," she whispered.

"What?" I leaned closer to her.

"I wonder if there are any lilies left in all of Atlanta. This is insanity."

"It still wouldn't be enough for her," I said.

Sadie laughed in the quiet manner of churchlike respect. "No," she said, "it would *not* have been enough."

My husband, Rusty, stood on my opposite side with his hand on the small of my back, and our nineteen-year-old daughter, Lil, was to the left of him. Sadie and I attempted to hold in our laughter, like the nine-year-old girls we once had been in the chapel at private school instead of the forty-seven-year-old women we were. The misplaced amusement bubbled up from places forbidden and grabbed our guts and throats with the release of hilarity. I don't know why laughter comes at moments it should be banned; I don't know why it rains when we least need it or why love leaves when we most need it. But there we were: laughing at death.

"I bet," I said as I stifled the rising and irresponsible laughter, "everyone thought they were being original and thoughtful, sending lilies to Lilly's funeral."

In her attempt to stop a choked chuckle, Sadie snorted, and it was then that we broke into full laughter over something that was only vaguely funny or maybe not funny at all. But just the way you find yourself wanting something worse when you know you can't have it, we were unable to stop laughter in the one place it is inappropriate —the middle of a receiving line at Mother's funeral.

Rusty glanced at me, which for a reason I still don't understand made me laugh harder. He reached out to touch me, and I pulled away. My daughter looked at me as if I'd lost my mind, and I wondered if maybe I had. Sadie squeezed my hand, and we returned to normal—our mournful expressions intact.

Of course, nothing about Mother's death was funny. It was sudden and awful and left our small family bereft and confused. I've discovered the finality of death in this: It remains unchanged and unmoved by loneliness, regret, or grief. My need for Mother, for some kind of redemption or reconciliation, came fresh with every thought and reminder of her absence. Missing her was the ache with which I woke and then fell into restless sleep knowing.

The funeral was a huge event, and Mother

would have been proud to see how many people came, considering we're a small family. Mother is an only child, and Dad has only one brother, Uncle Cotton—an elusive figure in my life, an author who is constantly traveling and in exotic locales, a writer about whom Mother rolled her eyes as if writing were a wasteful career that didn't even deserve a comment (much as any career in the "arts" is wasteful, which is an odd opinion for a woman on the High Museum of Art board). But that's my mother—contradictions seamlessly fitting inside one another like the babushka dolls my grandmother brought me from her trip to Russia. Mother's best friend, Sadie's mother, Birdie, walked through the crowd, making order of the crowd and the event as smoothly as if Mother were there doing it herself.

Our web of friends caught Dad, Lil, Rusty, and me, cradling us with their grief and respect. There were newspaper articles and monuments, trees planted, and a bench placed in front of the High Museum.

The last woman in line then approached us, holding a single lily in her hand as if she were a bride going down the aisle. I thought I'd start laughing again but found I was finished. The day was almost over, and I was lulled into that certainty that I'd done well, that we had made it through the worst of it.

"Ellie?" A voice behind me said my name. Softly. Perfectly.

A hand fell on my shoulder, and then I saw his face. Twenty years later, minutes and hours and days rearranged to allow me to see him again as if time hadn't passed at all. Mostly I saw his eyes: almond shaped and kind, brown with green underneath, as if the eyes had meant to be the deep color of forest ferns and then at the last minute changed their mind.

I reached for Rusty's hand to steady myself, but he was making large gestures while talking to his buddy Weston and didn't feel me groping for firm grounding.

Then I saw Hutch's smile, a little crooked and higher on the right-hand side.

He hates being late.

I smiled at him. "Wow, hello, Hutch O'Brien." My voice held firm and fast, and for this I was grateful.

He is witty with a cutting sarcasm.

He loves his eggs fried with buttered toast.

There is a scar on his cheek where a dog bit him when he was ten years old. For every person who asks, he has a new story for how he obtained this scar. I've heard more tales than I can remember.

"Ellie," he said, "I'm so sorry about your mother. I know how close you were."

"Thanks, Hutch." I took his hand and shook it

as if we were past and vague acquaintances.

We stood silent, holding hands. I felt tears rising and I wanted to place my head on his chest: I knew where it would fit.

"Don't cry," he said, and squeezed my hand.

I nodded.

"It's great to see your beautiful face. Even in your grief, you're adorable."

"Not true," I said. "But thanks."

"Did your mom tell you that I'd interviewed her last week for the Atlanta History Center exhibit?"

"Yes, she did." Proper sentences formed on my tongue with the well-practiced art of social graces.

He likes the cold side of the pillow and the aisle seat on the plane.

Hutch glanced around the sacristy. "I know this is an awful time and you probably won't even remember seeing me, but can I ask you a favor?"

"Anything," I said.

We were still holding hands, and I wouldn't let go.

"We—your mother and I—didn't finish our interview. Would you . . . talk to me when things calm down?"

I nodded.

"Okay," he said, and let go of my hand. "I'll call you? Is that okay?"

"Yes."

"I'm sorry, Ellie. I'm really sorry you're going through this pain."

"Thank you, Hutch. And thanks for coming."

Rusty tuned in; he'd heard the name. Hutch walked away, and Rusty took my still-warm hand. "Was that Hutch?"

"Yes," I whispered.

"What the hell was he doing here?"

I shrugged. "I assume he's paying his respects just like everyone else here."

Rusty turned back to Weston and released my hand.

We were leaving the church when I saw the wildflower arrangement: a glass vase shaped like a large fish bowl was full of cornflowers and black-eyed Susans, forget-me-nots and Texas bluebonnets. I stopped and slid my finger up the stalk of a cornflower, rubbing the petal against my cheek. A long inhale of the sweet jasmine vine, which poured out of the urn like wine, made me dizzy.

Wildflowers.

I lifted the card from the arrangement. "Condolences, Hutchinson O'Brien."

Rusty came from behind and hugged me, wiping the tears I hadn't realized were wet on my face. "I think the worst is over, baby. Let's go home," he said.

"Yes," I said. "Home."

I placed the card back in the flower arrangement, but it fluttered to the floor, where I left it with *his* name staring up at me.

Hutch.

We make our choices and then we live with them.

Everyone does.

Two

It had been only four days before the funeral, in the midst of my own art show, that Mother had said Hutch's name as dismissively as one would drop a crumpled napkin into the trash.

You are invited to the
ANNE LOMAX GALLERY
ATLANTA, GEORGIA
To Celebrate
Lillian (ELLIE) *Eddington Calvin's*
Forty-eight for Forty-eight
Forty-eight pieces of original artwork on
Ellie's forty-eighth birthday
Certain proceeds to benefit
Lilly's Love Charity

The crowded art gallery had throbbed as an erratic pulse. After painting alone in my attic, this show had been the ten-year culmination of my work. It was my forty-eighth birthday party and there were forty-eight paintings, the last ten of which I'd painted in a sleepless haze over the previous month. My actual birthday wouldn't be until September, and this party was in late July, but the coordination with Mother's fundraiser was a bit more important than my date of birth.

I paint flowers—all kinds. It thrills me that I could do this art for the rest of my life and still not examine every known flower. It had been Mother's idea—the forty-eight for forty-eight. She always had a gimmick, a plan.

But that was Mother—taking something she didn't approve of (my art) and turning it into a societal and charitable event with her name written all over it (literally, because ten percent of the money went to the charity she founded for homeless children).

I'd stood in my silk dress at the podium, where the Atlanta crowd took on a hazy quality, as if morning fog rolled over the room. There they were—friends, family, and strangers—touching and talking about my art, which until that night had been piled around my attic studio like discarded heirlooms. Rusty came up next to me and kissed my cheek; I turned to him.

"I am *so* proud of you," he said.

"Thanks." I held a glass of wine in my hand, but I was too nervous to drink.

I caught Sadie's gaze and she smiled at me. Then there was Mother—she hadn't moved an inch from my side all night.

Sissy Parkland approached us, her headband yanking her hair back so tight that she looked as if someone stood behind her pulling her hair. "Oh, Ellie, I bought the gardenia painting. I'm going to hang it in my sunroom. I am so thrilled. I wish I could buy *all* these paintings."

"*Gardenia jasminoides*," Mother said with a tight smile.

"Huh?" Sissy asked.

"The real name," Mother said, touching my arm. "Ellie here likes to call her paintings by their ordinary name, but all flowers have a botanical name; a real name."

"Well, ordinary or botanical, it's beautiful." Sissy waved at someone across the room and blew us a good-bye kiss off her palm.

I'd always insisted—either out of stubbornness or laziness—on calling all flowers by their ordinary name. Mother—either out of stubbornness or precision—always corrected me, explaining again and again how every flower had a first name and a surname, just like a person.

Lil came to stand with me. "Mom, they want a picture," she said, grabbing my hand.

Don Morgan, the *Points North* magazine photographer, set up in front of the podium. "The only daughter of an only daughter of an only daughter all named Lillian," Don said as Lil smiled, our heads tilted toward Mother. "Rusty, could you step away for this photo? I want to get the three Eddington women."

Rusty didn't move for a moment, and then he smiled—the charming smile. "Two of them are Calvin women, Don."

"Yes, they are, aren't they?" The flash went off.

Rusty stalked to the bar. My instinct was to go after him and soothe his hurt feelings, but then Mother tapped the microphone to make sure it was working. A high-pitched squeal brought the crowd to a quiet stop, and everyone turned to the podium.

There were many reasons the party had taken on a dreamlike quality, but the most striking of them was this: My husband and my mother had never been big fans of this art "hobby." We'd had fights and disagreements and quiet evenings of hostility over the time and effort I put into something they didn't truly deem worthy, yet that night they were my biggest fans.

The worst disagreement Rusty and I ever had had been when I forgot to pick Lil up from horseback riding. He'd thrown a jar of paint-brushes across my attic studio, where they'd scattered on the floor, skittering across the uneven floorboards as if to escape him, settling into the corners as if hiding. He'd compared my art to a drug, saying it was an escape. Maybe it was, but now that escape hung on linen walls with sold stickers on the frames.

Mr. Lomax, the art studio owner's husband, took the microphone and welcomed everyone to the party. I smiled, but my curls shivered with nervous shaking.

"Tonight we're here to celebrate Ellie Calvin, her birthday and her decade of work, but first I want to make an announcement." Mr. Lomax motioned toward Mother.

Mother placed her hand on my arm. "Oh, I was hoping he wouldn't do this."

"Today the Atlanta Historical Society announced their brand-new exhibit for the spring of next year. And our beloved Lillian Ashford Eddington will be part of this new display about the Atlanta Woman of the Year during the decade of the 1960s. We are so proud of her and look forward to the event."

Cheers and hollers came from the crowd. Mother took the microphone and blushed, looking out from under her eyelashes as a shy-girl. She wore a brand-new teal St. John suit with crystal buttons. Her silver hair was smooth and slick to her shoulders. She was a beautiful woman, and she knew it. We all knew it.

"Thank you so much. I am so proud to be part of this upcoming celebration of many, many women who have made a difference in Atlanta and in the South. This award was given to me over forty years ago and wasn't so much about me as it was my charity—Lilly's Love, which we are also benefiting tonight. So right now this party is about my daughter, Ellie—Lillian Eddington Calvin. For ten years, she has been painting in private." Mother looked at me with wide and proud eyes; fake eyes that could just as easily have been made of glass or plastic. "She's been holed up in her attic, and I have finally convinced her to show off her talent to the community, and for that we are all enriched."

Polite clapping filled the room, and Mother handed me the microphone. I'd prepared a speech about art and how creativity opens the heart and mind, but somehow all the words left my head and mouth. I smiled out at the crowd. There was my husband; there were my friends, my daughter, and my father; and I said the only words my tangled tongue formed. "I am grateful for all of you and for this night. Thanks for coming."

I handed the microphone back to Mother, who began the birthday song, and then there was the cake and the candles and the wishes and the hugs.

And just as anything wonderful does, the night fled away too fast.

Soon there were only empty plastic wineglasses, crumpled napkins, and the caterers cleaning and waiting for their payment. Rusty had taken Lil home, but Sadie stayed until the very end. We sat at a long conference table, laughing about how Mrs. Palo had bought a painting from the studio believing it was mine, but it had been painted by another artist on permanent display in the gallery. We wondered if she'd ever figure it out.

Mother sat with us. "Well, dear, I don't think that could have gone any better. It was a wonderful night. Truly wonderful. And you do look beautiful."

"Thanks, Mother. And congratulations on the history center exhibit. You didn't tell me about that."

"I was waiting for the right time."

I nodded, and Sadie kicked me under the table.

"And I meant to tell you this, too . . ." Mother clicked her manicured nails together, and it sounded like the skittering of a small animal's claws across a wooden floor. "The man who is doing the exhibit came to interview me yesterday. I couldn't place him, but then I remembered who he was—that silly old boyfriend of yours."

"Old boyfriend?" I asked, gathering my purse and cell phone.

"Yes, that college boy. Hutch something or other."

"Hutch O'Brien?" I asked.

She shooed her hand through the air. "I'd forgotten about him."

When I didn't answer, she turned to me. I

averted my gaze—I knew what she wanted. I always did. She wanted me to say I'd also forgotten about him.

I couldn't and didn't say it.

That night, Hutch infused my dreams. Like humidity in the summer air, his scent and memory filtered into the darkness and behind the curtain of sleep, where no one can control who or what shows up in the dream world. I sit on his lap, my legs wrapped around his waist. I bite his bottom lip, gently. He watches me paint, and then he waves good-bye from a plane's window. He walks me through a house with many rooms.

By dawn I rose and stood alone in the kitchen, drinking coffee. If I felt guilty, it was for allowing him into my bedroom, if only in dreams.

My need for Hutch had once been rooted deeply into my bones so that I'd felt the desire not as a part of me, but as me completely. But I wasn't that woman anymore. I'd been married to Rusty Calvin for over twenty years. I was a wife. And mother.

To shake off the night's ancient emotions, I read the article about the art show in the *Atlanta Journal-Constitution*. I took the newspaper back to the bedroom to show Rusty, but he was in the shower, so I set it on the dresser. I lifted the phone and called Mother. She didn't answer and I left her a message, thanking her for such a wonderful evening and reminding her to get the *AJC*.

Would I have said anything different if I'd known it would be my last message to her?

Of course.

Dishes clanged against one another as I emptied the dishwasher, when startlingly a cardinal slammed sideways against my kitchen window, her wing swiping the pane with red and brown feathers falling loose onto the outside sill. I stood, taking in a sharp breath and watching the bird fall. For the past twenty years of my married life I'd stood at that kitchen window, in that spot, for more hours than I could count, yet I'd never seen a bird fly into the glass.

The window overlooked the backyard—a manicured manifestation of suburban gardening and lawn care. Our swimming pool was still and quiet, the surface unruffled. A pot of geraniums had fallen over, and potting soil was a russet stain against the cream travertine tiles surrounding the hot tub. My hand lifted to the window in a late response, as if I could possibly tell the bird to stop.

I ran to the side kitchen door and out to the newly mowed grass; the blades slid between the soles of my feet and the leather sandals, smooth and slippery like worms. The cardinal lay in the grass, her wings not flapping but twitching. Her black eyes were open, and I wondered if this was an open death stare. My heart paused; I crouched down a few feet from the bird, tilted my head to stare. She blinked, her stick legs shivering in vain.

I sat, aware, yet somehow not, that the wet grass was seeping through my cotton skirt, that my legs were covered in shredded grass. The aroma of dirt and freshly cut pine washed over me, mixing with the sticky smell of a gardenia bush. The bird and I stared at each other, a kinship of stunned bemusement. Wow, we seemed to say, this has never happened before.

"Should I help?" I asked her. She only stared. I remembered hearing that one should never touch a wild bird in nature because the other wild birds will then have nothing to do with it again. This fact always made me think of *The Scarlet Letter*, of how once she was touched she was shunned.

"So," I said to the bird. "I won't touch you." She appeared relieved. "I'll give you a minute to get your wits about you."

I stared closely at her, never before this near to any small wild creature. I knew the male cardinals were the brightest red birds; the females were brown, with a shock of red bill and tail. A few wing feathers on the right were crooked, and I wanted to reach out and brush them into place. Two red feathers and one brown sat misplaced in the grass; she looked at them as if she knew they were a part of her that she'd lost.

I stared closer; her wing didn't look broken. Her eyes were bottomless and shimmering.

I waited.

I don't know how long I was there while this bird and I stared at each other in the damp grass, our eyes blinking and weighing the oddity of our situation, when I heard the house phone ringing. I was almost to the kitchen when the ring switched to my cell.

I grabbed my phone off the counter. "Hello."

"You never answer your house phone. Why don't you ever answer your house phone?" It was Dad, his voice loud and stiff.

"I was outside," I said. "What is it? Are you okay?"

"Your mother—" His voice broke like a twig off a tree during a wicked storm. The kitchen shifted in front of me like puzzle fragments coming undone. I reached for the desk chair, missed, stumbled backward into the corner of the counter.

"What, Dad? What about Mother?"

I wanted this to be a complaint: Mother went on a shopping spree again; Mother is angry I'm not coming for Sunday dinner; Mother is insisting on another dinner party and Dad wanted me to talk her out of it. A complaint.

Let this be a complaint.

"I found her, Ellie. In our bed. I found her. My God, why did *I* have to find her?"

I didn't ask another question, because some-times I don't ask the question I don't want to hear answered.

"Are you there? Can you hear me?" Dad's voice bellowed through the phone line.

"Yes," I said.

"She's dead, Ellie. Your mother is dead."

"I know," I said because I did know. When I heard his voice I knew. Maybe when the bird flew into the window I knew. But I knew. "I'm on my way." I hung up.

Rusty entered the kitchen in his fresh-pressed khakis, his white button-down. He held the *AJC* article about the art showing. The picture of Mother, Lil, and me stared out, mocking me for thinking all was well only twelve hours ago.

"Nice article," he said. "They did a good job." He then tossed the newspaper into the recycle bin.

I stared at my husband as if I didn't know him, as if a stranger had just walked into my kitchen and spoken to me.

He shrugged in a "What is it?" gesture.

"Mother died," I said in the same tone as if I'd just said, "Would you like some scrambled eggs?"

He came to me then, drawing me against him. "Oh, Ellie."

I jerked away and walked toward the recycle bin, pulling out my article. "I was going to frame this for her."

He cringed.

I threw it back into the bin. "Guess I won't now."

He reached for me, but I held up my hand. "I've got to get to Dad."

"I'll come with you," he said, and swiped the car keys off the counter.

That day lasted longer than any other I'd lived to that moment, as if all bad days were piled one on top of the other and time had expanded to fit into their width and depth. When I entered my home that night, I walked straight outside to check on the cardinal, hoping of course against hope that it had flown away.

On the grass, fallen and red, the bird lay dead, and I wept.

Rusty finally found me lying in the grass. He helped me up and walked me inside with soothing noises one would make to an inconsolable child. The hours in between that moment and the funeral were times I remember with only a blurry fatigue of "doing" what was necessary to say good-bye.

Although I understood that in many ways I would never say good-bye to Mother.

Three

When the phone rang a week after the funeral and HUTCH O'BRIEN appeared on the caller ID, I stared at it for the longest time, as if an apparition had filtered into my kitchen and into my life. Which in many ways it had.

I didn't answer that call, and I waited two full hours before I listened to the message.

"Hey, Ellie, I hope you and your family are doing well. I really don't want to put pressure on you to talk about your mom when I know how you must be grieving, but this exhibit deadline is fast approaching; I just need some final answers. If you can, will you please call me back?"

He left his number and I wrote it on a scrap of paper, folding it into a neat square and placing it in the side pocket of my purse.

I stood on a tightrope between the two choices —to call him or not to call him—unbalanced and sure to fall into memories. I know everyone has a love story. I don't feel any better or different that Hutch and I have one. I just know this one is mine.

We'd met in what would seem the most ordinary

31

circumstances. The most casual way people in their twenties ever meet—at a bar with friends. Nothing unusual or special about that. But everything was different—the way my smile shook; the way I wanted to touch the scar on his face; the way I stumbled over words inside my mouth; the way time stretched around us, elongating.

The bar and the friends and the noise faded, and there was only the man I saw standing in front of me. Sadie had approached me and hollered over the band and the noise, "I'm leaving." I nodded at her as if I didn't know her, as if she weren't my roommate and my ride back to the dorm.

I finally reached out and touched his cheek. "This scar. How did you get it?"

He placed his hand on top of mine. "A dog bite. I was ten."

"Oh," I said.

With his hand over mine, he pulled me toward his face and lips and toward our first kiss.

Three days after his message, I picked up the phone and dialed the now crumpled phone number. I sat on my back porch and stared out over the pool, which no one had swum in for almost a year. The phone rang until I was sure voice mail would pick up. I had a practiced message, but then his voice—live—came on the line and was breathless.

"Hey," he said.

"Hi, Hutch. This is Ellie Calvin. Is this a bad time?"

He laughed, a sound somehow both deep and melodic. "No, this is not a bad time. I just ran in from outside. My damn tomato plants are covered in some kind of boll weevil or demon."

"I think it's a demon," I said. "I mean, I think boll weevils only eat cotton."

His laughter rolled over my body. "Thanks for calling me back. I didn't think you would, really."

"Well, here I am, but I don't think I'm going to be much help."

"Let me tell you what I'm doing and maybe it will make more sense."

"Go ahead."

"This exhibit is about the ten women who won Atlanta Woman of the Year during the 1960s. Your mother, of course, won this for all her philan-thropic work, but in the old meeting minutes that I read, I believe what tipped things in her favor was her work with civil rights in 1961. I know she won the award in 1968, but it was partly because of her work in '61. But no one seems to be able to tell me exactly what that is or was."

"Huh?"

"Can you not hear me?"

"Hutch, are you sure you don't have her mixed up with another woman? Mother never worked in the movement. Ever."

He was silent long enough that I glanced at the phone to see if we were still connected. "Well, see, that's the thing. She was, but she wouldn't talk to me about it when I interviewed her. She said that one small summer had nothing to do with her Woman of the Year Award, but I think she's wrong."

"One small summer? I really have no idea what you're talking about," I said, standing to pace the backyard.

"Damn," he said.

"I'm sorry."

"No need for apologies. But maybe if we just meet and talk, I could find some more information that might help. Some pictures?"

"Dad has all the pictures."

"Yes," he said.

The silence between us was filled with a million words, all mixed up and upside down and inside out. Sometimes there's so much to say that nothing can be said.

"Well, nice to talk to you," he said.

"You too, Hutch."

I adored saying his name. I did. God help me, I did. When we hung up, I said it one more time.

But only one more time.

Later that evening, twilight—my favorite kind of light—fell across my backyard and I sat back on the lounge chair, talking to Lil on the phone.

"Mom, I swear I have no idea how she finds any of her clothes, they are all over the apartment. How does someone live like that?"

I laughed at my organized and precise daughter, who hangs her clothes by color and style. "Sweetness, I have no idea. But that's what makes the world so interesting—everyone is different."

"Ughhh, I like totally knew you were gonna say that. I swear I could have a conversation with you without you because I know what you'll say."

The back door opened and I turned to see Rusty sauntering, which is what Rusty does, across the lawn. I waved and smiled.

"Dad's home," I said to Lil. "I'll call you tomorrow. Gotta go. . . ."

"Tell Dad hey," she said.

Rusty kissed the top of my sun-warm hair. "Hey, darling. What's for dinner?"

I cringed. "I didn't cook tonight. I spent the day with Dad. He was in a bad way."

He came around and sat at the end of the lounge chair, squeezing my ankle. "Are you okay?"

Rusty had been asking me this same question every day since Mother died, as if he were checking to make sure I wouldn't disintegrate and disappear, as if there were a bubble on the edge of my tire and it might blow while I drive.

"I'm not sure what 'okay' is, but yes, I'm fine."

"Who were you talking to?"

"Lil."

He pouted. "She didn't want to talk to me?"

"You can call her anytime, Rusty. She was on her way out to some study session."

"Okay," he said, and stared off across the lawn. "We need to call the lawn service and tell them that the back hedges are getting too high and the fence is separating at the corner."

I didn't answer, and he looked back to me. "Ellie, did you hear me?"

I nodded.

"Seriously, are you okay?"

I stood up and looked down at him. "What do mean by okay?"

He stood and faced me. "I mean I'm worried about you. I mean I know this is hard, but why won't you talk to me about it? All you say is, 'I'm fine.' That's what I mean, Ellie." Anger was sprinkled on the circumference of his words.

"I don't know what to say. It hurts. It's a terrible relief, and I feel guilty about that. It's sad and it's sudden and it feels as if the earth has shifted beneath my feet, but I can't see what that changes. Maybe it doesn't change anything, but maybe it changes everything. I have no idea. I feel foggy and disconnected, but I'm okay. You ask if I'm okay and I'm okay."

He hugged me, holding me against his chest and running his fingers through my hair. "Let's go out to dinner. Okay?" he asked.

I leaned into his chest, relaxed. "Perfect."

Marriages, I thought at that moment, are made of these moments, as if they are the stitches that form a long hem at the bottom of a garment, holding it together just when it appears as if the frayed edges will unravel.

Four

After the funeral, Dad had demanded more from and of me than I could have imagined. Lil was back at summer school at Auburn University, and everything moved too quickly and too slowly all at once. Two weeks later, while packing up Mother's closet, I was sleep-deprived and restless. For the first time in my life, I was alone in her dressing room. Yet she was everywhere—inside that room, inside my heart, inside my head. Just everywhere.

For all her instruction, words, and lectures, Mother had never once told me what to do with her things when she died. She'd told me how to feel, where to go, and even whom to marry, yet never what to do at that moment.

I'd arranged her clothes by color and use, packed them in boxes and bins, labeled for the Junior League Newly New store. I'd thought I would take some pieces—the St. John suits, the

Prada shoes, the Chanel dresses—but I didn't. Not only because they wouldn't fit Lil or me, but because they seemed disconnected from my life. These things of my mother's were not of or for or about me in any way. I hadn't expected this feeling of not wanting my mother's things; I'd needed my mother in different ways and in so many times that I would've guessed I'd cling to her leftovers as I'd clung to her.

Finally I knelt before the locked bottom drawer of her built-in dresser. Her formal ball gowns, which hung in thick plastic coverings, dangled like the multicolored jewels on her charm bracelet: red, blue, bright orange. I held the key Dad had given me. He'd said, "This is the key to your mother's locked drawer. Please take care of everything. I can't bear to see or touch her things. Can you please deal with it?" Then he'd gone off to play golf with Rusty.

I flipped the key back and forth between my hands. I wanted to feel everything and be connected to the moment so I could enjoy this final and minuscule victory—the ability to open this drawer without her permission. Yet the act of holding the key didn't feel victorious; it felt like nothing, as if it were emptiness defined.

Her words (some of her many) echoed in my head, as if she were watching me (maybe she was): *With every wish fulfilled there is something lost.*

Yes.

The tumblers inside the polished wood scrambled. I slid my finger into the space between drawer and dresser and then pulled. There were only two items inside: a large leather book and an engraved fountain pen.

From its size I thought the book was a Bible, and I felt cheated. I pulled out the drawer and slid it into the center of the room, held the book in my hands. It was heavy and ancient with its warm weight. The silver fountain pen had a Celtic design engraved and etched into the sides.

The leather was worn smooth, a small dent in the upper left corner rubbed to raw, as if Mother had placed her thumb there and moved it back and forth over many, many years. Wrapped around the book was a leather string braided with twine and a blue stone knotted into its end. I undid the cord and opened the book to the middle. I've always done this when I pick up a book—I flip to the center, read a page to try to discover if the words on it resonate. I know some people open to the beginning, others to the last parts. Mother, if I had to guess, would have opened a book to the conclusion—to see how it ended before she agreed to begin.

I'd never seen this leather book I held in my hands. After moving into the well-lit bedroom, I sat on the bench at the end of my parents' bed and allowed the book to fall open in my lap.

Pages and pages of my mother's handwriting in black fountain ink were crooked across the thick cream paper. I flipped quickly through the pages. She wrote in an upward slant that left open space on the top left and the bottom right.

"What is this?" I mumbled the words aloud while my finger ran along the sentence in the middle of a random page.

I'm hiding inside this house tonight with a broken heart. I've never really known what brokenness was or what it meant. But it's not a broken feeling; it's an empty feeling.

My heart stilled like the breath I hold underwater, knowing if I inhale, I'll die. Then I shivered, lifting my gaze to stare across the room to the marble fireplace, where the framed oil painting of my mother in her wedding dress hung over the mantel. I flipped to the opening page.

To my precious granddaughter, Lilly,
with all the secrets and power
held within words.
—Lillian Rose Caulfield, 1952, December 31

This was a journal, a leather journal given to my mother by her grandmother, my great-grandmother. I counted backward to 1952—

Mother would have been twelve years old when she started this diary. I glanced forward and realized she had written in it only once a year—every New Year's Eve.

I read the first page:

I've always known I'm different. Grandmother gave me this journal because she knows this also—she knows how it feels. She told me I can "write" my life in here. She said that every New Year's Eve I can write everything I want for my next year.

Mother's twelve-year-old handwriting was loopy and crooked, sometimes hearts for dots above the i's. I held within my hands my mother's entire life journey beginning at twelve years old.

There were other items stashed in the back of the journal, and I lifted them in a detached, bemused way, as if I had been given permission to wade through the stars or breathe underwater. There was a drawing I'd made at nine years old; a torn piece of a letter with what looked like a poem; an envelope yellowed and crackling with Mother's address; another letter, but this one in Mother's handwriting, folded and inside an unsent and unaddressed envelope.

I had lost her to gain her.

I lay flat on my back, staring up at the ceiling of my parents' bedroom with a crystal chandelier above my head. I wanted to call Hutch and whisper, "I found a secret piece of my mother." But I didn't call him. Of course I didn't.

Mother's journal was under my left hand, and although I heard Dad's footsteps, I didn't move. He stood over me. "Ellie, are you okay?" I nodded, or I thought I nodded, but there was no movement. "Ladybug, *are* you okay?"

"Did you know Mother kept a journal of her entire life?" I turned my head to look at him.

"I suspected." He took my hand and pulled me to sit.

"What does that mean?"

"Well, every New Year's Eve she would write in that book"—he pointed to it—"in the same spot at the top of the stairs in that nook, and then she'd lock it back up. She only skipped once. It was why we never went out on New Year's. She made me promise in life or death that I would never read it. I promised."

"You didn't promise for me, did you?" I asked.

"No." He shook his head, looking away. "I don't think I could read it anyway. It's too much to have lost her. I can't . . . ." He stopped.

"Can't what? Get to know her more?"

He looked back at me with this pain I'd never seen etched around his eyes. "She allowed me to know all of her she chose to let me know. That was all I needed, Ellie."

"It wasn't enough for me," I said, my fingers closing around the journal.

"Is anything?" he asked, his hands held out in supplication.

"I hope so, Dad."

Silence filled the space between us until I asked, "How was golf?"

"Fine," he said.

"Beautiful day for eighteen," I said in the lingo I knew well. "What did you shoot?"

"An eighty-six. Not my best, but I had a par on fourteen. Yes, it was beautiful weather." He walked into the closet. There was the clang of empty hangers, and then he returned to the bedroom, his eyebrows dipped low and protective, as if this could stop any tears or grief. "Thank you," he said.

"You're welcome." I hugged him.

He returned the hug, but he was taut, as if he were responsible for holding his body together.

"Dad, I need to ask you a question."

"Anything, Ladybug."

"Do you know anything at all about Mother working with the civil rights movement?"

"She didn't."

"Are you sure?"

"Ellie, we've been together since almost the

43

beginning of that era, and . . . well, she cared, but she was never involved."

"Well . . ."

He held up his hand to halt my words and then stepped back and stared at me, and then at the leather book. "You can take that with you."

"I was planning on it," I said.

He shook his head. "It's like the world has turned upside down."

"I know." I kissed his cheek.

"Ellie?" He stared out the window.

"Yes?"

He gazed back at me now, tears filming his eyes. "What am I going to do about her garden?"

"I don't know, Dad. God, I don't know."

Five

I returned to my own home and held Mother's journal in my hand. Everything else in my life would wait. Rusty was out that night, and I'd canceled my dinner with Sadie. I sat on the chaise longue in the sunroom and began to read. What she'd lived in seventy years I would read in one night, because this much I knew—I would not stop until I was done.

In the early entries, I'd discovered there were

years when Mother didn't care about where she lived, what she wore, whom she married, where she vacationed, or to what country club she belonged. She swung on the monkey bars, spent all night writing a story, and cursed. She cared about and loved her mother; she needed her mother's love. There were moments and maybe even years when she cared about books and stories and laughter.

Then her entries moved into the years when she fell in love with this man who broke her heart. He was only called "Him," his name never once mentioned.

I continued to read, my legs curled underneath me; the sun was gone, and the only light in the house was the reading lamp over my shoulder. I read about her childhood and her goals, about her heart and her family, and about "Him"—the man she never named, but the man she desired who eventually recanted and withdrew his love.

I was on her twentieth year when Rusty came home. His footsteps echoed across the empty house, and I knew these steps as they moved into the kitchen and opened the refrigerator—he'd be grabbing bottled water, and then he'd move toward the bedroom, loosening his tie, yawning, rubbing at the beginning of stubble on his cheeks. He'd then walk quietly into the bedroom and maybe not even notice the empty bed as he moved to the bathroom to prepare for sleep.

I waited without reading because I knew eventually he'd come looking for me, which he did. "Ellie?" he called out into the hallway.

"I'm in the sunroom," I replied, and waited.

He then stood in the doorway and tilted his head. "You're reading?"

"Yes," I said.

He glanced at his watch. "It's midnight."

"I know," I said. "Go on to bed. I'll come when I'm finished."

"Okay," he said. "But I'm going to sleep. Try not to wake me when you come in. I have a huge day tomorrow."

When I closed the journal the sun hadn't risen, but its pre-light whispered into the room through the slatted wood blinds, thin strips of dawn gold announcing the imminent arrival of a new day. On the chair in the sunroom, I'd read and slept fitfully through the night and through my mother's life: a life I knew nothing about. I'd discovered a woman I'd lived with and called Mother and yet never really understood at all; a woman who wanted a happy life, who arranged her years better than most cities are planned and yet found this: You can *not* make someone love you.

She was a woman who participated in the civil rights movement and went to college and loved and drank and laughed and then finally decided that cold perfection was the answer to life.

Every New Year's Eve she wrote a summary of her year, a story sometimes and other years just a few lines, and then at the end of each entry she wrote her goals for the following year. She would check through the wishes and goals that came true or were met from the previous year's entry. From the age of twenty forward, some variation of this wish remained unmet and unchecked: This is the year . . . *He* will love me.

Her grandmother had told her to write in this journal every New Year's Eve in the nook below the stained-glass angel window in our family home. Often Mother wrote to this angel, but mostly she wrote to herself.

Then there was the sketch I'd made at nine years old, and the torn poem, but it was her handwritten letter I couldn't finish. It was meant for another, and I could read only the opening heartrending words before I folded it and vowed to someday give it to the man for whom she wrote the words. Why else would she leave all this for me?

I sat up straight, stretching. I cursed—a thing I don't usually do but that seemed absolutely appropriate for that moment.

"What?" Rusty's voice entered the room, and I looked up to see him standing in the doorway, squinting into the morning light, still wearing his linen pajama bottoms and white T-shirt.

"Shit," I repeated, tasting the word as if it were a foreign food or forbidden drug.

"What's going on? Have you been up all night?"

I nodded. "On and off."

He shook his head. "Have you lost your mind?"

"I don't think so," I said.

"Okay, then. I'm showering and off to work. I'll see you tonight?"

"Okay, then," I said, repeating him and yet knowing he wouldn't notice. For the first time in a long time, I was angry with him. No, worse than angry. I wanted to punch him or throw the journal at his face or toss his golf trophy through the sunroom window. He didn't see this, and he left me alone again.

The anger ran out of me as quickly as it had arrived, and I was spent, empty as the vase on the side table that sometimes held flowers, but only sometimes.

I didn't know what to do with these disharmonious emotions about my marriage and husband. There were, then, absolutely no words to define the mayhem of feelings, as if I had become the turmoil and fallen into a place where words and sentences didn't exist, explanations hadn't been invented, and only dread and anger survived. I wanted words to go with the emotion.

But as I'd been doing, I ignored the awful sensations and went on with the day. Twice that same afternoon, I picked up the phone to call Hutch and tell him that I had Mother's story in my hands, that maybe together we could figure out her "one small summer" in Alabama. I tried to ignore the need to call him, but although I could decide what to do and not do, I couldn't stop thinking about him. I tried, but my heart and mind wandered—like mindless, disobedient children—into the past.

And the past is where I found my present.

Through that day, I slowly understood that I was in many ways repeating Mother's story. She'd taught me so well that I hadn't even understood I was being taught, and the lesson was this: Choose the proper and appropriate way to protect yourself. I was now withering in a marriage and a life that had somehow killed the most precious quadrant of my heart—the part that felt emotion. If I put myself on automatic, there would be no wanting or needing, and the sheltered life would take on its predestined course that required no choosing or action on my part.

In reading Mother's story, spread as it was through pages and years, I saw that she had done this: When her heart shattered, when she broke and the pain was too much to bear, she'd shut her soul and made the one decision that never required another decision. If her heart was quieted, it could never again bother her with its wants and needs and longings.

My soul dropped to its knees, and I understood that if I wanted to live this very same way (Mother's way), I could: I was well on her path. But I had a choice. A real and definitive moment where I could choose love or safety; deadness or pain; risk or shelter. I wasn't sure how to choose or what I'd decide to do, but something had to be done before my heart was closed tight for good and all, before the drowning of my soul was complete.

My heart returned to a singular time—when I was with Hutch O'Brien.

After Hutch and I met at the bar that night, we were inseparable. Sleep and food seemed inconsequential, almost foolish. We believed we were the rare and lucky ones, the ones that found the Person that completed the incomplete parts of our souls. We'd finished each other's sentences. We'd read the same books. We'd listened to the same music.

I finally brought Hutch home to meet my parents, and maybe that's where the demise began, because nothing stays the same. Ever. Especially after meeting my mother.

Hutch and Mother met the Thanksgiving of my junior year. The dining room table of our family home was set, flashing with the family silver and Wedgwood china, the candles like those silly

New Year's Eve sparklers we lit as children. Hutch sat in the library watching football with Dad while Mother and I peeled the potatoes. Nat King Cole sang on the radio, where holiday songs dominated the airwaves.

"So, Ellie, where are his people from?" Mother asked.

"Linden, Alabama," I said.

She threw potato peels into the trash. "I've never heard of that place."

"It's a really small town outside Mobile."

"What does his daddy do?"

I stared at Mother with a knife held in my hand. "Why can't you just ask about him? I'll tell you how wonderful he is, how he cares about me, how he notices people and looks them in the eye when they talk, how he reaches for my hand at the exact right moment, how he never judges others, how his best friends would do anything for him because they know he would do anything for them."

Mother tossed a pile of potatoes into the boiling water. Her back was to me. "What does he want to do with his life?"

"He's a history major."

"What the hell's he gonna do with that?" She spun around and glared at me.

"Mother, my God, it's the same major as mine."

"What could he possibly *do?* It's different for you, Ellie."

"Different?"

"Yes."

I turned to walk out of the kitchen when I heard her. "You need to find someone more appropriate."

I stopped with my hand flat on the swinging kitchen door. "Appropriate?" I turned to face Mother. "I love him. Isn't that appropriate enough?"

"No, Ellie, it's not. I wish it were, but it isn't."

At dinner, after a few glasses of red wine, Mother turned to Hutch and asked, "So tell me about your people, son. I know you're from Alabama, but really that's all our Ellie has told us."

"I'm from a small town outside Mobile called Linden. Not even sure you can find it on a map." He smiled at Mother, but his charm and humor had as little effect as an ant on an elephant.

Hutch looked to me, and I rolled my eyes. This was the one and only subject I was hoping to avoid. I almost would have preferred the "Are you having sex?" conversation.

"Well," Mother said, taking another long swallow of wine. "What does your daddy do in Linden?"

Hutch didn't answer Mother for a longer time than was comfortable and then looked her directly in the eye. "Whatever he can. Usually works on cars."

"Oh." There was a triumphant note to Mother's voice. If there were subtitles to her words, they would say to me, "I told you so."

"And your mama?" she asked.

"She's been ill, ma'am."

"With?"

"The drink, usually."

"Mother," I said sharply.

"What?" She glared at me. "I'm just trying to find out about his life."

Hutch took my hand and squeezed it. "I grew up in that small town in a double-wide trailer and worked my way to Auburn, where I'm studying history and hope to work in a museum or library system. I moved to Auburn and fell in love with the most adorable and miraculous girl I've ever met, and here I am. Really, ma'am, that's all there is to it. A simple story about rural Alabama. Nothing that interesting."

"You're interesting," I said, and kissed his cheek.

Mother stood. "I'll be right back. I think I need more wine."

When she left the room, Dad looked at us both. "You just have to love her the way she is." He laughed and the room lightened.

*Excerpt from Lillian Ashford's Journal
New Year's Eve 1960
Twenty Years Old*

This is the year I met the man I will love forever; I know this. There are some things in life you know. I met him at Birdie's Summer House; the place everyone knows changes everything.

I am only twenty—I understand that I'm not in the experienced category but this is not something someone needs to be taught to understand: Love. When He shook my hand, I held on to his longer than I should have. His voice, my God, his voice washed over me like water. When he walked away my body shook for hours. I have done nothing the past few months but think of him, his touch, his voice, his strong hands, his long back, and the small space behind his neck where his hair meets his skin, where . . .

I think I have gone crazy with Love. Is that possible? When can I see him again—oh when? I will return to

Alabama no matter what it takes—I will find a job there and stay at the Summer House on the bay. I don't care what Mother and Dad say; I don't care if I must deny all that I've been taught. My best friend, Birdie, will be there for me.

If it is true what Grandmother told me—if it is true that I can mold my life with my words, then every year for the rest of my life I will write THIS: HE will love me. HE will always love me.

Always.

Six

I finally dialed his number, Hutch's number, to inform him that I knew a little more about those summers of '60 and '61. His voice mail picked up.

"Hey, you," I said, rushing my message. "It's Ellie. The weirdest thing has happened. I found Mother's journal and there was a little bit about those summers in there. Not much, but maybe it will help you. . . ."

I couldn't find the right words to say good-bye—I never can—so I hung up.

I stood in the middle of my attic studio because that is what I do when I need to think or to just be or to escape—I paint. The light was soft that day, the kind that comes when the clouds are thin and shielding without hiding the sun.

My attic studio was wide open. In the rest of the house I had walls separating each room one from the other, but I kept open the attic space that runs the length and width of the house. My cell phone rang, and I glanced at the screen—Sadie. I answered, and she was talking before I said hello. "Hey, I'm at the front door, can't you hear me?"

"I'm in the studio, just come in. It's unlocked."

Her quick and light footsteps echoed up the attic stairs and she entered the space, her high heels in her hand, her ponytail loose.

Sadie and I are second-generation best friends. Our mothers—Birdie and Lilly—had been best friends since first grade, and Sadie and I grew up understanding we were tied together by not only friendship, but also kinship. Now she is part of the Buckhead world in which we live, yet oddly separate. Her kind heart, soft voice, and simple ways keep me from falling directly into the conventional world in which I live, the way Alice fell into the rabbit hole. Her beauty is stunning and unadorned. If there is something beyond and better than "best friend," that is Sadie to me.

I hugged her. In her hand, she held a white box with a string around it. She stretched out her hand. "For me?" I asked.

"Food."

I opened the box and looked at Sadie, grinning. "What would I ever do without you? Please don't ever let me find out." Inside were my favorite cookies—madeleines from Henri's Bakery. I took out a sugary concoction and allowed the sugar to melt on my tongue. "Manna from heaven."

Sadie reached to hug me but accidentally knocked the box. The cookies scattered across my rough and paint-splattered hardwood floor, and we laughed in that remarkable way that best friends can and do. We knelt on the floor and gathered the food, dropping the cookies into the box. I sat cross-legged and let out a long sigh.

"Go ahead," Sadie said. "Whatever it is, say it."

"I had the weirdest thing happen yesterday." I picked up a cookie off the floor, blew on it, taking a bite and speaking with my mouth full because I could. "I found Mother's journal."

"What?"

I shrugged. "I know. I never knew about it. I cleaned out her closet and packed up everything for Dad."

"Of course you did. You are so sweet, my friend."

"Anyway, I found the journal in the bottom locked drawer. I've always, always wondered what was in there—I thought it was her good jewelry. You know, the jewelry she didn't want me to see or touch. I read the entire thing. There is so much I didn't know . . . and now so many questions."

"Wow."

"Yeah." I scooted back and leaned against the wall.

Sadie drew her knees up to her chest and tilted her head. "I have the most perfectly perfect idea. Why don't you get out of here for a while? Go to your family's beach house in St. Simons. Just take her journal and go. Read and rest."

"That's not what I need."

"What do you need?"

"To find a man. . . ."

Sadie lifted her eyebrows and laughed. "You need a man?"

"Not for me." I smiled because that is what Sadie can make me do even when I'm not in the mood to do so. "Okay, here it is: When she was twenty years old, Mother fell in love with someone. A someone who lived in Alabama. A someone who changed his mind about loving her. A man who was also friends with your mother. For two years, Mother spent her summers at your family Summer House."

"Isn't it funny how we still call it the Summer House and Mom lives there all the time now?" Sadie shook her head and her ponytail fell out; she slipped the rubber band around her wrist and looked at me. "I have no idea about a man, but I do know your mother didn't like to visit there. She used to talk all of us into coming to St. Simons."

"I guess I never thought much about it. I just knew that we always had a beach house in Georgia and that is where we went—there was no discussion about it. But then again, there wasn't much discussion with Mother about much of anything once she'd made up her mind."

"Exactly," Sadie said.

"But there was more to it than her just being

stubborn about St. Simons. There is, or at least there *was,* someone there in Alabama she was avoiding."

"Well, I guess my mom would know, but she never said anything to me."

I let out a long sigh. "I want to find out."

"Why?" Sadie placed her hand on my knee. "Why does it matter now?"

"I don't understand why she kept these summers such a secret. It's like she omitted two entire summers of her life."

"Yeah, for a woman who was intent on 'telling the truth,' she sure had her own secrets. Shit, remember that time we were grounded for two months for lying about Parson's party? She went ballistic about lies . . . she said, and I quote, 'Always speak the truth.' "

"Well, this is a truth she never spoke. And whoever this man was, he changed her life course. She—I think—also left a letter for him. And . . ." I paused. "For the Atlanta history exhibit they want to know more about that summer of '61 because that is when she supposedly helped with the movement. She never told me about it and she never told Dad and . . . somehow the history center knows something I don't. That is really weird."

Sadie smiled that knowing, smart-ass smile. There is this radar she has—this bullshit radar —and I know better than to try to sneak underneath it. "And exactly, Ellie, who is the 'they' that needs to know more?"

I cringe.

"Yeah, that's what I thought. Go to the Summer House, Ellie. Stay with my mother. Her heart will burst, she'll be so happy to have you. I bet she'll be able to tell you some stories. And . . ." She winked. "You know the legend—that everything changes at the Summer House. That truth is always revealed."

"Legend or fairy tale?"

"You'll never know unless you go."

"I can't just . . . leave."

"Yes, you can. Go to my mom's. You've only been a few times, what with your mother's bizarre allergic reaction to Alabama."

"You'll come with me?" I was hopeful yet understood the futility of that hope.

"You know I can't. Kenz and Connor both have full schedules with horseback competitions and baseball tournaments."

"Yes, I know," I said. Sadie's two teens were involved in more activities than any children I'd ever known. And if I didn't adore Sadie, I'd hate her for making it all look effortless and smooth and normal.

"I can drive down there with you and get you settled," she said. "And then you can stay as long as you like."

"I can't. I can't leave Dad. What if Lil wants to

come home and I'm not here? I have that fund-raiser for the church, and then there's that party for Tinsley's fiftieth birthday."

"There's my best friend with the list. Always the list."

I do have a thing about lists. I make them for almost everything: what I need to do; where I need to go. It helps me keep things in order, which is what Rusty needs: order.

"There's just no way," I said.

"The guesthouse is always open for you."

"I'll think about it. I promise."

But instead of thinking about going to Alabama, I found myself brooding (others might call it obsessing) about Hutch O'Brien, as if all the times I had forced myself not to think about him added up and came rushing at me like a wave with a wicked undertow. I remembered breathing the same breath, our limbs intertwined under the sodden air falling across our skin under an open window. I felt the longing and particullar knowing of loving someone so much that there were no words, only movement. Nothing was enough. And everything was enough.

For the past few years, I knew he'd been living in Atlanta, working for the Atlanta History Center: Rusty and I are members, and I read the newsletter. Hutch had been hired to manage and create all their special exhibits, which occur a few times a year. This time the new exhibit was about ten different women. I wondered if he would still have done the project if the show were about just Mother, about only Lillian Ashford Eddington, the woman he partially blamed for our breakup.

I know the reason Hutch and I have never run into each other—our circle of friends could not be more different. I'd once thought I saw him at the market, but by the time I made my way across the dog food aisle, he was gone. I found myself standing there for so long with shaking feelings of familiarity and desire that a stranger asked if I was okay. Yes, I was fine, thanks for asking.

There was one other time I'd seen him, but it was in Florida. I'd been in a restaurant in Seaside. Lil was ten years old and we were on a spring break trip. Sadie and I had taken the kids, as Rusty had decided there was no way he was leaving when he had Masters golf tickets. Sadie chased six-year-old Connor across the restaurant. Clams congealed on my plate, curdling in the heat, when I looked up and saw Hutch's face across the room. He stood alone at the entrance-way. My heart was an entire sea rolling toward the shore in instinct.

I stood next to him before I knew I'd walked across the room. He looked at me. First the smile —it's always first the smile. People's faces initially do what comes natural—and then comes the real reaction. Next his face was a blank wall, his eyes a calm bay.

"Hi, Hutch," I stammered, and pointed across the room toward Sadie. "I'm here, too."

He nodded. "I see that." And he laughed, but kindly. He doesn't know how to be anything but. Even in anger there is no meanness, just emptiness. Maybe rage is better—at least it's an emotion. What Hutch showed was complete indifference, or so it seemed.

I saw her then: a tall woman with curls walking toward him. He moved to her, kissing her in greeting. I backed away, stumbled into the table behind me, where a woman's iced tea toppled over in the same slow motion as my heart. When I'd finished apologizing, when I'd wiped my skirt, Hutch and his wife were gone, as if they'd never been there.

The restaurant's air pressed in on me with the weight of water pushing me down so I couldn't get to the surface where there was oxygen, voices, sunlight. I swam through the tables with the buoy centerpieces, past the shellac-thick bar, around the swinging lanterns, until I returned to the table with Sadie and the kids. She looked at me. "You okay?"

I nodded, and then I cried tears that had never been wept—tears pent up in some unknown place for over twelve years. I don't know why it sometimes takes that long to feel something, but that's how long it took to understand and feel what I had lost: that sweetness in Hutch O'Brien.

Move on. . . .

Which is of course what I'd done. Moved on. Right?

Seven

I made my mandatory appearance at the Broomes' fiftieth anniversary party because they are my parents' next-door neighbors, because they are my friend Annie's parents, and because, well . . . because the firmly grounded social graces I don't remember learning—I've just known them—were planted so deeply in my mental maneuvering that I dressed in a navy Tory Burch dress, pulled my curls into a loose ponytail, and swiped on my makeup before driving to the Broomes' home in Buckhead.

Buckhead. The part of Atlanta that is still Atlanta—meaning it has the mailing address: Atlanta, Georgia. There are what seem like hundreds of outlying neighborhoods—inside and outside of I-285—where people live and say, "Yes, I live in Atlanta." This is a point of contention with the old Atlanta crowd, those "from" Atlanta, those born at Piedmont Hospital or Crawford Long, those whose parents and grandparents belong to the Piedmont Driving Club or Cherokee Town and Country Club—preferably both.

OTP they call those who live "outside the perimeter" of I-285, and when their children move to Marietta or Duluth or Peachtree Corners, they act as if they must pack an overnight bag to drive under the asphalt circle of spaghetti junction and then stop at a rest stop before reaching their destination in a suburban-gated neighborhood.

There are those who say that Peachtree Street once stood for the real Atlanta, the Atlanta of *Gone With the Wind* and Mayor Hartsfield, yet now the road changes into Peachtree Industrial or Peachtree Parkway and then continues to run into forever. For now, though, Peachtree Street led only to the Broomes' driveway. I sat in my car for a moment and stared at my childhood home next door.

When my gaze returned to the Broomes' house, I saw Sadie and Annie were walking toward the front door. They stopped and waved, as if they were in a homecoming parade. I was meeting Rusty there, as he'd be coming from a meeting. I went to greet my friends.

"You look amazing," Sadie said as I joined them at the front door.

They were both dressed in understated casual

dresses that I knew cost more than most prom dresses. "Of course so do you," I said.

We walked into Annie's parents' brick home. The foyer shimmered with the up lighting Mother had also insisted on in every room, offering a soft glow to her chemically peeled and perfectly maintained skin. Caterers made clanging noises in the kitchen; rosemary aroma mixed into the atmosphere of the Broomes' home.

Mrs. Broome called my name as she entered the foyer. I held my arms open for a hug. She smiled in genuine relief: I was sane and on time. I knew Annie's mother well enough to know that she was worried that since I'd lost Mother and Lil had left for college, I'd be a new and different crazy person who forgot to do things like bathe and show up at dinner parties.

I hugged Mrs. Broome. "Happy Anniversary."

"Well, dear, you know I just like to find an excuse to have a party."

We all moved toward the kitchen when Dad came up behind me, gave me a bear hug. "Hey, Dad." I turned and gave him a kiss on the cheek. The aroma of sweet-sour whiskey surrounded his face.

"You look great, Ladybug. Really great." He said this with a raise of his eyebrows.

"As if you thought I wouldn't?"

"Wouldn't what?"

"Look great," I said.

"Well, these have been hard days for you, haven't they?" He smoothed the front of his Cherokee Town and Country Club polo shirt, which did not need smoothing.

"I'm good, Dad." I motioned to the bartender, Roger, whom I've known for twenty years and who knew exactly what my motion meant: martini, straight up, a little dirty, three olives. Now. He smiled at me and gave a single nod while Dad continued to talk. "Well, when I was playing golf with Rusty today, he said you were in a bad way when he saw you this morning. I told him—"

"In a bad way? Me?"

"He said you never went to bed, that you stayed up all night reading."

Roger handed me my martini; I took a very long swallow. "I'm fine, Dad."

There is a world that exists in this part of Buckhead, a world I've lived in but is separate, an empire, and a kingdom of men. It's not that Dad loves Rusty more than he loves me, it's that they've been playing golf with the same group of men for over twenty years. This is what the club men do—the same thing they've always done with the same people they've always done it with on the same day they've always done it on. They play golf on the manicured greens and then go to the men's bar upstairs—a place where the women are forbidden to enter. Seriously.

I smiled at Dad. "I need to go around and say hello to everyone." Couples had begun to fill the house, and if I understood anything, I understood the social graces required in the Broome home—they were the same ones required in my home.

"Hey, baby." Rusty ambled toward me wearing a crisp pair of khakis, a golf polo shirt, and a smile—his uniform.

I smiled at my husband and he hugged me, slipping his hand into mine.

"You look great tonight," Rusty said in a voice just loud enough to be heard, but not loud enough to suggest that he was trying to be heard.

He leaned up against the counter, waving to someone across the room. Sara Matthews sidled up to us, hugging simultaneously—one arm for each of us. "How are y'all?" she asked with a big smile. Her lips had grown since the last time I saw her, and the left side of her mouth was larger than the right, making me tilt my head.

"Good," I said. "You?"

"Great," she said, looking at Rusty and lifting her eyebrows, although her forehead didn't move at all with the motion. "And y'all?"

Rusty took her hand. "How's your dad?" Sara's dad had a triple bypass the week before, and Rusty remembered this.

Sara's eyes filled with tears. "Not good." She pouted with her crooked lips.

Rusty kissed the back of her hand. "Please

give him our love, and let him know we're keeping him in our prayers."

"What?" I said this before I knew the thought had formed itself into a word and been born on my tongue.

Sara glared at me. "He said y'all are praying for my dad."

I looked at Rusty. He is a man who prays only that his golf ball makes it in the hole for par; he doesn't pray for men who've had bypass surgery. I walked away, headed to the hallway bathroom, leaving Sara and Rusty to stare after me with the concerned look of the superior. I slammed the door shut and stared into the porcelain sink, which was hand painted with tiny yellow and pink butterflies.

What was wrong with me? I didn't want Rusty anywhere near me. I'd just begun to realize that the awful feeling of love having left our marriage wasn't going to pass. Something was desperately wrong with me. This had to be my fault, because if you can't love your husband, who, my God, can you love?

If I really looked at our life—we were the lucky ones. We had it all.

I would fix this just as I fixed everything else in our life. I would repair these feelings the same way I did a leaking faucet or a broken cabinet door. I turned on the sink, splashing my face with cold water.

Sadie called from the other side of the door. "You okay, Ellie?"

I opened the door, smiling at her. "Absolutely."

"Did Rusty say something mean to you?"

"No," I said, sidling past her into the hallway, walls lined with Broome family portraits framed in dark wood.

She lifted her hand and wiped at the side of my right eye with her pinky finger. "Mascara," she said as a simple explanation.

My purse vibrated, and I yanked out my cell phone.

Hutch.

"I've got to get this," I told Sadie, and walked toward the empty sunroom off the foyer.

"Hey, you," I said quietly.

"I've always loved the way you say that."

I laughed. "Say what?"

" 'Hey, you.' As if it couldn't be anyone but me."

"Oh." The word dipped down into a calm place.

The silence was full and empty as my stomach did that flip-flop thing it had once done at the sound of his voice. We'd always been able to lean into the quiet, rest in it, as if silence had its own language, a dialect only we knew and were content to speak.

"You got my message?" I finally asked, pacing the sunroom.

"I did. Is this a good time to talk?"

"Not really. I'm at the Broomes' fiftieth wedding anniversary party."

"Wow, when you can't find Mrs. Broome, just sneak back to the pantry and she'll be there sipping the Jack straight from the bottle."

I laughed too loud. "How do you know that dirty little secret?"

"I have my ways."

"You always have." I paused, embarrassed I'd slipped into our banter that was twenty years gone. "Really, how do you know this?"

"Don't you remember? You told me . . . when we were together and went over there after that Thanksgiving dinner. In college, you told me."

"That's right."

"Anyway . . ." He paused before he asked, "How about lunch tomorrow and you can tell me about those summers in Alabama."

"I don't even have a lunch's worth of information."

"Well, then the rest of the time we can talk about me."

"That sounds just perfect," I said. "Noon at Grace, okay?"

When we hung up, I was still laughing until I turned and saw Rusty staring at me from the doorway. "What's so damn funny?" he asked.

I pointed at the cell phone. "Lil."

He motioned for me to join the party, and we

mingled until I finally hugged the Broomes and told them I would see them soon.

Mrs. Broome took both my hands in hers as Rusty stood by my side. "Dear, one day you'll be able to have a fiftieth wedding anniversary and you'll understand what a beautiful thing it is."

"Yes," I said, and kissed her cheek. "I have to go now."

Rusty walked me outside. "Why are you leaving?"

"I don't feel well. I'll just meet you at home," I said, and tried my very best to smile at him.

"Please don't go," he said. "I hate being at parties without you."

"I know."

He pouted.

"Rusty, I found Mother's journal."

"Oh, wow. Did you read it?"

"Yes, that's what I was reading all night."

He stared off for a moment, as if he hadn't heard me. "I don't think I could do that—read someone else's journal. So . . . invasive."

"There's so much about her I didn't know."

We walked to the car as we talked. "Of course there is. There's so much about everyone we don't know."

"Well, there were these two summers—'60 and '61—when she was in college that she had a lover and was involved in some part of the movement."

"So what? That's way past, Ellie. Done."

"So what?"

"I just don't see how that matters at all now."

"Well," I said, taking car keys from my purse and opening the driver's-side door, "I do see how it matters. I think I might go to Alabama, to the Summer House, and talk to Sadie's mom. . . ." My voice trailed off.

He shook his head. "This is not a good time for you to be gone."

"Why?" I sat in the driver's seat and started the car.

"We all need you here."

"Yes," I said. "But I think I need to go there."

He stared at me for the longest time, as if I hadn't spoken at all. Then he dropped his hands onto the top of my car, looking down at me in the driver's seat. "Maybe you need some counseling or something, darling. I mean, losing a mother is one of the top five stressors in a life."

"Top five stressors?" I asked. "Like the top five songs of the week? Or the the top five investments for 2010?"

He threw up his hands. "Damn, Ellie, I'm just trying to be helpful."

I slumped into myself. "I'm sorry. I'm exhausted. I'll just see you at home, okay?" Even as I said the word—sorry—I wondered why I always ended up uttering those five letters in a row when there was nothing I had to be sorry about. Or was there? Confusion seemed to be the preeminent sentiment for me those days.

He nodded. "Yes, see you there." This was one of those times—those many times—when his words didn't match the meaning of those same words.

I drove home, and instead of figuring out how to assuage Rusty's foul mood, I found myself planning what to wear to lunch the next day. This should have been a warning sign, but it merely felt like a distraction.

One thing being called another . . . maybe that's where it all began.

Excerpt from Lillian Ashford's Journal
New Year's Eve 1960
Twenty Years Old

Mother has already agreed that I can spend another month with Birdie in Alabama this next summer. I have a job as a lifeguard at their country club pool. I didn't mention Him to Mother, but of course He is the only reason I want to go. This need for Him has somehow turned into a river in my soul, moving and carving places inside of me that only He can fill.

Five months. That is how long until I touch His beautiful face again.

This is our secret—oh Journal. Our secret. It must stay that way. If I am only able to write in here once a year and speak my goals and my wishes, it is here that I can speak this desire and write this— This is The Year He will love me as much as I love Him. We will be together.

Eight

The restaurant, Grace, was decorated to offer the feeling of an Italian villa: clean, creamy, and calm. I waited at the bar with a sweet tea, second-guessing this lunch, myself, and my outfit (white linen pants and an Henri Beguelin silk tank top).

I'd told Rusty I was meeting Hutch to give him the information about Mother. He'd stood in the kitchen with his briefcase at his feet. "You're serious?" he'd asked.

"Yes, I am."

"This isn't something you can tell him on the phone?"

"Well, I wanted to give him copies of the pages about those two years. This is about Mother, Rusty. This is about the exhibit. Not about me. Or Hutch."

"Are you sure about that?"

"Very," I'd said.

Rusty had slammed the door on the way out, which was his way of discussing Hutch with the same contempt Mother once had. Her campaign against Hutch had begun the moment she'd met him and continued after Thanksgiving and into that spring.

• • •

It had been the weekend before finals, the coming summer whispering its humid and seductive ease into our lives. Hutch and I had come to Atlanta for the final push-through in our studies. We sat on the back porch of Mother's house, our history books open, our pencils stuck behind our ears, as we quizzed each other. Facts I couldn't remember now at gunpoint came easily and quickly then. We were confident in our grades, in our lives, in our desire.

I found out later that Mother had hired a private detective to unearth a remnant of Hutch O'Brien, and it was Hutch's and my first fight. And in many ways our last, as it was what I used to explain my own betrayal.

Mother had come out onto the porch, her purse angling off the crook of her elbow. "I'm going to the garden club," she said. "You two okay alone here?"

"Of course," we said together, and then smiled at each other, at our identical words.

She began to walk away and then stopped and turned on her high heels. "Oh, Hutch, it's so weird that there is another boy named Hutchinson from your hometown."

He laughed and placed his finger on a line in the history book, so he could look up at Mother. "No, I'm it."

"Really? Are you sure?"

"Yes," he said, and glanced at me. "The one and only."

"Well, that's weird, because I wouldn't have taken you for the type to have spent a month in jail. There is no way you are that same boy." She pushed her hair off her forehead, although it had so much hair spray that there was no way it needed smoothing. She glanced at me.

"Mother," I said, "what are you talking about?"

She walked toward us and sat in a chair. "I'm sorry . . . I didn't mean to just drop that like a bomb. I thought surely it was another boy. I'm . . . sorry."

"No, ma'am, sure enough that was me. I was fourteen. It's actually a pretty terrible story, one I don't usually like to remember or talk about."

She nodded. "I understand." Mother then left Hutch and me there in the backyard facing each other over an iron table and history books.

Hutch stared at me for the longest time while this blackness of dread spread inside me, as if the news were an oil spill in water. "It's not what it sounds like," he said.

"Okay," I said.

"My God, how did she know? The records have been sealed for years."

"So . . . it's true?" My heart sped; my mouth was an arid desert of fear.

"Ellie . . ."

I stood. "Seriously? She's right? And you never told me? Are you kidding me?"

"Sit down and listen, please. I'll tell you the entire story."

I stayed standing. "I'm listening, Hutch. Go ahead."

He stood with me, taking my hands. "Sit down."

When we once again faced each other over our notes and class papers, he did tell me the story. A terrible story that had once changed him and then changed us.

"Ellie," he said, regretful but resolute, "I am so sorry I never told you about this story. It's terrible, and in trying to forget it ever happened, I pretend it never happened."

"That doesn't work," I said. "Pretending something didn't happen doesn't work."

"I know, and I should have told you. But when you are finally where you want to be, you try to forget where you were."

"What happened, Hutch?"

"I was with my cousin." He paused. "Anyway. He wanted . . . no, he needed some Jack Daniel's. I was fourteen, but I drove. We all did. We were in the country. Mama hardly left the trailer and Daddy was never home . . . so we all learned to drive young. Edwin had me take him to the liquor store, and I did. I waited in the car, not knowing that he wasn't buying liquor but actually demanding it at gunpoint."

He was quiet for a long while, and I waited, wanting to go back in time—only five minutes. To the five minutes ago when I didn't know this about him. When this darkness hadn't entered my awareness. "Go ahead," I said.

"Even when he ran into the car, I didn't know. Even when I saw the gun, I didn't realize what he'd done. It wasn't until the liquor store owner came running out and Edwin shot at him . . ." Hutch looked away.

"My God, did he hit him?"

"Yes, he hit him. But I didn't know that. I swear I wouldn't have driven away if I'd known. Edwin was screaming at me to drive. To drive. To step on it. And I did."

"So . . . then what happened?"

"All the horrible things you imagine. That man died. Edwin is still in jail and I went to juvenile. Your mother was wrong, though—I wasn't there for a month. I was there for a year. And I don't know who'd I'd be or where I'd be if it weren't for Mr. Bartow."

"Who is he?"

"He is the farmer I worked for. He is the man who believed in me. He is the man who hired a lawyer and finally got me acquitted and the records sealed. He is the man who paid for Auburn. . . ."

"Why did he do all that for you?"

"He believed in me. I'd worked his farm since

I was twelve, but every evening we sat in his library and talked about books and history . . . he'd give me books to read and then we'd discuss them. He . . . lost his son and he sort of adopted me."

"That's who you stay with when you go home, isn't it?"

He nodded. "Yes."

"When were you ever going to tell me any of this?"

"I was going to tell you. I was."

"When?"

He exhaled. "I don't know. But not here and not like this. I wanted to be able to take you home; let you meet Mr. Bartow and . . . not like this, where it looks like I'm hiding something from the person I love the most."

"You *were* hiding this from me," I said.

He shook his head. "Not hiding. Waiting."

I dropped my head into my hands so he wouldn't see my tears. He came to the side of my chair. "Ellie, please don't. I promise this has nothing to do with us or how much I love you. I promise."

"Then what did it have to do with?"

"I think maybe I was worried you wouldn't respect me if you knew."

I lifted my head. "You didn't trust my love?"

"No, I just—for a little while longer—wanted you to believe in my goodness and not know the darker parts. I was afraid it would change things if you knew."

"It does change things, Hutch. Not because that happened to you, but because you kept it from me." I lifted my head and allowed him to see my tear-filled eyes. "Was it terrible for you? Was it awful?"

"Yes," he said. "Do you want to hear about it? Or would it be better if you didn't?"

"I want to hear it. I want to know everything of you. Everything—not just the good parts."

We sat up most of that night while he told me of the harrowing life that was juvenile hall, as he told me all that he'd hidden from himself and from me. I adored him more because of it. I loved the soft, wounded, broken pieces of him in a way I never had before.

When I left for school that next morning, Mother stood on the front porch staring after me. I threw my bag into the car as she hollered toward me, "You cannot leave without saying good-bye, Lillian Eddington."

I stared at her for the longest time, wondering how a woman who claimed to love me as she did could desire to inflict pain. I didn't find an answer in her face or angry expressions.

I walked to her. "Mother, I don't understand you. Why did you do that? Why did you do that to Hutch? To me?"

She placed her hands on my face; I withdrew. "Because I only want the best for you."

"What if he's the best for me?"

"Oh, he's not, Ellie. I see things you don't see. He's not for you."

"You are cruel and mean and you have no idea what love is, Mother."

She shook her head. "I do know. And if you can't see what I'm trying to do—protect you—then you can go get hurt. But don't come crying to me when you do."

"I wasn't planning on it," I said.

We didn't talk—Mother and I—for a full three weeks. I didn't answer her calls or frantic messages on the answering machine. When we did finally speak, her speech contained the same sentiments with new anger and inflection.

And with Hutch: What Mother had meant for harm only brought us closer together.

For a time. For a short time.

Later, when our breakup was over, I wondered if it would have made a difference if he'd told me the awful story from the beginning, if I hadn't heard it from Mother. My insecurity over our solid relationship, something I thought as secure as the world anchored in space, rocked me sideways. I had believed there was nothing significant he had ever kept from me or from my heart. Somehow this one omission wormed its way into my soul like a virus of doubt. If this, then what else?

What if I hadn't met Rusty right after that

weekend? What if I hadn't felt the ridiculous want to have someone else need me? Or maybe really nothing would have made a difference— as if Fate had decided we weren't meant to be and it didn't matter what order or how events were told or said or done.

Hutch walked into the bar, glancing around and then waving at me. He wore jeans and a white, slightly wrinkled button-down. He gave me an awkward hug, and we followed the hostess to the table, our words overlapping as we searched for a rhythm of conversation.

"Yoo-hoo, Ellie," I heard behind me. I twisted to see Belinda and Eve waving at me from the next table. I excused myself and greeted them with a hug.

"Who is that?" Belinda asked in a whisper.

"An old friend doing that history center show about Mother."

"Ohhh." She glanced at Hutch and then me. "Well, have a lovely lunch."

"You two also," I said.

I returned to the table and sat across from Hutch.

"Friends?" he asked.

"Yes, friends and megaphones."

"Huh?" He opened his menu.

"Meaning everyone, by two o'clock today, will know I was at lunch with you."

He looked up at me with those brown eyes. "Is this going to be a problem for you?"

"No problem at all." I shook my head, pulling out the Xerox pages of Mother's journal from 1960 and 1961. "So here's what I have. It isn't much. She mostly writes about heartbreak."

He raised his eyebrows and his smile lifted at the same time. "Your mother was heartbroken?"

"I know. I know it doesn't seem possible, but it's true. It seems there was a group of friends that were involved on the fringe of the civil rights movement. For example: They'd meet protesters at the end of the Freedom Rides, but they didn't go on one. She did a sit-in and went to planning meetings, but I don't think she was ever in danger. Mostly I think she was obsessed with this man who happened to be involved. The first summer was quiet, nothing really. They met in '60, and then she went back the next summer to be with him and that's when she got involved with the movement."

He took the pages from me, glanced at them. "How do we find out more? I mean, not a lot. I don't want to intrude, but enough that I can put something substantial in the timeline?"

"Can I ask you something?"

"Sure."

"How did you know . . . I mean, who told you that she'd been active in this way?"

"Well, when I started doing the research on all

ten women, I started first with the paperwork and voting records. It seems that your mother was nominated for her philanthropy work, but someone told the committee about her summer of '61 and this tipped the votes in her favor. The records don't show who provided the information, so . . . I don't know who to interview except you."

"And Mother didn't tell you anything?"

"She pretended I didn't ask, glossing right over it and continuing the story about her Lilly's Love charity."

I shook my head. "Wow . . ." I opened my menu. "Let's order and then I'll tell you what I'm thinking."

He closed his menu. "I've already decided what I want."

We ordered, and until our food arrived we talked about how the history center had just joined with the Margaret Mitchell House and random small talk to fill the empty places where meaningful words hadn't yet arrived.

Our food came—roasted chicken for him, ravioli for me. We thanked the waitress, and then he lifted his silverware. "Now tell me what you're thinking about how to find out more about your mother," he said.

"Well, when Mother spent those summers in Alabama, she stayed at the Worthingtons' Summer House in Bayside with Sadie's mom,

Birdie. Birdie lives there full-time now. I thought I'd go down there and talk to her, ask a few questions. . . ."

"I'm coming," he said, and took a bite of his roasted chicken.

I laughed. "No way. That's just not a very good idea."

"Funny how a lot of what I do isn't a very good idea, but turns out great." He took another bite and leaned over the table. "I'm serious. My best buddy, Drew, lives there now."

"Drew Irving?"

He nodded. "He's a vet there." He planted his palms on either side of the table. "So when do you think you'll go?"

"I think . . ." I stared off and knew, looking back to him. "Tomorrow."

"Perfect," he said. "So now let's talk about you. How are you?"

"That's boring. First, tell me all about you." I smiled, cutting into my ravioli. "Please," I said. "Tell me what and how you've been doing." I paused, weighing words before saying the truth. "I've often wondered."

"Okay . . ." He leaned back in his chair, staring up at the ceiling as if his story, the years and days between our good-bye and this moment, were etched there. This offered me the chance to stare at him, to find the Hutch I loved and knew. His face was wider, his eyebrows lower, his mouth was lined around the lips; but when he looked at me, stared at me, *he* was there behind his eyes. I remembered once in college when a new sorority sister had looked at a photo of Hutch on my bulletin board, she'd said, "He's so cute," and I'd been surprised, not because he wasn't good-looking, but because it was never the thing I noticed about him. I loved the Hutch who hid behind his eyes.

He gave me the facts. He'd been married six years to Ginger, whom he'd met in Atlanta after we broke up. Divorced when she slept with her personal trainer—a cliché not worth talking about, he said. No kids. He was inspired by his work at the Atlanta History Center. He lived in Virginia Highlands and for six years had been dating a woman named Hillary. "Life," he said, "never turns out exactly the way you think. And sometimes that's good."

"You've been dating her a long time . . . ," I said.

"Is that your polite way of asking why I haven't married her?"

I tried to hide my smile but couldn't. "Probably."

"I wish I had a really good answer for you . . . and for her. Because I do love her. But I promised myself I'd never marry again unless . . ."

"Unless what?"

The waitress dropped our bill on the table, and Hutch grabbed it. "My treat."

"Thanks," I said. "Now . . . unless what?"

He placed a credit card on the bill and slid it to the end of the table. "That is an entirely other lunch, okay?"

I nodded. "Okay."

After he paid, we walked outside, then stood at the curb in that awkward moment of finding a way to say good-bye.

"Thanks for feeding me," I said, smiling.

He took my hand. "See you in Bayside."

I let go of his hand and slid my sunglasses over my eyes. "Hutch . . . I don't know . . ."

"I do."

He waved over his shoulder, and once again, we didn't say good-bye.

I made a list of all the things I would take to the Summer House the next morning. I didn't doubt, for one second or even a half second, my decision to go to Ms. Birdie's. After the last pair of shoes were thrown into my suitcase, I wondered if I should bring another bathing suit. I rubbed my hand across the leather journal and then tucked it under a cotton T-shirt.

I'd recognized a few names in Mother's journal, people she'd remained close to in the tightly wound world of Buckhead. She'd talked about landmarks and places, and although her life was gone, the places she mentioned were still there —the Pink Pig still exists (not in the same place, but I went every year as a child, and I've taken

Lil every year since she was born). We continue to be members of the Piedmont Driving Club and the Capital City Club. I'm a member of the Junior League, as was Mother and her mother before her. Some things just don't change.

I grabbed my cell phone and called Sadie, told her that, yes, we were going to her mother's house in Alabama. I had some questions for Ms. Birdie Worthington. A rebel for her time, Birdie had kept her family name and never took her husband's last name. Sadie, of course, was thrilled because she knew all along that I would go, and she'd be there to pick me up in the morning.

I hung up as Rusty walked into the bedroom, staring at my suitcase as if it were a man naked in our marriage bed. "What the hell?"

I waited. I've learned to do this—wait—because I want to see which Rusty will show up, the angry or the sweet. I hate this about myself, that I do this, that I base my reactions and answers on his moods, but I've learned. In a marriage we all learn, I think.

"Ellie." His voice was soft, sweet. "Are you going somewhere?" He came next to me, kissing me.

"I am. I tried to call you, but I couldn't reach you."

"I was on the golf course."

"I know."

He sat on the edge of the bed and patted the

place next to him. I joined him and he placed his arm around me, pulling me closer, where I dropped my head on his shoulder. "I know how hard this has been for you. I know I'm busy, but you can't just up and leave."

"I'm not up and leaving." I lifted my head and kissed his face. "I'm just going to Birdie's Summer House for a few days."

"Huh?"

"You see, there are some things I want to ask her."

"We have a telephone, Ellie."

"Rusty, please. I really need to get away for a couple days, and I want to sit down and talk to Birdie. There is nothing wrong with that. Lil's at summer school. You're crazy busy. It's just a few days. . . ."

He rubbed his hand up and down my back. "You poor thing. You're hurting so much, aren't you?"

"I am."

He released me and took my face in his hands, gently. "I'm sorry that you are, but I don't think running away is the answer."

"I am not running away. Please try and understand. Please." I leaned into his palm. "I'm going."

He yanked his hands away and threw them in the air, as if he were a referee at a championship football game and someone had just scored the winning field goal. The veins in his neck bulged; his lips were thin and white; his brow furrowed with squinted eyes. My stomach flipped over and my throat clenched. I looked away and across the room to the oil painting of Lil and me. She was two years old in this picture and she sat on my lap, her face lifted to mine, smiling.

The silence with Rusty was another language completely. It wasn't so much about the words and sentences that would come after the silence, it was what grew inside him and in the unspeaking space between us: rage.

"I really don't want you to go," Rusty said, and stood. He walked over to my suitcase, calmly threw a pile of clothes toward me, then dumped the remainder onto the floor.

I buried my face in my hands; I couldn't watch him do this. He walked out of the bedroom with a slam of the door that shook the oil painting. I walked toward the frame and straightened it, and then I knelt onto the plush cream carpet and repacked my suitcase.

The house was quiet with the hum of the air conditioner, which was a white noise to the pain across my chest as I then carried a pile of clothes to the laundry room. He'd say sorry; he always did.

And this is what I saw in that moment standing in my tiled laundry room: a huge block of marble, one I had given Rusty on our wedding day—a pure white block of flawless marble. With every temper tantrum, with every cruel word and disregard, with every time he held up his hand and told me not to argue, he had chipped away a piece of that solid rock. In my hand now I held a single crushed pebble.

I stood in the laundry room writing a list of things that needed to be done while I was gone when his footsteps approached. I stopped and waited. He entered the laundry room and came to me, pulled me into his arms. "God, baby. I'm sorry. That was ridiculous, throwing clothes. I'm an idiot. I just can't stand to think of you not being in this house. If you need to go to Bayside, please go. But know how much I'll miss you."

"Thanks." I pulled away and tossed a load of whites into the washing machine, then yanked a pile from the dryer and began to fold.

"Let's have a glass of wine and sit on the back porch. It's a gorgeous night."

I nodded with my back to him. "Sure, in a minute."

"Forget it," he said.

I turned to him. "I wish I could."

"What the hell does that mean?"

"I wish I could forget your temper tantrums, Rusty. I wish I could. God, how I've tried."

He shook his head. "I apologized."

"I know," I said. "I know."

He took my hand. "Come on, you can fold laundry later."

Together we walked out to the backyard.

Excerpt from Lillian Ashford's Journal
New Year's Eve 1961
Twenty-one Years Old

This was the year everything came together and then fell apart.

The summer started with Him as I wanted, as I knew. This summer held the most beautiful minutes of my life. Being near Him was the only time I wasn't lonely—in my whole life this was the only time I wasn't lonely.

I want to find the moment it all fell apart—but it must have started at the beginning—what brought us together and what tore us apart were threaded together in that one day when we were planning to meet His friends from Alabama who'd gone on a Freedom Ride. He picked me up from Tech—I'd just finished exams in May. Of course I knew these Freedom Rides were dangerous—but I only knew it in theory, just something I saw on the news. We were going to greet the bus in Montgomery—show our support with a group of friends. But by the time we got there, the beatings had already happened. The highway patrol had abandoned the bus, let it ride into Montgomery where a mob beat the riders. It was and is the most terrible thing I have ever seen. How can, Oh, how can humans do this one to another?

Nine

It was two in the afternoon when Sadie and I crossed the Alabama state line. Sadie drove behind me, and on our cell phone headsets we'd talked our way down I-85 through Peachtree City, Newnan, and LaGrange and into Auburn. Our conversation only barely kept me from dwelling on Rusty.

His fury was infrequent, but blazing like the burst of a flame in a bonfire when gas is thrown —quick, hot, and then subsiding. In the beginning of our marriage, I'd just put this anger into the "hotheaded Calvin" category. He didn't hurt me when he got mad; he didn't hit or call me foul names. Yes, he threw things, and sometimes he let out a stream of curses that I didn't know could be strung together, yet . . . when the anger was over it was as if it had never happened. As if the kind man didn't know the frenzy-mad man.

But of course I knew and lived with both men.

"So," Sadie asked, and I could hear Alison Krauss on her CD player, "how did Rusty take the news about this trip?"

"Fine. Of course he didn't want me to go, but he understands."

I didn't fully comprehend why I lied to my best friend, but I knew it had something to do with someone not understanding an event he or she doesn't normally see. Like trying to explain viewing a ghost or hearing voices—the only human you'd want to share this with is one who had seen and heard the same thing. Even I doubted my knowing, in the same way someone might disbelieve an after-death experience.

There were swaths of dark land within Rusty that only I have seen, and I can't explain them to anyone who has viewed only the beautiful landscape. We all have a cavern and an abyss inside, I told myself.

"God, it's so hot," Sadie said into my headset. I agreed.

The Alabama summer sun wasn't a kind friend; it was a clinging, damp, overly needy companion that followed me through the landscape. Heat shimmered through the pine trees, moving in waves off the pavement. My car pumped the air conditioner in vain. My hands slipped on the leather steering wheel as I turned off the exit onto College Street and into Auburn. We'd decided to stop and say hello to Lil on the way to Bayside.

"Sadie," I said into my headpiece, "I'm going to hang up now in reverence as we pass the War Eagle Club."

Her laughter was loud and full of memories. "Fine, I'll follow you to Lil's."

I drove toward the low concrete building on the right, slowed, smiled, and honked, as did Sadie. The broken sign out front was exactly the same as it had been twenty-five years ago, announcing the band for the weekend. The side lot was composed of dirt and generations of college students' spilled beers. I was sure alcohol was the glue preventing the parking lot from disintegrating. A short bus was parked in the lot; the words *NO DUI/War Eagle Club Shuttle* were painted on the side. They hadn't had that bus twenty-five years ago.

I slammed on my brakes and made a quick right into the dirt. Sadie laid on her horn, barely missing my back bumper, and she then drove up to the Arby's parking lot to make a crooked U-turn and return. I stood waiting for her, leaning against my car, the heat nestled in between my shoulder blades and pressing as a hand on top of my head.

Sadie jumped out of her car. "What are you doing?"

I nodded toward the building. "Let's have a beer."

"No way."

"Come on, just one."

She laughed. "That is exactly what you used to say to get me to come out with you when I'd have a test or project due. Just one, you'd say. It was never just one."

"It will be this time."

"I bet it's not even open. Ours are the only cars in the parking lot. It's only four in the afternoon. What will they say when two women in prissy sundresses and sandals come walking in for a beer?"

"I don't care. Do you?"

"No," Sadie said, "I don't care, and thanks for reminding me that I don't care."

We picked our way through the parking lot, stepping around cigarette butts, empty Jim Beam bottles, crushed beer cans—college, exactly. I pushed open the red-painted wooden door and stood still, waiting for my eyes to adjust to the dim light, my nose to the rank odor that had once been the aroma of a good night out. If I closed my eyes and didn't look at my body, or my face, or my outfit, I could feel eighteen, invincible, my entire life ahead of me with wide-open possibilities that I didn't even bother to think about because at that moment I was along for the wild ride that was preadulthood. It had been a time when only the absolute present mattered: what band was playing, who stood next to me in the crowd, a test grade, a touch, a kiss—all so important.

"May I help you ladies?" a deep male voice called from inside.

Sadie pushed me from the lower back, nudging me into the bar area. I emerged, blinking. "Yes, we'd like two Bud Lights, draft, cold."

He laughed. "A little early, but I think I can accommodate."

He must have been twenty-one to be serving drinks, but he looked much younger—which was the obvious and awful thing that happens when you get old: You think legal adults look like toddlers.

I sat on the sticky bar stool, and Sadie sat next to me. Neither of us spoke as the dark-haired bartender poured the beer. As if in agreement, we spun around and surveyed the room. Posters advertising beer, vodka, bands, parties, and even cigarettes were taped crooked to the chocolate-colored panel walls. The stage was in complete darkness, and the tables were scattered in a random pattern.

Sadie spoke first. "This is a time warp. Nothing has changed. So weird. But then again, I've never been in here when it's empty."

The bartender placed our beers in front of us. "You been here before?" he asked.

"A long, long time ago," I said.

He squinted at me. "Then you must have been an infant."

"No," I said, blushing and thankful he couldn't see me clearly. "We were here in the eighties."

"Oh," he said, and I imagined him going back, back, back in time to before he was born and he couldn't grasp the concept.

Sadie took a long sip of beer. "Those were the days of scrunchies and leg warmers, of kegs and Mick Jagger and—"

"Stop," I said. "You're freaking him out."

He laughed. "No."

He walked off to clean the tables at the back of the room, and Sadie and I sipped our beers in silence. Finally she looked at me. "You two—you and Rusty—never came here together. It was always us girls."

"He didn't like to go out with me when I was in a crowd or with other people. He liked for us to be . . . just us. I thought that was so sweet. So damn sweet. I mean, he wanted me all to himself. He must have really worshipped me."

"Funny how we get confused about what's love and what's freakish control."

"Exactly," I said, and swallowed my urge to cry with a long, cold swallow of Bud Light.

Sadie, as she always can, heard the sadness in my voice anyway. "I'm sorry. I didn't mean it like—"

"No, it's true. I thought all those ways of keeping me to himself were his ways of loving me."

"Change of subject."

I stared at Sadie for a moment. "I think Hutch will be in Bayside, Sadie."

She placed her mug on the counter. "You think?"

"Well, he said he would go because he's

finalizing this exhibit about the '60s Women of the Year and he wants some last-minute facts about Mother. But I told him it wasn't a good idea, that I'd tell him whatever I found out."

"Finalizing the exhibit? You really think that's what he's finalizing, Ellie?"

"Yes, I do. He has a girlfriend. I'm actually stunned he doesn't hate me. For God's sake, we haven't spoken in over twenty years, and the last time we did talk . . . it wasn't good."

"Ellie . . ."

"What?"

She shook her head. "You're a wise, grown woman. I don't have to give you advice. Hell, you're the one everyone goes to *for* advice. There's nothing I can tell you that you wouldn't tell yourself."

"Exactly," I said.

The hum of the air conditioner was all we heard until we set our mugs down, empty. "Let's go see Lil and get on to Bayside," she said.

I nodded, dropped a twenty on the bar, which was overpaying, but I knew college students weren't good tippers. We hollered good-bye to the bartender, and he shouted out, "Later," as if we'd return to hear the band that night.

"The thing," I said to Sadie, "that strikes me right now is how awful and dark this place is and was and yet . . . didn't we have the best times here?"

She paused at the door, and her gaze settled into the dark room. "Yes."

"So it doesn't always have to look good to be good."

"Maybe someone should have told us that what it looks like doesn't always have everything to do with what it feels like."

"Yeah, and who would that have been?"

"Not our parents." She placed her arm around my shoulder and we walked out the door, squinting into the sunlight.

The aroma of Lil's apartment was a combination of soap and mixed-up perfume—too many girls sharing a single small space. Dishes were in the sink, but the living room was clean because I'd given Lil a warning I was coming to visit. She sat on the couch with her legs curled up underneath her bottom like a comma. Her hair was pulled back in a headband, her curls falling free down her back and over her shoulders. The bronze streaks in her hair, which were scattered misplaced threads, were a gift from my mother—a gift given unknowingly and yet one Mother often mentioned, as if she'd sacrificed something of great value.

Lil's face was unadorned, and my heart squeezed at her simple beauty, at the many ages she had been and would be with and in that face of hers. The curves I knew better than I knew my own, as I've looked longer and harder at her eyes, her mouth, her slanted eyebrows, than I have ever stared into my own mirror.

We, Rusty and I, hadn't ever discussed or planned our family. We weren't the type to sit down and say, "Okay, let's have five kids." Or one kid. I remember a time at a dinner party when someone asked Rusty if we were planning on having any more kids, and Rusty had answered that *we* thought one was more than enough. I'd nodded with the dull thought that I didn't remember any such conversation, but with a newborn I was too exhausted to even think about disagreeing.

Later, I'd asked him about that comment, and his response had been surprise, saying that he thought we'd talked about this, about how we wanted only one child, how we weren't the type to have a household full of screaming brats, and how we'd agreed that we were so lucky to have healthy, beautiful Lil that we didn't need to take any more chances. "Oh," I'd said. Just "Oh." Then I'd wondered if I was crazy to not remember such an important conversation.

I'd decided, through the years, that Rusty wasn't exactly lying in that conversation, but that our discussions about other couples' kids and about children in general had led him to believe that this was how I felt.

Lil—Lillian Eddington Calvin—is the most

open portion of my heart; she is the most creative piece of my soul.

"Mom, Mom, Mom," she said in that exasperated tone of the eternally irritated young adult.

"Yes?" I smiled at her.

"Did you hear anything I just said?"

"Yes, you said that chemistry sucks, that Billy Morton got a DUI, that you hate your new roommate who took Indie's place while she's at home over the summer . . ."

"Oh," she said, and smiled back at me. "You just weren't . . . well, talking back."

"I was listening," I said. "And just absorbing all the sounds of you."

She rolled her eyes, but her smile remained. "So, I guess enough about me. Me. Me. Where are you headed with Aunt Sadie?"

Sadie had gently excused herself with the excuse that she wanted to go to Toomer's Corner and buy a T-shirt for her son from J & M Bookstore. Although she wasn't Lil's aunt, because Rusty's brother Matt was far from active in our lives, living in Memphis, Sadie has been Lil's "aunt" since the day Lil was born.

"I'm finally going to stay in Ms. Birdie's guesthouse on the bay. You know she's been inviting us to for ages. I'll be spending a few days—or maybe a couple weeks. I haven't decided."

"Wow. That's not like you."

"What's not?" I asked as I wondered how my

daughter perceived me—what is "like me" and what is "not like me."

"You know, not deciding. You always know where we're going and why and for how long." She shrugged. "That's all I meant."

I reached over and took her hand. "This is different."

"I know," she said, and didn't pull her hand away, which made my heart grow larger. She glanced at a poster of the Auburn baseball team, their schedule posted at the bottom of the torn paper.

"How's Chad?" I asked, gesturing toward the poster. Her boyfriend was the starting catcher for the team.

She smiled now, and then she released my hand to make a wide gesture of open arms. "Great. Just great. I hate that he's at that stupid Cape Cod league all summer—but . . . he's great."

I leaned over and gave her a long hug. "I need to get on the road, but Lil, I'm only about three and a half hours away. Please come visit me if you have a break from class or want to get away. We'll head over to the beach or something fun."

She nodded. "Okay." She paused for a long time before she finally asked what she must have wanted to ask all along, because the question was rushed, soft, the way she asked or said the things that were important to her. "Are you okay?"

"Yes."

"You're not just saying that to make me feel better?"

I kissed her cheek as Sadie opened the front door as if she'd been standing outside listening, waiting for us to finish our conversation, which she probably was. She carried a J & M bag and entered the room. Her usual entrance was boisterous, loud, full of light, and she'd toned down her enthusiasm for us.

"You ready to go?" she asked.

"Yep." I stood and stretched. Lil rose also, hugged me again.

"I love you," I said.

"I love you, too." For a moment she didn't let go.

And even as I walked to the car and then drove toward Bayside, I didn't let go of her, of that simple, complicated love.

Excerpt from Lillian Ashford's Journal
New Year's Eve 1961
Twenty-one Years Old

We found His best friend in the road, bleeding and unconscious. We took him to the emergency room, where the nurses and doctors were scared to take him because he was black. A Negro, they said. My rage was so intense that when it was all over, when the hospital took His best friend, when we left and began the drive home, I shook. He took me in His arms that night, our love-making was something I never knew it could be—it was all of me and yet I was empty of anything but my need for Him.

Yet His wounded pain followed us this entire summer—He blamed himself for not getting to Montgomery on time; I tried to soothe and heal this guilt in Him, and I thought I had. I believed I had.

On the night of the Jubilee—the night when all is forgiven, when new

*beginnings are offered, we made love
at the edge of the bay, and I thought
He had forgiven Himself.*
But I was wrong.

Ten

Day slipped into night, covering me in comfort, loosening the knot that had been my gut for the past months. Sadie and I were on the guesthouse back porch. Her eyes were closed as she leaned back on the rocking chair. "The knot is gone," I said.

She answered without opening her eyes. "What knot?"

"The one that had replaced my stomach."

She sighed, this long sound of exhaled air and relief. "I hoped for just that. I just hoped."

We'd arrived at Birdie Worthington's Summer House in the evening. The bay houses of Bayside, Alabama, stood stalwart *against* time, hurricane, development, and too many visitors' admiring eyes, and yet they stood *with* tradition, family, and beauty. The houses are scattered as pearls sewn along a wedding dress hemline down a thin, miles-long road born in Bayside and then extending parallel to the bay's coastline. I had a nagging sadness when I thought about how I would never know all the beautiful stories in each summer home, about each life that lived on the water-blessed street. Gates and hedges hid most of the homes from sight, and as Sadie's car slowed, I wondered what she was doing, as she seemed to be turning into a nest of shrubs and magnolia trees. And then I saw it—the hidden driveway. I slammed on my brakes, skidding in behind her, and I assumed she was laughing at me.

I stopped the car and absorbed the beauty. All the houses were situated so the rear of the house faced the street. Birdie's house was white with shutters of pale blue set against the siding like ponds of water against tumbled white clouds. Covered porches surrounded the lower level of the house—swings, rocking chairs, and plants so abundant that they flowed outward and upward throughout the entire area. A hand-painted and crooked sign was propped in the dirt next to the walkway: SUMMER HOUSE.

We parked and Sadie exited her car, waving to an identical but much smaller home to the left. "There's your guesthouse." Then she pointed to the Summer House sign. "And I made that when I was twelve years old. Mom found it in the attic last year and put it out."

"Oh," I said, beauty stunning me into silence. "I barely remember this place."

"I know, because you only came once, and that was with your dad. It always broke Mom's heart that this home wasn't part of her lifelong friendship with your mother."

"I don't get it," I said, just as Birdie came out to the porch, welcoming us with her warm smile, a cold sweet tea, and a long hug.

"You've finally come here, Ellie. Oh, finally. Your mother is looking down on us, smiling, I'm sure. Welcome to my summer home." Birdie's accent was so thick, it was as if it were drenched in both butter and cream.

"Well, you're sure living one long summer." I kissed her cheek.

After dinner and one too many glasses of cold Chardonnay, Sadie and I sat on the back porch of the guesthouse, quiet.

Sadie reached over, touching my knee. "Get some sleep. We'll talk tomorrow. I'm going over to Mom's so you can have this place to yourself. Are you sure you're . . ."

"Okay alone? Are you going to ask if I'm okay alone?"

"No, I know that you are."

And she was gone into the night, and I was alone.

Not lonely, just alone.

I entered the guesthouse and allowed it to surround me as wrapped arms holding me. I walked back to the single bedroom, where my suitcase was open on the hardwood floor but still packed. I dug around for my PJs and toiletries, entered the white-tiled bathroom to wash my face, brush my teeth—all the functions one does before bed no matter where you're located or where you've run. For the first time in months, years maybe, I fell onto a bed without anxiety.

There was a gentle rapping on the door, and I believed it was a branch or a foraging animal, but then I heard the voice through an open window.

"Ellie."

My name crawled into sleep, tenderly awakening me. The clock read 4:10 A.M. I went to the door, and there was no fear in this, although at any other time, in any other place, my name and a knock at four in the morning would cause panic.

Sadie stood on the porch in mud boots, a T-shirt with a faded Crawfish Joe's logo, jeans shorts, and a baseball cap. The overhead light fell onto her exposed skin. She held a pair of bright pink Wellie boots and another baseball hat. At her feet there was a cooler, a spearlike stick called a gig, and a fishing net. I stared at her, absorbing all these sights in the slow-motion way of one who wakes to another world.

"A jubilee," she whispered, holding out her palms as if whatever this jubilee was, it rested in her hands.

"Huh?"

She leaned down and picked up a thermos to pour a cup of coffee into the top, then handed it to me. "Caffeine. Now go put on a pair of shorts and your ugliest T-shirt, and I'll explain as we walk."

I did as I was told, blurry. I slipped the baseball cap onto my head, the boots onto my feet, and then I swallowed the coffee. Together we carried her paraphernalia toward the bay as she explained. "This is it. A jubilee. It's here for you; I know it. Everyone else will think it's for them, but I know it's for you."

"I'm still confused. I'm sorry. Can I go back to bed?"

"Could it be any more perfect? It's a sign. It's a gift."

"What?" I squinted into the darkness, as if this could make shapes come alive.

"You have no idea, do you?"

"No."

"This is when a mystical world appears, when weather, wind, and water come together exactly right. The entire town will run to the water now. There will be so much sea life to catch that it won't be able to be caught."

"I don't think I get it."

"You will. Grab the other side of the cooler." She gave me directions, which I obeyed without question. We reached the water's edge, where other people had arrived before us. The bay was a blue and fading bruise against the night sky. The crescent moon sent only the thinnest line of reflected light onto the surface of the water. I stood at the bay's edge, wearing Birdie's mud boots, which were too small, and my toes went numb crushed up against the tip of the rubber. I didn't care one bit because I was immersed in the middle of an enchantment I'd never experienced and hadn't known existed.

There were the shadows and solid bodies of people up and down the shoreline, half-lit in the night: supernatural. Children's voices called across the water with squeals resonant with such wholesome and utter delight that I could imagine the echoes were what heaven sounded like in the middle of the day. Sadie stood next to me, and in words wrapped in laughter, she explained how to gig the flounder and then net the crabs crawling at my feet. We had an Igloo cooler behind us, denting the marshy sand with its weight.

"What's going on?" I asked.

"All of them—the shrimp, the flounder, the crabs—they're all coming up for air. Somehow, for reasons that take a scientist to explain, the oxygen level at the bottom drops too low and everything rushes to the surface."

My eyes adjusted and I saw a sacrifice of the sea in such abundance that I was sure I was fantasizing. The flounder swam over one another, almost seeming to creep up the pilings of the dock. The crabs scurried toward the shoreline, three deep in places. The shrimp were translucent in their panicked rise to the surface. Each creature was in total disregard for the others. They, each and every one, were fighting for oxygen and attempting to leave their life-giving bay to do so.

"All they're trying to do is come up for air," I said. "Poor things, they're in a panic."

Sadie whispered into the night, "Come on. Let's get this thing started. Only take as much as Birdie can eat and freeze, only to the top of that cooler."

"You know," I said, "when we were driving in from Mobile, I noticed that some of the businesses were called Jubilee this or that. I get it now." I stood still and quiet.

Sadie poked me. "Come on, girlfriend, why're you just standing there?"

"I don't get this. . . ."

"It's overwhelming until you let yourself fall into it. It's nature's gift. It's not something you have to understand, silly. Get moving. We don't know when it'll be over or when we'll have another. You have to grab it when you have it."

I waded deeper into the water and watched this miracle: fish coming to the surface, ready to be trapped. The flounder's scales reflected the scattered flashlights; the laughter and "camaraderie" of strangers echoed across the water. There was no competition because there was enough for everyone. There was more than enough. Even the crowd at the water's edge could never catch or hold what came to the surface.

A teenage couple bumped into me, and the girl was squealing as the boy told her to "gig it; just spear it. You can do it." She tried and laughed and held on to him all at the same time. I reached down, gigged a flounder, lifted it, and stared. I touched the scales; its life squirmed below my fingers.

Sadie and I netted crabs, screaming and yanking at the one that snatched the end of her T-shirt. I held my hand out over the water and stopped.

"What is it?" she asked.

"The water," I said. "Look. It's not reflecting the light; it is the light. Moving light. Water-light."

The crab released, dropped to our feet, and scurried into deeper bay, safe for the moment. "It is," she said. "You're right." She dipped her hand into the water and allowed the light to run through her fingers, dripping onto her shirt and shorts. "Wow."

"Is this real?" I asked.

"Of course it is."

"It feels too much, like more than real. Like life will never be the same after this." I paused before I told her, "You know, Mother wrote about this."

"About you?"

"No, about a jubilee. I had no idea what she was writing about—she saw it as an omen of her new beginning, of a fresh start. That she would be with the man she loved forever. It was their beginning."

"That's what a jubilee is. Mom can tell you more about it, but it has something to do with letting go and with forgiveness, too."

The sweet salt-smell born deeper in the bay rose to the surface as we inhaled the unseen. Standing in the water surrounded by fish and crab and shrimp, I sensed a presence next to us, an appearance I hadn't felt all night—one I knew. I looked up to see *his* face: Hutch, standing next to Sadie and me, looking down at us as if we were mermaids or something even more mysterious than that.

"You just never know what a jubilee will wash ashore, do you?" Hutch asked in this voice surrounded by and drenched in fascination.

In this simply mysterious night, in a moment of sheer surprise, I jumped to my feet and threw my arms around Hutch. A flashlight in his hand blinded me.

"Hutch," I cried in abandon until I remembered who I was—not an eighteen-year-old girlfriend swimming in the bay, but a married forty-something-year-old woman. We pulled back, quick shame filling my heart and face with blood as warm and light-stricken as the bay water. "Fancy meeting you here," I said with that hint of sarcasm I knew he'd hear.

"Fancy indeed." He motioned behind him, where a man sidestepped a small child to come to Hutch's side. "You remember Drew?"

"I do," I said. "Hey, Drew. . . ."

Old college friends, Sadie, Drew, Hutch, and I stood in the moonlit water.

Sadie walked closer. "Hutch, how are you?"

"I'm good. Running into you two." He shook his head. "A jubilee is a mysterious thing."

Sadie splashed water toward both men.

"You live here?" I asked Drew, whom I would not have recognized twenty pounds heavier and bald.

"Yes, I live here. Have since vet school."

"Lucky you."

He glanced at Sadie holding a cast net. "You catching any shrimp?"

"I was just about to show Ellie how to use it, but I'm a terrible teacher."

"Ah . . ." Hutch puffed up his chest in mock manliness. "I am a pro."

"I'm sure you are," Drew said.

"No, really, I am." Hutch held out his hand. "Let me teach you."

Sadie shook her head. "Show-off."

The net was nylon, pearl colored, with small silver gray weights sewn around the edges. When

Hutch threw it over the water, it was as if a full moon with a tarnished outline settled into the bay, sinking beneath the surface to surround the school of shrimp. He raised the net and dumped a squirming mass into the bucket. "Wanna try?" he asked.

I shook my head.

"Come on. I'll show you. This is a small-cast net; you can do it."

"I don't think I'm very good at stuff like this."

"Won't know until you try." He stood behind me and put his hands on mine, instructing me how to anchor the net's rim to my left wrist. His pulled me back to rest, and in my mind's eye I could see every bend and line of his body, warm and familiar; I sank back into him. Then, grabbing the net halfway down, I held the bottom between my teeth. It tasted of mud and salt and all that forms this earth. He took my right hand and we threw the net over the water like a Frisbee, but it bunched together, landing in a mass of tangles on the water's surface, slowly sinking. Together we laughed.

"Told you," I said.

Hutch lifted the net. There were two shrimp; I took them in my hand. The sleek, pale white, almost see-through bodies slid between my fingers. The whiskers tickled my palms and wrists. I tossed them into the bucket.

"So," he said. "Can we meet sometime tomorrow and make a plan?"

"Absolutely. . . ."

He lowered his voice as Drew and Sadie talked to each other. "Listen, Ellie. This is about my job. About the exhibit. Nothing else at all. I want to make this the best work I've ever done. This is the last thing I have after six months of work on the show."

I nodded. "Okay, just let me talk to Birdie and find my way into this thing."

"Great."

I'd almost forgotten about Sadie and Drew when Drew's voice announced, "We'd like to catch up, but we've been sent on the cooler run."

"Cooler run?" I asked.

"Not the kind you remember," Drew said. "This is an empty cooler full of ice for the fish. Good to see you, ladies." He tipped his baseball hat, and Hutch and Drew were gone as if they'd never been there.

For long moments Sadie and I stared at each other, and then together, as if on some cue, we broke into laughter. I allowed the amusement to flow out of me, through me, and into that bay that was more moving light than moving water.

This was how the jubilee seemed to work; people came into and out of your space and water and then disappeared. You couldn't feel them come, and you didn't see them leave. A stranger turned into a friend and then vanished. Sadie and I sat on top of our cooler at the water's edge —no longer trying to stay dry.

"I feel like I'm part of the bay," I said in a soft whisper.

"We are. Tonight we are." Sadie ran her fingers over the top of the water, shrimp scattering.

There are nights when the places and spaces in a life shift, disassemble, and then reassemble in the sliver of time between moments, between seconds. There are people who enter or reenter a life, who touch you or laugh with you in the middle of a jubilee, in the midst of nature's sacrifice, so that your life couldn't be the same even if you wanted it to be so.

That is what happened that night.

Excerpt from Lillian Ashford's Journal
New Year's Eve 1961
Twenty-one Years Old

After the Jubilee, our love was stronger than any force of man or nature. Or so I'd believed. We swam in the ocean and sat around the pool drinking ice-cold gin and tonics with slices of cucumber floating on the top. We held hands and made love—or I was making love, I don't know now what it was for him. And this is the sorrowful part. When I look back, I hear myself in the middle of it telling Him of my love, and I know now He never used that word: love. He said "adore" and "What would I do without you?" and "best friend," but never that, never love. How could I have not noticed that He never said that word?

Because here is why: I felt Love in every touch, in every motion, in every look. He couldn't stay away from me for even an hour, finding me at the shoreline or the dinner table or the back porch of the Summer House. Our skin made of magnets that drew together with and against our will. How could that not have been love?

We whispered and sat in the back of bars and secret meetings to help the movement, our fingers entwined, our skin moist with need.

I want to write everything we did and said all summer, but I can't—my heart can't bear to write what will never be again.

Which means we now come to the worst part of the year—the sorrowful part—the part that butts up right next to the joyful part; one on top of the other.

Eleven

Morning came in a quiet whisper; even after the chaos of a jubilee, there was the calm of simple beauty. An undemanding day began with sun, warmth, and water sending cloud-filtered shafts of soft light across the bay to a backyard swathed in live oaks old, gnarled, and ancient. I cradled my coffee cup, walking through the grass and opening the gate with the letter *W* forged into the iron where moss and leaves were caught in the curls of the scrolling. My bare feet hit the wooden pier worn smooth by storm, wind, and running feet. I reached the end of the dock, where there was a grill, a white wooden table, scattered chairs, and lanterns with half-burned candles.

The plank boards shimmied under my feet, and I turned to see Sadie walking toward me, holding a coffee cup. I waved with my free hand. She reached my side and hugged me with one arm; no words were spoken. I sat on the hanging swing, patted the seat next to me.

She sat and we listened to the water, to the screeching gulls, to the boat motors we could hear but not see. There were a few bloated flounder floating on the surface of the bay; dead shrimp at the edges of sand and water; a crab floating past us as the tide moved to sea—jubilee remnants. Finally I spoke. "Thank you," I said.

"For?"

"Bringing me here."

"You're welcome. Please stay as long as you need. Mother says you can stay for a hundred years."

"Hmmm . . . a hundred years. I don't think that's long enough. Can you ask for more time? Please?"

Sadie laughed softly, as if it were a secret that we're able to laugh. Then I saw Ms. Birdie standing at the back gate. The feeling was disconcerting, as if you realized a car was following you or someone had tapped your phone. She waved at us as we walked up the cobblestone path back to the house. Grass and moss grew between the stepping-stones, anchoring them to earth as surely as if they'd grown there. The heat was already intense, and sweat ran down my back below my tank top.

We reached the stairs and she smiled down at us. Her dark and gray hair, which she'd stopped coloring years ago, was pulled back into a barrette. Her face was naked of makeup, showing her years of wrinkles set and formed around her sweet spirit. "Breakfast is ready," she said as a greeting.

"Oh, you didn't have to cook for us," I said.

She laughed. "Of course I didn't. But I wanted to do so. And don't be thinking that I'll do it every morning now."

We entered Ms. Birdie's kitchen—a conglomeration of so many colors of yellow, I thought the sun had taken residence. The countertops were pale vanilla ice cream yellow, the walls canary, the cabinets bright. The sweet smell of eggs, sausage, and something spicy I thought was cilantro filled the room.

Birdie placed the dishes on the kitchen island. "Dig in."

We filled our plates to overflowing and sat at the round glass top table in the corner of the room.

"Are you happy you moved here full-time?" I asked.

"Yes. Yes, I am. You know, I moved here right after Lyle passed away." She stared off and her eyes flashed with tears, and just as suddenly were dry. "He was devoted to this place, but he didn't ever want to live here full-time. He was so tangled in the Atlanta world." She swiped her hand through the air. "So, the jubilee . . . did you enjoy it?"

"It was amazing. Truly. I've never seen anything like it," I said.

Birdie opened a drawer so full of junk, I didn't know how she found the pink pad of paper she

129

placed on the kitchen table. She licked the end of a pencil (I've never understood why people do this) and started to make a list. I wanted to laugh—a soul mate, I thought—but I didn't make a noise, I just watched and listened.

"So here's the explanation," Birdie said. "No one is really sure why the jubilee happens, but there are certain things that *must* happen."

She wrote, *The Bay of the Holy Spirit*, and then she looked up at me. "That's what the Spaniards called this Mobile Bay. And this is the only place you can find a jubilee."

"Mother," Sadie interrupted, "there's another."

"Doesn't count," Birdie said, and leaned toward me. "They say it happens in Tokyo Bay, but it doesn't matter because you can't eat the fish or shrimp. Not a real jubilee if you can't partake of the sacrifice."

Then Birdie wrote, *1860*. She didn't look at me when she said, "That is the year of the first known jubilee, but of course there were ones before that one. Just because something isn't known doesn't mean it isn't or wasn't already there."

Then she wrote: *1. There must be an eastern wind.*

"Now," she said. "The old ones, old like me, and the small children—the innocent—can tell you the air feels like silk. The softest silk. We feel it coming. I was gonna say something last night, but, well . . . I wanted to wait for it to

130

really be here. You seemed too sad to tell you that something that wonderful might happen and then it not happen. Because you see, sometimes all the right things can be here and the jubilee still not happen."

Then she wrote and related the following points as if she were a teacher and there were a blackboard on the wall:

2. *There must be a low water-surface temperature.*
3. *There must be an incoming tide.*
4. *Predawn.*
5. *Summer.*

"All these things *can* add up to a jubilee, but they don't have to. Scientists say it's the low oxygen level that makes all the shrimp and fish and crab run to us, run to the surface, to sacrifice. But they can't explain why sometimes it's just a shrimp jubilee or just a flounder jubilee. That's the thing of the Holy Spirit—you can try and explain it all away, but then there are some things that have no explanation, that are mystical and perfect, things that no list in the world will make clear." She looked directly at me now, her face young. "Life . . . exactly the same. Some things are beyond our understanding."

I nodded, because that was all I could do.

"Some people use this list to remove the

mystery. But there is only so much that can be proven. Why would anyone, ever, want to remove the mystery of life?"

"Not me," I said. "Never. Not that. What's left without the mystery, the unseen?"

Birdie smiled at me as if I were twelve years old and I'd brought home a straight-A report card.

"When I was little," Sadie said, "I used to have bad dreams about being lost underwater where I couldn't find my way up or down, and I couldn't breathe."

"Unfortunately that sounds like my real life," I said, attempting humor but missing by a million galaxies.

"I always woke up before I burst through the surface of the water." Sadie smiled at me. "But, you—you'll burst through any day now."

"Yep." And the laugh was real. "And get caught in a net."

Birdie laughed in that quiet, sweet way of a mother. "Most swim free," she said as she ripped the paper off the pad and headed for the trash can.

I touched her arm. "Can I have that?"

"The list?" Birdie asked.

Sadie laughed. "Remember, Mom, Ellie is obsessed with lists."

I poked Sadie with my foot. "That's not why. I want it to remind me that some things can't be explained with a list."

"I couldn't have said it better myself." Sadie stood. "In fact, I think I have said that."

Birdie picked up our plates, but Sadie intervened, clearing and washing the silverware, then dropping it in the dishwasher while listing the activities I could participate in in Bayside after she left that morning. Then she turned to me. "You'll be okay."

"Of course I will. What with all the multiple activities you just told me I could do here. . . ."

She smiled that cute, closemouthed smile she's always had—the one where she is trying not to smile, but it wants to break through anyway. "You're making fun of me," she said.

"Never," I said. I looked to Birdie, my heart near my throat. "Do you mind if I ask you a couple questions about Mother?"

"Isn't that why you're here?" Birdie's laugh filled the bubble of silence, and she leaned against the counter, her hands behind her back holding the counter, her smile wide, as if whatever question I had would be received into that grin.

"I don't know how to do it or where to start."

"Just start like you did that time you were afraid to jump off the high dive in second grade." Ms. Birdie lifted one hand in the air, a movement of blessing.

"Yeah, well, Sadie pushed me. I didn't exactly jump."

"Precisely."

"Well, I found Mother's journal. In it she would summarize her year—no real details of names or exact dates, just a summary of the year that had passed with her goals for the next year. She believed if she wrote her wishes down, they would all come true. And oddly and terribly, most of them did come to pass. But one. Except for one."

"Him," Birdie said.

"Yes. Who is it?"

Birdie looked away. "Him." She sighed and turned to the window, staring out at the bay for the longest time in an emptiness that held the answer I wanted and needed. When she did turn back to me, her smile was gone, her face closed and placid. "Don't go there, Ellie. It's not important anymore. It's something that she went through a long, long time ago. She reconciled it into her life and moved on. I can tell you whatever you want to know about the activities we did that summer, our help with civil rights, but not Him. I won't talk about Him. Why didn't she burn that journal?"

"I think she meant to hide it or put it away. But, Birdie, the life she wrote and the life she lived were two different things. The life she lived was one of organized perfection, but the life she wrote was one of brokenness and heartache."

134

"I'll tell you the story of that summer, but not His name. That's not fair to Him or to your father."

"I read some of what happened . . . but it was a summary more about her broken heart than the circumstances."

"We'll talk." She nodded in dismissal, and I realized that as much as I wanted and needed to hear the story at that moment, I would have to wait. She took my face in her hands. "It is amazing to see you. I am so glad you're here. You have always been—for me—a daughter."

"Don't make me cry," I said, but laughed and kissed her sweet cheek. "Thank you so much for having me."

Together, Sadie and I walked across the wet grass to the guest cottage. I stopped halfway, turned to her. "You know that list your mother just made? It's the same as my marriage. But different."

"How so?" she asked, shielding her eyes from the morning sun with her palm.

"That damn list. You know, everything that *must* be there was there—the solid families, the jobs, the health—a Norman Rockwell painting of the Appropriate Atlanta Family. The 'must' list was made, checked twice like Santa would do. Same friends, same Lutheran background, same college, similar upbringing, stable parents. It was all so 'Appropriate.' The checklist went on and I filled in every box." I made check marks in the air as if the list were hanging in the wet atmosphere.

Sadie reached for my hand. "Oh, Ellie. What do you think is wrong, then?"

It was time, I knew, to put words to my fear. "I can't peg it down. It's just this awful feeling in the pit of my stomach, like someone is twisting my stomach in an Indian burn move we used to do to each other's arms as kids and then at the same time they're grabbing my throat, clenching down. Rusty walks in the room and I want to walk out. He touches me and I pull away. It's awful. I have no idea what's happening to me. I feel . . . sick."

Sadie stopped on the grass. "I know."

"What do you mean, you know?"

"Seriously? I see you almost every day. I've watched you disappear into some kind of quiet cocoon. I've watched Rusty yell at you and seen you make excuses. I've watched you stay home when you should go out. You think I don't notice?"

"I just haven't found the words to talk about it, but I know something is wrong with me. I can fix this. If I can just get quiet and figure out what's wrong with me, I can mend it."

She stopped me and placed her hands on either side of my shoulders. "Nothing is wrong with you. Sometimes enough hurt is just enough hurt."

I started walking again and then looked to Sadie. "I've never spoken those words out loud. They've been stuck inside me. Maybe now the sick feeling will go away."

We walked in stillness, and then when we arrived on the porch she picked up Mother's book where I'd left it on the front porch table. The journal fell to the porch, open and face-down, the pages scrunched up like a woman who has fallen in her tulle party dress, the pages flattened and folded, pressed outward and inward.

She grimaced. "Sorry."

I leaned down to pick it up, but she beat me to it, handling the book with care and brushing off the moss and leaves. A page fluttered out, yellowed and folded into a square, settling into a crack on the floorboards. We both stared, as though the paper might rise and fly away, as if it were a living thing.

"This is a picture I drew when I was nine years old." I picked up the paper, unfolded it, and pointed to the top right corner to show Sadie the date.

"What is it?"

"It's called *A New Cinderella*." I handed it to her.

"It's a crayon drawing of Cinderella leaving the castle with a suitcase. You even threw the shoe on the ground." She pointed. "In the dirt. It's like she said, 'Forget it, I'm outta here.' "

"I hated the picture in the book where Cinderella is sitting by the fireplace ashes, crying and crying and crying. I remember thinking, You're a grown-up, so why don't you just pack up and leave?" I stared at the picture for a moment. "I know I wrote a story to go with it, but I don't know what happened to it."

"And your mother kept this and only this drawing of yours?"

"No, she has an entire box of old drawings, but this one was with her journal. I've tried to find the box, but I can't. I asked Dad to look for it."

"I wonder why she put only this one in her journal."

"I have no idea. It was an odd collection of things she kept locked up."

"What else?"

"This poem," I said, and handed her the torn paper. "Well, it's not really a poem—but I think it was meant to be, or it's part of something else."

She took it and read. When she looked up, she said, "Whoever wrote this loved her deeply."

I took the poem. "I know. That's why it's confusing. I mean, how does a feeling like that just go away? Just leave?"

"That's what you're trying to figure out, isn't it?"

I nodded. "Partly."

"Take your time. Talk to Mother and call me a

hundred times a day or not at all—whatever you need. Flirt with Hutch."

"I wasn't flirting with Hutch. I don't know how to flirt anymore. And trust me, he probably still cringes at my name." I paused. "Is there a way to thank you?"

"Take care of yourself," she said, and she hugged me good-bye, leaving me with Mother's journal and my own choices.

The New Cinderella
By Ellie Eddington
Nine Years Old

The Torn Poem Found in Lillian Caulfield Eddington's Journal
"What You Feel Like"

You feel like . . . all I've ever wanted.
You feel like . . . my meant-to-be;
my all; my destiny;
my happy ending.
You feel like . . .my love story
that changed the world.
You feel like . . . what I've always
wanted and didn't know I wanted.
You feel like . . . the one I've been
waiting for.
You feel like . . . the destination to
which all my roads have finally led.
You feel like . . . you live in my heart
and you'll never leave; home;
my forever.
You feel like . . . what they all call love;
the lock and the key—both.
You feel like . . . my softest place; mine;
my gentlest heartbeat.
You feel like . . . you've embedded
yourself into my soul.

You feel like . . . the reward for making
  it this far, being this brave.
You feel like . . . the answer to every
  prayer—every one.
You are . . . . . . the reason for
  everything that came before.

Twelve

Bayside seemed built for just this: complete loss of time and self. I don't know if that was the founder's goal, and I didn't have to give in to it, but this gift was there for the taking. I resisted the making of *the list*. Oh, the list—I wanted to make one for all the things I needed to accomplish that first day. I should have taken the pen out of the house just like you'd remove the liquor bottle from the house of an alcoholic.

During that morning, I'd called Rusty four times, but there wasn't an answer.

I hung up, frustrated, and then drove into town. The unexpected and sudden appearance of the bay from behind trees and street signs took my breath away when I rounded a corner and wasn't ready for the sight of sunlight's sequins spread across the waves.

I thought of Mother in Bayside and then in Atlanta; I wondered what those two very separate lives looked like. I needed to see her on Peachtree Street, at the Piedmont Driving Club, in her house wearing a dress with a ribbon around the middle. A timeline would help me—an artistic timeline built of her days in '60 and '61. Other people found meaning inside their words, but I discovered mine within drawing. I'd get to the bookstore and dig up a book about Atlanta history, but my first stop was to buy the vegetables Birdie asked me to pick up at Pappy's Vegetable Stand, which Birdie told me was "the absolute only place to buy fresh veggies."

The minute I met Pappy, I smiled; he was older than anyone I'd personally known.

"Hey there, missy," he said. His white hair stuck out in opposite directions, his top pate bald and shining. The wrinkles embedded in his face seemed to hold a story I might one day be lucky enough to hear. There was a scar that ran from the corner of his right eye, like a lightning bolt, to the temple of his right ear.

"Hey, Mr. Pappy," I said. "I'm a friend of Ms. Birdie's and she told me this was the only place to buy veggies."

"Ah, yes. She would know."

I chose two fat tomatoes, a cucumber, and an onion the size of my fist and then dropped them into the brown paper bag. I handed money to Pappy. "You making an onion, cucumber, tomato salad today?"

"You got it," I said.

"My wife, now, she knows how to make a salad." He stared off at the sky and then smiled. Birdie had told me he would do this—mention his wife in one way or another, even though his wife had passed ten years before.

I nodded. "I would bet her salad is better than mine," I said, and left the change on the wooden counter, which was really just a piece of plywood over two ancient kegs.

He counted slowly and then smiled. "Thanks."

"See you tomorrow." I gathered my bag.

"Tomorrow for sure," he said. "Now you go do what you need to do today and have a good one."

I wanted to turn around and holler at him, "If I knew what to do, I'd do it." But I just grinned.

I parked on the side street next to the bookstore and realized I could've walked the two blocks. I entered the store, and the dusty-sweet smell of books filled my senses. I was back in elementary school, hiding in the library during lunch hour because this meant I wouldn't have to make conversation with the smiling, beautiful people. Back then everyone in the school seemed to know what it meant to be a happy person. I only knew how to have twisted knots in my stomach, which prevented me from opening my mouth and speaking anything that made any sense. Of course I got over this by junior high, but not without a sheer and utter force of will pushed from behind by Sadie.

The bookstore was quiet and buzzing in the

same way as a forest: Activity is evident, but done in the most quiet and efficient of ways. Throughout the room, bookshelves were pushed together like an overcrowded party of shy people waiting for someone to talk to them. I wound my way through the aisles, passing a few women picking books off the shelves, reading the back blurbs. I mumbled, "Excuse me," and made it to the checkout counter, which was empty.

I stood on my tiptoes and scanned the room for someone who looked like a salesperson, and then a teenage girl popped up from behind the counter, startling me into laughter. "Hey," she said. "You need some help?"

"I didn't see you." I leaned over the counter to see from where she'd actually emerged.

"Filing . . ." She pointed to the floor, where papers were arranged in piles.

"I'm looking for a book on Atlanta history, especially the time from about the 1950s through 1970s. With pictures," I said.

"Hmm . . ." She stared off past me, toward the street. Her long dark hair fell down her back, and her blue eyes squinted against her thoughts.

"Got it," she said, walking out from behind the counter and motioning. "Follow me."

She walked and talked at the same time, and I held in laughter because she was obviously an adolescent with her jaunty step, swinging hair, and cut-off jeans, but she talked and acted as if she owned the store. "We have a variety of history books, but I'm thinking the best for what you need is called *Atlanta and Environs*. Then we also have these lovely picture books that are done for all the places in the South. We have one from the 1960s, I do believe. If we don't have it, the library will, or I can order it for you." She stopped in front of a shelf with piles of large books; she pulled one off the shelf. "Here."

This book was as big as the family Bible, and I opened the cover. "Thanks," I said.

"No problem. You can browse through these if you want." She ran her finger over the spines of the books as if they were children. "And if you have any questions, my name is Ashley and I'll be at the front desk."

"Okay, then, Ashley. Thank you."

I tried to imagine my Lil or Sadie's daughter, Kenz, speaking like that, but I couldn't. I had always bit my tongue so as not to tell Lil to eliminate "like" from her vocabulary. I chose two books and then noticed the pungent aroma of oil paint, which I followed like a perfume to the back room to hit upon treasure: an art store connected to the bookstore.

The building itself was a cat curled in sleep, bending around the corner so that the bookstore resided on the main street and the café and art store on the side street. I placed the books on a café table and then browsed through the art supplies to find poster board and paper for a timeline. When Hutch's voice filled the room, I was already smiling.

He wasn't saying my name, but I knew his voice. "Ashley, you're late for swim practice. Come on. Your dad is gonna kill you and then me."

Then Drew's voice. "Ashley, come on."

I stood with this smile, this silly, openhearted smile, while wearing no makeup, ratty shorts, and a tired linen shirt. They didn't see me until they turned to the door, motioning for who I assumed was Drew's daughter—the jubilant Ashley.

Hutch's smile was genuine and free; it always had been. He stopped short, laughing. "Well, hey, Ellie. I was just about to call you."

His voice made my heart skip that little extra beat it once had when he'd said my name. Sometimes a voice can change a heartbeat.

"Hey, Hutch." I pulled at my shirt as if this could change the fact that it had a large tomato stain from Pappy's stand on the middle of my abdomen. "Seems like I keep seeing you at my absolute best."

"Of course you look your absolute best. You couldn't look otherwise."

Ashley walked up now, a bag with dolphins etched in the nylon flung over her shoulder.

"You know each other?" She looked between her dad, Hutch, and me.

"Yep, old friends," Hutch said.

"Very old," Drew said.

"Cool," she said, turning into a teenager. "I'm late, Dad."

Hutch pointed at the books I held. "Research?"

I nodded.

"Anything from Birdie?"

"Not yet," I said.

"Hey," Drew said. "We got to go, buddy."

Hutch turned to me. "See you later, right?"

"Yes," I said.

Hutch walked off with his large steps and his languid movements, and then he was gone. I wanted to remember, really remember, why we'd said good-bye. Of course, as with anything, there was a culmination, an event plus another event, moments adding up, but when had the end begun?

It was after my three-week standoff when I did what I was trained to do every week: I called Mother on Sunday afternoon. She'd been brusque and short with me. "What is it, Mother? Are you okay?"

"I am just so worried about you and Hutch."

"We're fine. Why would you be worried?"

"I mean, seriously, Ellie dear, do you realize you're dating a boy from a trailer park who has been in jail? Have you really given this any thought?" Anger was on the ragged edges of her words.

"Yes, I realize that. I love him. And it was juvenile detention, not jail. And it wasn't his fault. Really, Mother, do you think he chose where to grow up and who to grow up with?"

"Do you actually think he could be part of this family?"

"Stop it," I'd said. "Stop."

"I've lived longer, Ellie. I know the consequences of loving someone inappropriate. You make a decision and then you have to live with it. That's how it works. Don't you see how awful this could be? Can't you see?"

"No." I'd started to cry but stopped myself. "This is crazy. Stop it. Hutch is the most amazing man I've ever met. Stop making him into someone else."

Then Mother started to do something I'd never heard her do before: She began to weep. Words came between sobs. "Don't hate me, Ellie. It's not me you should hate. I just know." She caught her breath with the skill of a catcher in a baseball game: victory the only goal. "He's not right for you."

A small meanness in me pictured Mother crying tearless and dry, her sobbing in sound only. "I don't hate you, Mother. But I do love Hutch."

My anger consumed me for days. I called Dad and asked him to please have a talk with Mother, to please make her understand that she was wrong and hurting me by not believing in me or my decisions. Dad proceeded, in his calm voice, to tell me that talking to Mother would do no good and only anger her further. Really, he told me, just let it go. She'll get over it.

But she didn't. She would call and plead with me, leaving long messages on my machine about my future and my decisions, about how I didn't know how one decision would change everything. I chose the cruelest of all the actions I could have: no action. I ignored her, and I knew, of course, that this would make her insane. The anger between us grew as a living and fanged animal we couldn't get past. Finally she called and apologized with words as dry as parched soil, telling me, "I hate for you to think I've been cruel. I will now respect you enough to let you make your own mistakes."

That was as close to any apology as I would ever receive from her, and I made the choice to forgive because I knew there wasn't anything more to come from her. That half-worthy repentance was the best she knew to do.

Soon after that, Rusty approached me in the library. Did my wandering start with Mother's words or with Rusty's invitation?

Where does anything begin?

I remembered these things as I wandered in and out of the art shelves, choosing papers and charcoals, pencils and paints. My pile on the café table grew beyond my two books until a woman came to ask if I needed any help. I glanced up at her and thought I must be looking at her the same way I would if she had woken me from a nap or dream—confused and bleary.

"Help?" I asked.

She smiled as if she'd seen this look before—lost in the art store. She was tiny; a sandpiper was what came to mind. She had deep brown hair like feathers brushing the wind, a small mouth chirping her greeting. She held her hand out to shake mine. "I'm Leona Riordan. Can I help you with choosing any supplies?"

I shook her hand. "Hi, I'm Ellie. I think I've got it all. Guess I just need to check out."

Leona, who appeared to be my age, talked quickly but with that southern accent that made it seem as if she were talking slower than she was. "Well, you must be an artist."

"Or an artist wannabe," I said.

"No, no." She grabbed some of my supplies and headed toward the checkout counter, talking over her shoulder. "Like a writer—if you're writing, you're a writer. If you're painting or drawing or . . . whatever . . . you're an artist."

"Are you?" I grabbed a handful of charcoals and followed her.

"An artist? No. A writer. I try."

I followed her.

"Research?" She pointed to the books.

Only, I thought, in the South is such nosiness considered polite, and even I wasn't used to people asking so many questions. "Yes, that sweet girl Ashley helped me find these."

"Our best employee by a million miles," Leona said.

"I knew her dad in college." I reached for my wallet.

"So, you're visiting Bayside?"

"Yes, I'm staying at Birdie Worthington's for a while."

"Oh, yes. I've heard you were there. Vance Hillman told me."

"Who?"

"A local. The pharmacist." She pointed out the window, as if I should know exactly where the pharmacy was and who Vance Hillman was.

I shrugged.

"Oh, he doesn't know you. He heard it from Bitsy, who is friends with Birdie's caretaker."

I laughed out loud.

"I know, I know," Leona said. "Small towns."

"It's great, I guess. In a way."

"Well, welcome from Atlanta. Glad you're here."

"This is an amazing store. It's brilliant to combine art and books. They're so simpatico."

"Exactly." She smiled at me in such a way that I believed I'd said the right thing to make us friends forever. "That is exactly what I meant to do," she said.

"Oh?" I asked. "You own the store?"

She pushed buttons on the cash register, entering my purchase into the computer, the tip of her tongue sticking out of the corner of her mouth in concentration. "Yep. Own it. Worry about it. Pay for it. Run it. If only all our employees were like Ashley." She clicked a key on the computer. "Okay, your damage is two hundred twenty-five dollars and sixty cents. You like the nice paper, don't you?"

"The thick cotton. Yes. It's my favorite." I handed her the American Express card.

I waved good-bye, and when I reached the front of the store, I stopped to read the poster propped up against the window: BOOK FESTIVAL. MOBILE. SUNDAY. The festival would be in three days. I smiled.

I carried my bags to the car and threw them in the backseat, avoiding the vegetables. I tried one more time to call Rusty, but once again I got only his voice mail. What saddened me most? That I was relieved to get his voice mail.

Excerpt from Lillian Ashford's Journal
New Year's Eve 1961
Twenty-one Years Old

Which means we now come to the worst part of the year—the sorrowful part—the part that butts up right next to the joyful part; one on top of the other.

We said goodbye, promising our love: I vowed to graduate and return to Him. We kept our plans a secret so when my best friend came to me to tell me of His betrayal, of the truth, my heart was torn apart. The sickness that comes with heartbreak is like no other sickness known to man because there is no cure for betrayal.

None.

I took Mama's car and told no one where I was going or why and I drove to Bayside. It was October and the record-breaking cold temperatures kept the streets empty. When I reached His trailer, I burst through the door and found Him alone, reading. When

I confronted Him, he admitted everything Birdie had told me—His betrayal
was true. And yet He told me that it
was before He loved me, and He'd
been with others when He was with
me but He said that once he knew He
loved me He never touched another.
Now He loved only me. It was the first
time He said the words "I love you."
And then He added the part that
matters most. "And you alone."

I know these are only six random
words said in a row. Just words "I love
you and you alone." Yet they are
words that mean everything.

Thirteen

With late afternoon light moving across the bay, I'd taken a swim. Climbing out of the water and onto the dock, I saw Ms. Birdie standing at the back fence, a glass of wine in her hand. I waved and she smiled in return. "Come on over," she hollered.

I waved at her. "Coming." My hair dripped like new rain onto a white linen cover-up. "How was your day?" I hugged her.

"Wonderful. How was yours?"

"Amazing. It's so peaceful and wonderful here."

"Good." She poured me a glass of Chardonnay, and we walked out to the screened-in porch. "I only treat myself to wine when I have guests. So you're just an excuse." Her voice was hidden underneath laughter.

I smiled. "I'll be any excuse you need."

Her words then came from far off—from the past to the present—words about Mother and her love. "They first met at the very end of summer in 1960. Your mother immediately figured out how to come back the following summer by getting a job at our club pool as a lifeguard. They didn't know each other well until that summer of '61, when the world turned inside out. You can't really know. I understand that you can read about it and watch movies and listen to the historians, but you can't really know because you weren't there."

"What do you mean?"

"The civil rights movement. Here. In Alabama. The world was on fire, or about to be. Nothing was real and everything was too real. We were caught up in it—your mother and I—in a way that is still hard for me to understand."

"Mother wrote about a sit-in and the Montgomery Freedom Riders' riot, but not in detail."

"Oh, we wanted to change the world. We wanted to make everyone see the error of their ways. That summer, we became involved with a group here in Bayside, and when you're doing something like that, you're so on fire, filled with such purpose and righteousness, that everything is heightened—desire, hate, joy, sadness—it's as if each emotion stretches itself out inside you. Want becomes more than want. Hate becomes more than hate. And she fell in love during this time. With him." Birdie looked away but continued talking. "He was beautiful." She shook her head. "He is beautiful."

"Ms. Birdie, is he alive?"

"Oh," she said, and smiled at me. "Most

definitely alive. But that isn't what we're talking about, is it? If you want to know the story, you have to listen to the story, okay?"

"Okay." Yet I wanted to blurt all my questions.

"We were in our own world that summer. We plotted and talked and schemed and went to speeches. Although we lived in Atlanta, this house has always been my family's summer home, so we lived here from May to September. Your mother came to live with us. We traveled to Birmingham and Montgomery and told my parents we were going to concerts and movies while we were in bars and honky-tonks."

"Tell me about one time. Just one."

"The Freedom Ride." She shook her head. "That was the most awful one. He had gone to pick up your mother from Georgia Tech and go straight to meet the bus in Montgomery, but they had a flat tire. I was there—in Montgomery —waiting for them. My parents thought we were all going to the beach for the day—May twenty-first. Do you know anything about that ride?"

I shook my head. "I'm embarrassed to say so, but I know very little. I can't believe Mother never . . ."

Birdie held up her hand. "She tried to forget those days the best she could, and sometimes to forget the bad parts we have to forget the good parts." She paused and then took a deep breath.

159

"You see, the Freedom Rides were designed to test the desegregation laws. Whites would sit in the back and blacks in the front. Everyone knew there would be trouble . . . everyone. Even we did. God, we hoped there wouldn't be, but there was."

"How?"

Birdie shook her head. "Oh, how I hate that these stories are lost to your generation." She laughed then. "I sound like an old fogy. Anyway . . . the governor promised to protect the bus."

"From?"

"Oh, Ellie, from the KKK, from snipers and angry southerners and mobs. They say the bus drove over ninety miles an hour down the highway, being protected by the Alabama Highway Patrol . . . and get this . . . right when the Greyhound reached the Montgomery city limits, the highway patrol left the bus alone. At the bus station—where we all waited—mobs beat the riders. The police didn't even stop them. Even the newspeople were attacked."

"Mother was there?"

"No, see, that's the thing. Not right away. They were late. When they got there, the beatings were done. Over. What she did, Ellie, was help get the men to the hospital. The police wouldn't even help with that. She was an avenging angel, taking men to the hospital, screaming, hollering, helping."

"You must have been enraged." My wineglass was empty by this time.

"Enraged and alive. Yes, we were the most alive we'd ever been. I didn't realize my best friend had fallen in love. That is how it was then—we all were in the throes of passion, and I didn't notice what had happened with her. Now here is why: He was wrong for her." Ms. Birdie stopped and stared at me. "He was wrong. And I thought she'd know better, know that it couldn't work, that it wouldn't go anywhere past a steamy Alabama summer. She was a smart woman— the smartest one I knew—and how could she fall for a man so wrong?

"We were in a bar after the riot, and it was when I looked over at her that I knew she loved him. Not the way you have affection for a puppy or the way you are fond of the beach or your best friend, but the way you love when there is nothing else in the entire world but the man in front of you: his touch, his voice, his presence. The way you desire when there is nothing you wouldn't do for him. She was gone and I saw it too late to help her or stop it."

I leaned forward. "Why was he so wrong?"

"He was a wild child. A boy in a man's body, loving everything and everyone. Your grandparents—her parents—would never have approved of him. He would have never become a real part of the family. She would have had to separate from all she knew to be with him. He lived a . . . different life."

"Well, maybe that's why she loved him."

"Of course it's part of why. But this was not a man you marry. But she gave her heart to him. When I realized her heart was gone, it was already too late for both of them."

"How?"

Birdie stood now. "That's enough for now, Ellie. Because here is the thing—you need to take what I've told you and find out if it's enough."

I heard my mother's voice in this woman. "I know. Mother always told me that I wanted too much, that I was too much, that with me—everything was too much. You think you can want too much?" I asked. "Really want too much so that nothing is ever enough?"

"Of course." Birdie held up her hand. "Absorb this, Ellie. It's a lot to know and feel and understand. Can't it just be enough to know that your mother loved and lost?"

"I don't think so," I said. "I really don't. But I'll try. But maybe, Ms. Birdie, maybe you can also want so little that you settle for something that isn't even close to enough."

"Maybe so, Ellie."

"Will you tell me a little bit about the legend of your Summer House?"

"Legend?" She laughed and shook her head.

"Rumor is more like it. They say that when you stay at this house the truth is revealed, that you see your life in a new way and understand. I just think that being by the bay does that. Nothing magical. Just a searching people usually come here with. But don't tell anyone I think that—it's a nice legend to pass down. Really that's what happens—rumor becomes story becomes legend. So let's just keep it that way." She winked at me.

"I'm in."

I walked across the lawn to the guesthouse, hearing Birdie's question in the rustling palm fronds. *Was it enough?*

Mother lost; everyone does. When she was in love—when anyone is in love—the heart cannot imagine its loss. When I first met Rusty, I of course could not imagine hurt or loss would come from his words, which had then been nothing but sweet.

Rusty had come to me when I'd been studying for a history exam. The air in the library was full of that beautiful combination of dust and paper. I sat in a cubby in the far back corner, my hair in a ponytail, a pencil under the rubber band. I was lost, reviewing the Battle of Waterloo, when Rusty Calvin tapped my shoulder. "Hey, cute Ellie."

He always put the word *cute* before my name;

it made me blush. I knew him. Everyone knew Rusty. He was from the frat-boy party set; the Atlanta elite; the boys who allowed only the most beautiful into their crowd. He'd dated well over half my sorority, and I knew him only on the periphery of my life. He needed a pencil. He needed to know if I had the outline to chapter 4 for the test. I gave him both.

He studied in the desk cubby next to mine, and when I folded my papers and books, when I packed my backpack and stood to leave, so did he, casually inviting me to the party he was on his way to at that moment.

Crossroads. We all have them, and they are so often seen only in hindsight. This was mine. Hutch was out of town for the intramural rugby team he played on, and I'd finished studying. Nothing complex. Just that, and then everything changed.

Being inside the beautiful group was never a goal; it was never an aspiration or even a need. Then the seductive need to be there again and again crept into my life. The slow ruination of my relationship with Hutch was never about diminishing feelings for him. Or maybe it was, but I claimed it wasn't. I'd said that our distance was only about me spreading my wings, wanting to do new things and have new friends. Newness.

Rusty was patient during his relentless pursuit of my heart. He said he accepted that I loved another and that he just wanted to be friends. He invited me to every party, every road trip, every lake excursion, saying, "Come on, just as friends." He invited; he flirted; he presented gifts and trips and heartfelt conversations of depth that I haven't had with him since that time. Of course he knew there would be that day, that very moment, when we wouldn't be just friends, and he waited.

I understand that decisions are a combination of smaller choices built up over time, so to say that I suddenly and unexplainably kissed Rusty Calvin at a band party is partly true and completely not true. What is true—I did not mean to hurt Hutch; I did not want him to drive past the lawn party and see me with Rusty; I did not want to "cheat." But I did, and Hutch saw, and he hurt.

Excerpt from Lillian Ashford's Journal
New Year's Eve 1961
Twenty-one Years Old

I know these are only six random words said in a row. Just words. "I love you and you alone." Yet they are words that mean everything.

How was I to believe Him? I huddled cold and empty in that trailer and let His words soothe me into believing Him, calm me into understanding that He did love me and me alone.

When we were curled and warm in his bed, He then told me the most horrible thing: He was leaving for a year. That He must. That He'd signed on with the Peace Corps to go to Africa for one full year.

He said that He needed to do this—He understood this about Himself—that He had to try and make a difference in this world and what He'd done that past summer had only hurt people. He begged me to wait. He told me to wait for Him. To just believe and wait.

But how was I to believe Him? First He betrayed me and then when He'd wooed me back to His bed and THEN, He tells me He is leaving again?

How was I to wait?

How was I to believe Him?

Fourteen

Back in Birdie's guesthouse, I sat in the large chaise longue facing the window that opens to the backyard, offering a view to the bay, and was absorbing Birdie's story when there was a knock. I stood and rubbed my eyes as I walked toward the door.

Hutch stood on the front porch, scraping mud off his shoes onto the side of the patio wood. "Hey." He looked up and smiled, embarrassed. "Didn't think you were here; knocked a couple times."

"Hey." I smiled back at him. "Sorry, I didn't hear you."

"Oh," he said, standing there, his arms swaying back and forth almost as if he had a child he was swinging. Then he clapped his hands together. "I hope it's okay that I stopped by. Drew and his family had some fund-raiser thing in Mobile and there's no Braves game on tonight. . . ."

"Last resort option?" I asked, but smiled. These are the words he'd used with me when he'd left me. I didn't think I'd remembered this—their saying seemed cruel at the time, and I'd buried the memory—Hutch standing on an apartment walkway, telling me that he was tired of being "the last resort option" when I'd done everything else I wanted to do. I had vehemently disagreed even as his words rang true. I'd said this to him: "That's not how I feel." And he'd replied, "Well, that's how you act."

Hutch just stared at me now with his smile still present, but no words.

"I was kidding, Hutch. A joke."

He nodded.

"Wanna come in?" I held the door open.

"No. Probably not. But you want to go get a beer at Crawfish Joe's?"

"A beer?" I laughed. "I haven't had a beer in . . ." And then I stopped as I remembered Sadie and I in the War Eagle Club. "I haven't had a beer since the War Eagle Club."

"My God, woman. Are you serious?"

"A few days ago."

"Is this something I want to know about?" He laughed, rubbing the stubble along his chin. "Seriously, a couple days ago?"

"Silly story . . . I was with Sadie in Auburn last week. Just let me change clothes real quick, and we'll go," I said. "Is that okay?"

"Sure."

I motioned for him to come in. "It'll take me two seconds. Come on in."

He hesitated and then entered, but stood at the

entranceway. I walked toward the back of the house and hollered, "One minute; I promise."

I decided on a spaghetti-strap sundress and simple flip-flops. I loosed my hair from its ponytail, but didn't brush it. I put mascara quickly on my eyelashes, pink on my lips, and then I stepped out of the bedroom. "Let's go," I said. "Ready?"

"Sure am."

French doors were flung open so it felt as though we were inside and outside at the same time. But these weren't like any French doors I'd seen—these were pieces of plywood with panes of glass crooked and fragile in the middle. The room was crowded and too warm.

"Fancy, ain't it?" Hutch asked as he guided us to a table near the bar and against a wall.

"Very," I said, sitting in a rickety chair. "Just like I like it."

"I don't believe you," he said. "I have a feeling you're used to something much different."

"Doesn't matter what I'm used to; it only matters what I like."

"Sit," he said in a quiet voice. "I'll go get us two beers."

When he returned he held two cold beer mugs and menus. "Thank you," I said. He sat across from me and we perused the menus in silence, and then I closed mine. "I'm not that hungry."

He looked over the top of his menu. "You gotta get the hush puppies. Just try them."

I nodded in agreement. "Okay."

He shut his menu and ordered for both of us and then said, "Tell me all about yourself, Ellie."

"Well, what do you really want to know? You know the facts—I've been married to Rusty for twenty-two years. We've lived in Atlanta—same house, even—for that whole time. Lil is nineteen already and in summer school . . . that's about it, really." I finished the facts just as our food arrived.

"No way is that about it. I saw the article in the *AJC* about your art. Tell me all about it." He popped a hush puppy in his mouth and leaned back in his seat, smiling.

"Yes, that. Well, about ten years ago I started. It all began because I wanted to surprise Mother with a painting of her garden. She was obsessed with her garden."

"Oh, I remember."

My heart reached for Hutch, and I looked away to continue. "Anyway, I was trying to paint the entire garden, but found I would get consumed with a single flower. And that is how it started, and I'm still going. I guess I could never stop, really. There are more flowers than I could ever paint. Even when a flower looks ordinary, close up, each one has something extraordinary about it."

"Just like you." His voice was quiet and true. He meant those words; he'd said them before.

"That's . . . sweet."

"Did you take classes or anything like that?"

"I did. I've taken a few at the art institute. But the truth is I've always done it for myself—for the time in the studio and attic. For how I feel when I'm painting. That's why—for how I feel when I'm doing it. Don't get me wrong—the art show was one of the most special nights of my life and also the last night with my mother—but mostly I paint for the feeling I have when I'm with it."

"I know."

I tilted my head.

"I get that way with my projects . . ."

"Like this one? The Woman of the Year project?"

"Exactly. So, did you find out . . . anything?"

"I did." While we ate hush puppies and drank our cold beers, I told Hutch what Birdie had told me.

"Wow. Your mother."

"I know. I can barely imagine this woman."

He picked up the empty basket. "So." He smiled. "You weren't hungry?"

"Should we get more?"

"Yes." He motioned for the waitress and two more beers, and another basket landed on our table.

His hand rested on the top of the table, his left leg stretched out. He smiled at me with that same genuine affability that had opened my heart all those years ago, an unmeasured kindness that filled empty places. The languid humidity of the outdoor restaurant loosened that tenuous grip on the disappearing line between past and present.

"That's all I know," I said. Silence pulled us apart, the gap that had closed between us opening wide again.

He laughed and I looked at him; his gaze was across the room. "Old Tommy-boy over there." He nodded toward a man at the bar. "Has no idea what he's getting himself into tonight."

The bar was a long scarred piece of plywood with one too many layers of shellac covering the surface, as if the shine could possibly make up for the cheapness of the wood. A woman who was my age, beautiful in the way of entitled coastal southern girls, held a shot of tequila. She smiled at the man next to her. I couldn't see his face, but he must have been smiling.

"What?" I asked.

"That guy. He's messing with the most dangerous of all pathologies." Hutch leaned forward and whispered in my favorite voice of his, "the good girl come undone. The most dangerous of all women in the wild."

"What?" I wanted to touch Hutch, but I didn't.

"That is Bitsy Morgan—a friend of Drew's. I met her the other night. The ultimate good girl. You know—straight A's in high school; graduated from University of Alabama with honors; never did drugs or got in any trouble to speak of; married her college sweetheart and gave him four beautiful blond-haired blue-eyed children. Joined the Junior League, heads the PTA, jogs her three miles a day, teaches Sunday school. That kind."

I sighed. "Doesn't sound scary to me."

"Ah, that's because you don't know the rest of the story."

"Seems to be my biggest problem lately."

He grinned. "Seems Bitsy Morgan has discovered that her sweet husband is sweet on more than just her. On more than just women, actually. So now, and only now, does this latent pathology come roaring to life."

"Meaning?" I did touch him then, but only the back of his palm, the place above his wrist.

"Like a sleeping cancer cell come alive with the proper catalyst, she will officially come undone here and now. With tequila."

I laughed too loudly, and both Bitsy and this man turned to stare at us.

"I need to be getting on," he said, pulling his wallet from his back pocket and dropping a twenty on the table. I stood and Hutch did also.

We were standing in the middle of the parking

174

lot, his car parked next to mine. "So, I'll see you around?" I asked.

"Of course. This was fun. Please just call me if you find out anything else. But I think I'll take a trip to the museum in Montgomery tomorrow and dig through old film files and see if I can find a photo of the ride . . . you want to come with me?"

A dome of silence fell over us, and I leaned into it, rested for a moment.

"Do you?" he asked with a grin.

"Yes, that's a great idea. And I'll try and get more names."

"Great. I'll call you in the morning."

He smiled, and then we hugged in this awkward way where we didn't know what to do with our arms, with bodies that had once come together with ease. "Bye, now," I said, and slid into the driver's seat. I waited and allowed him to drive out first because my hands were shaking.

Excerpt from Lillian Ashford's Journal
New Year's Eve 1961
Twenty-one Years Old

It is when I return home that the facts of His betrayal begin to worm their way into my soul like maggots eating away at my belief. I don't believe Him. I am frantic. He is gone and being without Him hurts all the way to the inside of my bones. How does someone not DO something when they hurt this way?

How does a broken heart wait for the man who broke it?

My belief in Him turned to doubt and then the doubt to anger and the anger to despair. I told myself that I would never again be the girl who believes in love when it isn't there. I will never again be fooled. Never, ever again.

This is what I believed: that His love was tepid water compared to my scalding need and desire.

I decided that I would love someone

safe who would love me back and not love anyone else.

A thing inside me closed. I almost heard it: a click like a lock. Then after that vow, after that promise and shutting off of my desperation, came the need to show Him how this feels; how it is and how it feels to know I am loved by another.

Last week at the Bradfords' Christmas party I found the chance: Redmond Eddington, who has been flirting with me for over a year, found me alone in the dining room. I moved, took his hand, and whispered in his ear that we should go for a nice walk outside, be alone for a while. This seduction in his Ford was quick and a little sad. After a girl knows what it is like to really make love, anything else is . . . empty.

Now it wasn't that it was bad or even unpleasant, just hollow. If I looked at him just right, it could be Him, I could pretend it was Him. But that wasn't what mattered to me. What mattered was that He would know, really know, where I was and what I'd been doing. Redmond and I returned to the party, holding hands, smiling in that way.

But this love-making had nothing to do with love, and everything to do with getting even. There was no victory in this. I hate myself for what I did. I hate that I slept with a man I don't love. I hate all of it.

And that is what I mean about becoming and doing something that awful. I can look at that girl who was in that car with Redmond and wonder who she is and why she is there. I, me, Lilly Caulfield Ashford, would never do that. Ever. Who was that in that car? A girl who came alive in the hurt and pain of losing Him to other women and then to Africa: that's who.

Fifteen

It was the hum of a lawn mower that woke me that next morning after dinner with Hutch. It had been a night of half-sleep as my body tried to find a place to rest after sitting with Hutch and feeling his kindness, as if time had never passed and yet a million years separated our skin from touching. Finally giving up on the elusive reprieve of sleep, I rose early, and Birdie found me on the dock. "Good morning," I whispered, not wanting to disturb nature or air or morning.

"Ready for breakfast?" she asked.

"Yep," I said, and then motioned to the bay. "How lucky you are to wake up to this." This was not a question.

"Very blessed. Now you can see why I left Atlanta, right?"

"Absolutely."

Together we walked back to her house, through the yard and back gate, and I thought how the mother I knew would never have left her beloved Atlanta. Yet the woman in the journal would have. Mother, once, had trusted in love, and yet I knew the woman who told me Hutch

O'Brien was from the wrong kind of family, the wrong kind of boy for me. How could I, she'd once asked, be with a boy from a broken, poor Alabama family when there was so much more for me?

I believe words have a way of working their way into a soul and forming that soul into a shape and vessel it might not have otherwise been. How many times can a mother tell a daughter what is and is not good for her and that daughter not believe it? But where did those words and beliefs come from in the first place—in the beginning?

There was a day when my mother didn't believe in inappropriate or appropriate love. There was a day—an amazing day and time—when she believed in only this: love. And when she stopped believing in that, she passed that disbelief on to me and into my life.

And maybe she was right—Hutch might not have been "right" for me.

Birdie and I sat at the kitchen table, and she placed a plate of scrambled eggs and sausage in front of me. We sat in silence, watching the chickadees nibbling at the seed in the bird feeder outside her window. I waited.

She smiled at me. "It wasn't enough, was it?"

"No," I said. "I'm not trying to be nosy and push my way into your life's story. I just want to know what you know about Mother. That's all.

How did he betray her? Why didn't they come back together when she came for him? What else did she do to help change civil rights?"

Birdie sat to face me. "After that summer of '61, life settled down. Everyone returned to their real lives—to college and families and reality. The summer seemed like a dream to everyone except your mother. I didn't know it at the time, but she went home plotting how to get back to him. When I told her . . . some things he'd done, she got in her car and went to find him. I never knew what happened that day, but when she came home, she was different."

"I know what happened," I said.

Ms. Birdie stared at me with wide eyes.

"She confronted him about whatever the betrayal was and he admitted it, but told her that whatever it was he did it *before* he knew he loved her. He professed his true feelings, but then told her that he had to go . . . and he asked her to wait for him. Then in her brokenness or heartbreak or anger—whatever you want to call it—she slept with Dad."

"I figured that's what happened—but you see, this man had already committed to the Peace Corps. He was out of college—older—and didn't yet want to get a job. He said he couldn't imagine putting on a suit and walking into a building every day, said it would kill his soul. So off he went."

"That was his betrayal? That's what she thought was betrayal?"

"No." She shook her head. "This boy . . . this man loved more women than just your mother. She didn't realize this about him; she didn't see or know that he . . ." Birdie paused, closing her eyes. "That he—in your generation's words—slept around. She thought she was the only one. When I told her, she was shattered in ways I didn't expect."

"You told her?"

"Yes . . ." Birdie released a long sigh, as if this word held more than three letters. "Ellie, please stop. This really is enough. Your mother loved a man who loved her. He betrayed her and then asked her to wait for him, and she didn't. She chose someone else, and here you are. It is the most common story of man—love and loss. There is nothing new in here for you."

"But there is—because there was something else. You just said it."

"Listen, Ellie, when a heart is hurting, it makes its own decisions."

"I don't want to be her, though. I don't want to shut down my heart and live a life of cold perfection."

"You think she lived with a closed heart?"

"In many ways, yes."

"We all make our decisions about what our heart can live with and can live without. She

182

made her decisions, and you can make yours."

Avoiding all conversation about my own life, I changed the subject. "Tell me more about the things you did that summer when your parents thought you were at the club or swimming pool."

"Ah—" She laughed into the word. She sat at the table again and patted it as if it were a child. "We didn't do anything to brag about. Most of our time we thought we were changing the world—and maybe we were, but only in the smallest ways. Remember, this is Alabama and we were smack-dab in the middle of the drama and fire. Martin Luther King Jr. George Wallace. Desegregation. It all seems organized and logical in hindsight—you can learn about it in school in a nice little timeline—but we were in the middle of chaos. We only knew to do what we knew to do—the little things, which we thought were big things."

"Like?"

"Sitting with our black friends at the lunch counter or walking them into the voter registration at Town Hall or standing with them while they used the public water fountain. The laws had changed, but the people had not."

"Were you ever in . . . danger?"

She smiled. "We thought we were. And maybe we were. But this is a small town and everyone knew our mamas and daddies, and no one was gonna touch us. After Montgomery we stayed local."

"In the end, though—you did make a difference. You did."

"We'd like to think so."

"Will you at least give me the names of the group y'all hung out with that summer? I promise I won't use your name or anything. I just want to see if anything rings a bell or if I recognize a name or—"

"It won't do you any good."

"Please."

"Please don't ask me again."

"I don't understand why his name is such a secret."

"Well, I don't understand why you so desperately need to know his name. So, let's just say we don't understand one another and let it go at that?" She had this sweet smile on her face.

Birdie cleared our breakfast dishes and placed them in the sink without rinsing before speaking again. "So, what is on your schedule today?" she asked as if we were never talking about Mother, as if the conversation we'd just had was in the distant past and I'd just walked into the room. When Birdie was done, she was done.

"Well, I'm headed to Montgomery with Hutch to look at old film in the archives."

The sink water splashed and the plates rang against one another like wind chimes as Birdie rinsed and placed them in the dishwasher. She turned and smiled at me. "Your old boyfriend. The boy from Linden?"

"Yes."

She turned around and then looked over her shoulder. "Oh, I forgot to tell you. Tonight I'm having a party to cook all the food from the jubilee. I've invited almost everyone I know."

"I'll be there," I said, and kissed her on the cheek on the way out.

I buckled the seat belt in Hutch's Saab convertible, a car that had definitely seen shinier days. The once dark brown leather was faded like an ancient saddle seat. The dark blue color on the outside was now a weakened sky.

Hutch looked over to me. "I know it's not the fanciest chariot in the world, but don't worry, old Bette has done just fine for me. She'll get us where we need to go."

"I never said I was worried." I slipped my sunglasses over my eyes and wrapped my hair in a rubber band.

"Ah, but I saw you give her the good once-over."

"Why Bette?" I asked.

"No real reason other than I like the name. Sounded . . . trusty."

I laughed. "Let's go, you."

He revved the engine and laughed. "Look at that, she's showing off for you."

"Go," I said, shaking my head.

The music, whatever we could find on his crackling stereo system, blared and blended with the outside noises: cars, horns, squawking birds, wind.

"No XM for you, huh?"

"What?" He leaned closer to hear me over the wind and music.

"Nothing," I said, and patted the top of his hand resting on the gearshift. He lifted one finger and wound it around my pinky. With Rosanne Cash singing the old "If You Change Your Mind," we held fingers. As we crossed the Bayside bridge into Mobile, heading toward Montgomery, a flock of egrets startled and flew over the car, a mass of wings and feathers. I sighed in contentment.

"You okay?" he mouthed.

I nodded and slipped my hand under his, releasing his single finger and taking the whole of his hand into mine as if it were the exact right and not exact wrong thing to do. He squeezed and then let go. I folded my hands into my lap, and for the two-and-a-half-hour drive we talked very little. The sun settled into the car, slipping into the cracks and empty spaces like syrup.

"Ellie . . ." Hutch's voice sifted into my consciousness, and I startled, opened my eyes.

"Did I fall asleep?" I straightened my sunglasses and stretched. "I'm so sorry."

"Why are you sorry?"

"It's just been such a long, long time since I've been that relaxed. I wasn't very good company, was I?"

"You're always good company."

We climbed out of the car, then Hutch put up the top and locked it while I tried to make some semblance of order out of my wind-whipped hair. "What first?" I asked as he walked toward me.

"The Civil Rights Memorial, and then we'll hit the library and see what we can find in the archives. Also, I thought we'd go see the bus station—the Greyhound bus station where your mother would have gone that day of the beatings." He pointed. "There's the memorial."

We moved toward it, and I absorbed its beauty the way one would a sunset or an opening flower. Water rose from the middle of a round black granite stone, flowing over names that were carved and radiated outward like many hands of a clock. The memorialized names were of those who had died defending civil rights. On a curved gray stone wall behind the table, Dr. Martin Luther King Jr.'s paraphrase of a Bible verse was carved into the granite: "We will not be satisfied until justice rolls down like waters and righteousness like a mighty stream."

"This is spectacular and . . . sad," I said, shaking my head. "I just don't understand why she never told me about any of this. It is so . . .

important. It's such a part of our lives now. I mean, we can try and forget it ever happened . . . but it did happen and it changed everything."

"Ellie, if you're trying to forget something or someone, the last thing you do is talk about it, especially to your kid."

Standing then in front of the memorial, I dipped my hand in the flowing water, ran my finger over a single name. "But she could've at least told me about this. . . ."

"Maybe she just couldn't separate *this* from *him*."

"Maybe so," I said.

The water sent a spray around Hutch's face and I reached up, touched the scar on his left cheek. He placed his hand over mine and leaned into it and then just as quickly released my hand. "Let's go to the bus station."

"Just give me a minute," I said, standing in front of the memorial. I began to whisper the names etched on the stone, names of people I'd never met, yet I still felt an odd and disconnected kinship.

Hutch sat on a marble bench and leaned back, closed his eyes, lifting his face to the sun. I stared at him for a few moments, allowing myself to drink in his face and body with the luxury of his closed eyes. I went to him and sat quietly. Without opening his eyes, he reached over and placed his hand on my leg.

My cell phone rang inside my bag, and in digging for it, I dropped my purse's contents onto the ground. Out rolled lipstick, a wallet, loose change, two Sharpie pens, and some crumpled receipts. I fumbled for my phone and the paraphernalia. "Hello," I said, not even looking at the screen for a name.

Hutch jumped up and ran after a rolling lipstick, and I laughed out loud.

"What's so funny?" Rusty's voice echoed through the line.

"Rusty."

"Yes, Rusty. Your husband." His voice was robotic.

"Hey."

"Where are you?"

"Montgomery."

"What the hell are you doing in Montgomery? Tell me it's because you're on your way home."

"No, I'm here looking up some information about Mother. I'm at the Civil Rights Memorial. I can't believe we've never come here. It's just beautiful. I wanted to see what I could find maybe in the library or—"

"Oh, God, Ellie, you've become completely obsessed, haven't you?"

"What?"

Hutch was walking toward me, holding out my lipstick in triumph. He bowed and handed it to me. "Thanks," I mouthed, and pointed to the phone.

"Okay," Rusty said in exhale. "I used the wrong word. You're not obsessed, but do you really think you needed to go look up something you already know?"

"I wanted to find a picture or article or something."

"Why?"

"For the exhibition." I started stuffing things back into my purse, avoiding Hutch's eyes.

"You're with him, aren't you?"

"Who?"

"Your old idiot boyfriend. I can't even remember his name. Huck Finn or some southern shit like that."

I looked to Hutch as Rusty's words crashed down on me like hail: cold and harsh. I shivered before I answered. "Yes, Hutch is here."

Hutch turned away at this and walked toward the memorial, standing with his back to me.

"Seriously?"

"Rusty, please stop it. Why did you call? Surely not to yell at me about doing research."

"I called because I miss you. Because I love you. Because I want you to come home. But obviously I'm an asshole." There was a click and then silence. And my only thought, oddly, was that with cell phones the recipient of a slammed phone never knew it was slammed. It's hard to slam shut a keypad.

I walked to Hutch and touched his back. He turned. "I'm sorry if this is causing problems for you," he said.

"This"—I swept my hand across the memorial and around our bodies—"is not what caused the problems. Come on, I'm hungry. . . ."

He nodded. "I know just where to go."

After lunch at a barbecue joint I would never have found with GPS or on any map I owned, I settled back into Hutch's passenger seat and groaned. "Okay, I usually don't eat that much in two days, much less one sitting."

"We still have a lot of work to do. I needed to fortify you for the rest of the day. Bus station first."

We pulled up in front of the now shut-down Greyhound station and parked. It was clean and sparse, and I could barely imagine the horror of what went on that day, the scenes of blood and fire and hell. We walked toward the building and stood in front of the brick façade, a pewter greyhound still poised on the top right of the building, stretching in its eternal leaping posture. A storyboard—orange, red, and white—stretched down the edge of the structure. We looked at every board, read every quote, and gazed at each picture until we reached the end of the story, which of course only started a new story not written on those walls.

We sat on a bench and I turned toward him. "Wow."

"Not much else to say, is there?"

"Hutch, tell me about your parents now. Where are they?"

He looked at me for the longest while, so I thought he wouldn't answer, and then he exhaled. "It doesn't—in some weird way—seem possible that you don't know everything about me. That you don't know . . ."

I looked at the ground as if I needed to study the cracks in the concrete.

"They both died six years ago, Ellie. Mother drank herself into oblivion, and Dad had a heart attack a few months later. As much as it seemed that they couldn't live with each other, the truth is he couldn't live without her."

I closed my eyes and leaned into his shoulder. "I am so sorry for you."

He placed his hand on top of my head. "I know."

After the silence ebbed away, we stood as if on cue and walked back to his car.

The archives room of the library was empty yet somehow still demanded hushed voices. Hutch spoke to the librarian while I wandered around and looked at the framed photos of Alabama dignitaries, mayors, and governors.

Hutch returned with a few rolls of film. "There's more than we could ever go through in one sitting, but I think I narrowed it down to the local and Bayside papers. If your mother would be in anything, it would be those."

"Okay."

He threaded the microfilm machine and handed me another roll. "You take this one."

I sat at the machine next to him, and together we scrolled for over half an hour before I stood and stretched. "Nothing," I said.

He looked up at me, grinned. "Don't give up so quickly."

"I'm not. . . ." I squeezed his shoulders and sat back down, scrolling through grainy black-and-white photos of that awful day when the Freedom Riders were beaten and left bloody in the streets. My heart rose up and stretched toward compassion.

I reached over for Hutch. "Oh, what humans do to one another."

"It's awful," he said, still looking into his viewer. "And worse is, we do it over and over again in different forms with different reasons. History."

"These images are awful."

"Just concentrate on looking for a little white woman. She shouldn't be that hard to find if she's in there."

Another hour passed and my legs ached, my

eyes burned. Leaning back in the chair, I stretched.

"Ellie . . ." Hutch reached out his hand without looking up. "C'mere."

I took his hand and bent over as he slid his chair to the side. I glanced at a grainy and fogged black-and-white photo of a white woman kneeling in the street next to a bleeding man. Above her there was another man, his hand on her shoulder, his back to the camera. She looked up to the camera with tears on her face, her mouth distorted with whatever angry words were flowing forth. Her hair was falling into her face and down her back. She wore a flowered sundress cinched at the waist but obviously covered in dirt and blood.

I took in a quick breath. "Yes, that is Mother."

"Thank you so much, Ellie. This is exactly what I needed to make a difference." He sat back in his chair and kissed my hand. "Exactly. There is nothing like a picture. You can tell someone the history, but to show them is fantastic."

I smiled. "Good."

After we made copies and returned the film, we were back in the car. "You want me to drive?" I asked. "I mean, I'm the one who napped on the way here."

"No, I like to drive. Sit back."

The highway shimmered in a bluish evening haze while the car filled with the sweet smell of cut grass and wet earth. "We have to get back for Birdie's party," I said.

"Yep, Drew told me about it."

"You coming?"

He nodded. When we hit the highway, a few fat drops of rain landed on the windshield and then splattered on my face.

"Rain," I hollered, laughing.

Hutch looked up to the sky. "It didn't look like it was gonna rain, did it?" He pulled to the side of the road, and then a deluge dropped from the sky with a furious force, as if the rain were meant just for Hutch on the side of the road, frantically pulling on a convertible top. When Hutch got back in the car, he was as soaked as if he'd jumped into the bay and then the car.

"Oh, you." I reached over and wiped his shirt. "You're drenched."

He looked at me and laughed. "That was not the first or last time that will happen. The hazards of trying to live with the top down as much as possible."

I shook my head. "You're crazy. You know that, right?"

"I do. But I hope it's in a good way."

With blacktop disappearing under our car, I turned in my seat. "Listen, I talked more to Birdie this morning. She said that after the bus beatings, they mainly helped locally with voter registration, lunch escorts, and such. But after

1961, Mother went home, married Dad, and . . . had me. So really this event might be all you can find."

"It's like this tiny slice of her life that she deleted."

"Exactly. I wonder if she ever told anyone."

Water dripping down his face, his hair wet with rain, he looked straight out the windshield. "I doubt it. Your mother chose what she did and did not want people to know."

"We all do, I think."

His face changed; a flinch. "Ouch."

"Huh?"

"You meant me."

"Oh, God, Hutch. No, I didn't. That's not what I meant at all."

"It was our problem, Ellie. It was what started . . . the end—me not telling you was the start of the end."

"But that's not what I meant right now. And it was just as much—"

"Stop. We aren't going to talk about this. It's been a perfect day." He smiled at me and looked back to the highway.

I leaned into his shoulder. "I'm sorry."

"Don't be. Please don't be." He placed his hand on my damp hair, and I was content. For that moment, I was content.

And maybe, I thought later that night, that is all we can ask for: moments to be content.

Sixteen

I stood at the window, watching as the crowd gathered on Birdie's dock in the twilight. Laughter flowed toward the guesthouse through the open windows and screen's spaces, and then into the living room, a comforting sound.

I opened Mother's journal and flipped pages to these words: "This is the year I met the man I will love forever."

Love. Maybe there should be a hundred words for that one word. It seems too complex a thing to write in four letters. We have it; we don't have it. We need it; we lose it. We win it; we want it. We weep for it; we let it go.

When I was with Hutch, I'd loved him so completely that I couldn't have imagined any other man entering my heart. We were complete in a simple way, just wanting to be near, our voices within range. Before cell phones, before texting and e-mail, we found a way to find each other in every spare moment between classes, obligations, and other friendships.

So our breakup was like ripping skin from bone.

●●●

All breakups are awful, just by definition—the word *break* defines this, as if it couldn't be anything but awful. And ours—Hutch's and mine —wasn't any different.

Rusty's charm had worked its way into my soul, and then there was this small part of me that wanted both—of course we all want everything at the same time, don't we? For as long as we can have it.

There I was at an outdoor band party with Rusty as Hutch drove by. Of course I didn't know this—how could I have? But does it matter what we do or don't know as we make our choices?

And that night I did make a choice.

The band had been playing Rolling Stones cover songs, and somewhere in the middle of "Wild Horses," Rusty pulled me close. The first kiss wasn't tentative or soft—it was a claim made. I belonged to him. I knew this with certainty even as I wouldn't admit it to anyone else for months. I had started to like Rusty; I knew the feeling—the need to be by his side, the need to touch him, taste his kiss, hear his voice. I fought the emotions, knowing that in dating Rusty, I would lose Hutch. Even now I don't fully understand how my heart wandered, but somehow Mother's words about what was and was not best for me became a seed that grew into a solid tree of doubt.

A few nights later, Hutch and I stood on the outside staircase of my apartment. I shivered in my winter coat covering a thin nightgown. "Ellie, go inside. You'll get sick." His voice was as cold as the pewter air.

"Please, Hutch. Don't go. I'm sorry."

"Don't make this worse. It's obvious where you want to be, Ellie."

"I'm sorry. I'm just so messed up, so confused."

"I'm not a last resort option. I never will be."

"What? You don't love me anymore? Can you say that?"

"This has nothing to do with how I feel. This has to do with what I have to do, not with how I feel. You obviously want to be with him. And I'm not here to be the second-place winner. I'm not here for you when there's nothing better to do; when you've been to the fancy lake house and the fraternity formal ball and the black-tie fund-raiser."

"You don't trust me." I threw the accusation at him, as if he'd been the one to kiss another girl on the front lawn of the fraternity house.

"I just saw you making out with Rusty Calvin in front of a hundred people. Yes, Ellie, trust might be an issue."

"Me? Me? You dated me for two years without once telling me you'd been to jail. You want to fight about trust?"

He stood still and mute, and when he walked

away from me, he didn't say good-bye. I stood shivering and alone on the staircase until Sadie came outside to retrieve me, soothing me with words about how everything works out the way it should, how it would all be okay, that things happen for a reason.

Yep, a reason all right—a selfish reason.

I hadn't yet walked back inside the warm apartment when I knew, in the darkest and veiled corners of my heart, that I had made a monstrous mistake. I didn't love Rusty as I had Hutch, and I never would. I *could* love Rusty, but never in the extraordinary way I did Hutch.

I called Hutch's apartment five times a day, apologizing, stalking the places he went. But he almost seemed to disappear—I'd see him across the quad or in the cafeteria, but as soon as I came near him, he was gone.

Finally, after I'd stood waiting outside his lit class, he entered the hallway and stopped. "Ellie, please, you are making this so much harder than it needs to be."

"Please talk to me. Please let me apologize."

He stood in front of me while my back was against the student council bulletin board. "Go ahead," he said, coming closer.

"I'm sorry. I am so sorry. I didn't mean what I said. It came out wrong. Please can't we talk about this and fix it?"

"Ellie, you *are* dating Rusty Calvin. Right?"

"Yes, I go out with him, but we aren't steady or exclusive. Not like you and me."

"Why are you here, staring at me with those eyes?"

"Because I'm miserable."

"You want me to fix that?"

"I don't know. I just know I can't stand this terribleness between us. I only love you, Hutch. I can't eat . . . you didn't even say good-bye."

He took another step closer and kissed me long and sweet. "Good-bye, Ellie," he said.

"What?" I grabbed at his shirt.

"I shouldn't have left without saying good-bye. So that was good-bye."

"Hutch!"

He walked away, and anger finally replaced pain. Fine. Just damn fine. If that was what he wanted . . .

It was at the lake party that night that I told Rusty, "Yes, we can definitely go steady." He gave me his fraternity pin, and we made love in an empty canoe on the side of the lake under a cloudy, dark sky. When I cried, Rusty believed it was from affection and relief, and I never told him otherwise.

The choices we make when we're broken are sometimes the most awful of all our choices.

While the jubilee party continued outside the guesthouse, I glanced down at Mother's words.

Outside, someone turned the music up: Kenny Chesney sang about his blue chair on a beach somewhere.

I'm hiding inside this house tonight with a broken heart. I've never really known what this is or means. But it's not a broken feeling; it's an empty feeling. I don't know why they call it broken—it's emptiness, not brokenness that hurts so very much. First there is this falling, falling, falling feeling. I never knew, until now, that this is how lonely feels. I thought I knew, but I didn't.

A knock resonated through the room. I closed the journal and opened the door to a man I knew but couldn't find the name inside the names darting through my head. He had a wide grin. "Hey, girl. You cannot and will not stay inside on this perfect night while we party twenty yards away. Get out here."

"Uncle Cotton," I said in a voice that sounded a lot like the child who once would have called his name. I hugged him and stepped back to look at him. "What a wonderful surprise. It's so great to see you. What are you doing here?"

"I'm speaking at that book festival this weekend and Ms. Birdie invited me over tonight. I'm staying in Mobile."

Uncle Cotton somehow had all the most handsome parts of my father, yet it was almost as if those elements were exaggerated—as if he were Dad, yet drawn more distinctly or brighter. He was two years older than Dad, mid-seventies. His white hair was thinning but still carried the hint of curls that once surrounded his face in the photos I'd seen of their younger days. He was taller than Dad by a few inches. It hurt me to think this, but Dad was almost a watered-down version of his older brother.

"You too, Ms. Ellie, it's damn good to see you, too. It's been way too long. I'm sorry I missed your mother's funeral. I was in Europe. . . ."

"I know." I stepped back to let him in the room. "Come on in," I said.

He stepped into the cottage. "This place is great. I've stayed here before. Isn't it the best?"

I nodded. "Just right. Which is why I've decided I'm staying here and not going out there."

"Oh, you're going to the party all right."

"I am?" I glanced down at my shorts and T-shirt.

"Let me explain something to you," he said with this smile of such warmth, I couldn't help but smile in return.

"Explain away."

"We don't know, never have, when another jubilee will come. You can't hide in this house and say, 'Next time, oh, next time I'll celebrate the jubilee.' No way. You have to say, 'This time. Yes, this time, because I don't know when there will be a next time.' "

I laughed. "You sound like you are giving an inspirational speech at a high school graduation."

"Did it work on my only niece? Did my smooth talking finally have an effect on someone?"

"Yeah, right, like it's never worked before?"

He smiled at me, quiet, and then said, "Let's go. There's a party outside."

"I'll be right back," I said, and walked down the hall toward the bedroom. I grabbed my flip-flops, brushed lip gloss across my mouth, and slipped on a sundress.

We walked out the door and onto the wet grass. The dock shimmered in the distance like a mirage, waving and moving against the dark with the lanterns as pirouetting fireflies. I followed Uncle Cotton to the place where grass met wooden planks, and he stopped, turned to me. "Let's go."

I followed him into the party; and that is just how it felt—*into* the party, as if I were swallowed into something alive and breathing, as if I were Jonah and this were the whale, but a whale with a party inside. The difference between Jonah and me was that I didn't want to be spit out. Ever.

At the crowd's feet, the shrimp's pale pink

discarded shells were scattered on the dock. The broken backs and claws of the crab and the bones of flounder were piled in metal trash baskets. I saw Pappy and talked to him about fresh vegetables and tides, about his wife and how she adored a good party. I sat with Leona and talked about her art store and how to make it more attractive. We laughed, and my heart and stomach were so full that I leaned back on the bench and groaned.

Uncle Cotton found me alone at the far end of the dock, watching the party. He settled next to me without words. I wanted to ask him about Mother, how well he knew her, but I never wanted him to know that his brother's wife had once loved another so deeply. I searched for the right words.

"Uncle Cotton," I said, "how well did you know Mother?"

"Ellie, that's a tough question. I knew her well, and then I didn't know her at all. I knew her when she was young, younger than you. But I rarely saw her in the later years. So did I know her well?" He turned toward me and shook his head. "No, I don't think I did."

I sighed. "Yes, that's the thing. I don't think anyone did."

"Why are you asking?"

"I found her journal," I said, and then looked out into the night, searching for the way to continue, as if the answers were written in the outline of stars. "And there was this group of friends she hung out with—Birdie included—and I just thought . . ."

"Thought what? That if you knew that girl, you could know the woman who was your mother?"

"Yes, exactly."

He shook his head. "We all become the person we are from the person we were—if that makes sense—and I don't believe your mother was any different. Does it really matter how she became that way?"

"Yes, it does. For me it does."

He sighed.

"It matters more than I can explain." I turned to him and grabbed his forearm. "You see, she changed. She was this wide-open loving girl who believed she could fly and write words that could change the world, and then she became cold and calculating, and her only goal was a perfect and appropriate life. She closed her heart. And that could happen to me. I see it happening to me, and I want to know why it happened to her—how. I want to stop it in myself."

Uncle Cotton sighed. "Your life is yours. It doesn't matter what closed her heart. It only matters that you don't close yours."

"Oh, I know what closed her heart."

"What?" he asked.

"Love. Rejection."

"Your dad loves her more than any man I know has loved any woman."

"Not him." I held up my hand. "I'm sorry." I looked away, searching in vain for some way to reverse the words I'd just spoken, to take them out of the air and put them back into my mouth. I looked at him. "That's not something you need to know, and it's not something I should have told you."

He smiled, but even in the dark I could see it was a sad smile.

We were quiet long enough for me to wonder if he was angry or upset. Then he spoke. "I knew her only during those summers we were all involved in the movement."

"You were there, too?"

"Of course. I thought you knew that."

I shook my head.

He pointed toward Birdie. "I thought she would have told you."

"No, she didn't."

"It was a long time ago, Ellie."

"Yes, I know. Who else was there? Can you tell me?"

"Sure I can tell you. Let's see, there were Micah Reynolds and crazy Otis Shepherd. Margaret Parsons and Celia Babcock."

"Wait here. Wait—I'm gonna run and get some paper. I want you to tell me some names."

"No, go enjoy the party, Ellie. We can talk about this any ole day."

He hugged me and faded into the crowd and candlelight, greeting friends as I stood against the railing with a bit of something I might call hope.

The sun moved to the other side of the earth, the moon a mere thin smile above us, when I turned and saw Hutch's back; he was talking to a man, his voice lost in the noise. I tapped his shoulder. He turned and smiled at me as if he knew I was behind him the entire time.

"Hey, Ellie."

"I was wondering when you'd get here."

"I saw you across the dock, but was waiting my turn to say hello." He motioned to a bench at the dock's edge, and we moved toward it, away from the stereo. We sat and he faced me. "I had that picture of your mother blown up. I was hoping I could see the other faces . . . but I can't." He pulled a photocopied paper out of his pocket and held it up to a lantern. "Can you see it?"

"Wow."

He sighed and stared at me. I looked at him again, and I was stunned with the need to touch his face. I had to turn away in order to keep my hands at my side. Twenty-five years—I could not and would not allow myself to become one of those women who escaped that far into the past to fix her future.

A figure appeared before us, and I looked up to see a woman. She was tall, her brown curls flung around her face and head with the breeze. Her smile was closed but wide. "Hey, Hutch, Drew and I are gonna take Ashley home. She doesn't feel well; I think she ate too much shrimp. I warned her. . . ."

Hutch stood and put his arm over her shoulder. "Becky, I want you to meet an old friend. This is Ellie Eddington. Ellie, this is Drew's wife, Becky."

I stood. "Hi," I said, and held out my hand. "I'm Ellie Calvin."

"Calvin, that's right," Hutch said. "Ellie Calvin."

"I've heard about you from Hutch and Drew also. You all were the very best of friends in college."

"Yes, we were," I said.

She nodded at Hutch. "We'll just meet you at home." She glanced at me. "Nice to finally meet you. See you around town, I'm sure."

"Yes."

Hutch and I sat again, and I smiled at him. "Best of friends?"

"We were. That's true."

"Yes, it is." I looked out over the water. "I'm sorry, Hutch. I'm so sorry for anything I ever did that hurt or wounded us." I looked directly at him. "I am sorry."

"Thank you, Ellie. That was sweet, but unnecessary. I don't hold any—"

"I know, but I'm sorry about the pain I caused us; that I caused me. I'm sorry I was that girl that would've lied and cheated in her confusion."

"We were twenty years old, Ellie. We were all confused about everything all the time. We thought we knew it all, but we didn't, did we?"

"No, we didn't. And I think I knew less than most." I tried to smile, but my lips shook with the effort.

We talked, Hutch and I, for so long that the party emptied. Birdie blew out all the lanterns but the two by our bench. We discussed random and out-of-order events from the past twenty-five years—family and kids and births and deaths. We talked about Auburn football and careers, about art and history and everything except Rusty and Hillary.

When I yawned, Hutch laughed. "Okay, I think the party is over."

I glanced at the empty dock, the full trash cans, and the dark night. "Yes, I think so." He stood and held out his hand for me to take. "Thanks for talking to me for so long," I said.

Resting, like we do in that silence, until I asked, "Listen, on Sunday there's this book festival in Mobile. Any chance you want to go?"

"Go?"

"With me. I'm planning on going."

He stared at me for a moment; I wanted to kiss him. I wanted to taste his kindness. I wanted him.

He gave me a smile like a gift. "I'd like that."

"Good night, old friend," I said, and turned away before I ruined anything good I'd healed in that night.

"Good night," I heard him say, but I was already five steps ahead, moving toward the guesthouse. I felt his gaze on me until I opened the door and turned to wave good-bye. But he was gone; I'd imagined him watching. I leaned my head on the doorpost and looked into the night. Then I saw him. He was standing at the end of the dock, still watching. I waved and, wishing I didn't have to, I shut the door.

I'd actually shut the door to him a very long time ago and as much as I wanted or needed to, it was way past time to open that door.

Excerpt from Lillian Ashford's Journal
New Year's Eve 1962
Twenty-two Years Old

It was the end of last January when I started throwing up. All the time. Not just in the morning or when I smelled something bad or when I moved too fast—just all the time. I kept calling in sick to Mrs. Prinkle until she finally pulled me into the office. I know how I looked—I'd seen myself in the mirror all pale and skinny and sad.

I'd been walking through my days in a kind of black and white and gray fog. Everything seemed so pointless and meaningless and well, boring really. Nothing that had once seemed fun was fun anymore. Laughing was completely out of the question. I didn't know how anymore. All the decorating jobs were so stupid—didn't these women have anything better to do than ask Mrs. Prinkle about their blue-green fabric swatch for their sitting room club chair?

Mrs. Prinkle had stared at me for a long time and then asked me outright, like I'd been asked this question a hundred times, "Are you pregnant?" Now this had not even crossed my mind for half of one-half second. Really it hadn't. That night with Redmond was a memory I'd erased in that way I do when I can't stand to look at something. Not that I didn't like him, or that it was bad sex, just because of the reason . . . the reason itself.

But here we are with this—the reason doesn't matter sometimes. The result does.

Only sometimes.
Like this time.

Seventeen

I woke in the predawn dark that Sunday morning, unable to fall back asleep. My life swirled around me with its choices and its beginnings, with its endings and its sorrows. I finally abandoned the hope of unconscious bliss, and by the light of a single lamp, I sat down at the dining room table and spread out the art supplies I'd bought. With the charcoal I drew a horizontal line across the middle of the poster board, smudging the edges and then dividing the line into three parts: 1960; 1961; 1962. The journal was open at the end of the table and I started with June 1960, writing only what I knew, placing words like "met Him"; "back to school"; "returned to Bayside." I ended with a bright yellow star on my birthday in 1962. With nature's music my only companion, I began to fill in the blanks between.

The history books provided photos and details, my imagination offering images. I'd sketched the Summer House, Georgia Tech, her childhood home in Atlanta, and a faceless Him. By the time I reached the 1961 bus burning, my eyes burned and my hands ached. The late morning sun sent stripes of dust-dancing light onto the table, and I stretched. The bus burning seemed the pivotal point in their lives and a perfect time to take a break in mine.

My swimsuit on, I grabbed the towel off the hook by the front door. The walk to the dock was my favorite part of the morning; a silent prayer of gratitude was the only thing on my lips or mind. The dock still held remnants of the jubilee party: a beer can, a few shrimp shells squashed in between the dock boards, half-burned candles with melted wax on the wooden side tables. I smiled thinking that I'd been a part of what remained there.

My swim was silent. I emptied my mind and allowed only the swish of water, the hum of a motor under the waves coming from far off, the thump of a boat against a pillar, the squawk of a seagull, to fill my thoughts. After the swim, I crawled out onto the dock and saw Birdie standing at the fence. I waved. She waved back.

Birdie came toward me. "You really slept in. I'm so glad."

I smiled and yet didn't correct her.

"You want a late breakfast?"

"I'd absolutely love a late breakfast."

She had made hash browns and scrambled eggs that morning, and I sat in the yellow kitchen with my bay-soaked hair and worn T-shirt and shorts.

"The party was great. Really great. Did you know Uncle Cotton was gonna be here?" I said.

She grinned as if she held a deep secret. "Yep. I knew he was speaking at the book festival, so I invited him. He's not usually one for parties, but when I told him you were here, he wanted to surprise you."

"He did. It took me longer to recognize him than it should have, which is embarrassing considering he's my uncle. My only uncle. How . . . synchronistic that he's in town."

"Well . . . he's actually here quite a bit."

"He lives in Asheville."

"Yes. . . ." Birdie turned away and changed the subject. "So, did you meet anyone new?"

"A few people."

"Did you meet that journalist?"

I shook my head. "What journalist?"

"There is this woman from *Coastal Living* who is doing an article about 'Coastal Houses with Legends,' and she wants to do a bit about the Summer House. I've been nervous about letting someone come asking questions about my home, but I guess it's better coming from me than from rumor."

"Oh, I think that's fantastic. I bet you have great stories."

Birdie shrugged. "We'll see."

"Well, can I ask you something?"

"About the house?"

"No . . . do you know Micah Reynolds or Otis Shepherd?"

Birdie squinted at me. "Why are you asking?"

"Why didn't you tell me Cotton was part of that summer group y'all hung out with?"

"The names don't matter. Only what we did matters."

"Well, he told me those names and I just wanted to talk to them. You know . . . just talk to them."

"Well, Otis died years ago, but Micah lives out on Route 66. His office is downtown. He's an incredible man; he's our county commissioner, with eight kids and untold number of grandkids who still live here and are involved in the community."

I moved my eggs around without taking a bite. "Do you think he'd care if I asked him about that summer?"

"No, he's very proud of what happened. He believes we changed his life and the life of his family. He has great stories. I'm sure he'd be happy to meet you. But, Ellie, don't expect him to tell you what you want to know. He won't. He just won't. If you want to know about what we did, what that summer was like for all of us with the movement, he'll tell you."

"Is he African-American?" I asked.

"Of course."

I nodded and stood to kiss her. "Thanks for the breakfast."

She nodded toward the plate. "I'm not cooking you anything anymore if you're not going to eat it."

I returned to my seat. "You're right. I'm excited about the day and here I am running off without finishing." I took a bite of my now lukewarm eggs. Birdie and I talked about the weather and the party, about town gossip and the local election.

"You know what I think?" I asked.

She laughed. "I have no idea."

"You are the most amazing woman I've ever met, and Mother was blessed to have you as a best friend."

"Now don't you go getting all gooshy on me. Get on out of here and start your day."

I was at Pappy's stand buying vegetables, discussing the weirdness of seedless watermelon, when Rusty called. I stared at the screen of the cell phone, because it didn't—in some other-worldly way—seem possible that Rusty could call me while I talked to Pappy, while I bought produce in Bayside.

Questions chased after one another inside my head, too rapid to answer: *Is he here in town? What does he need? Should I answer?* I answered on the last ring before voice mail. "Hello."

"Where are you?" His voice was clear, as if he stood next to me, his breath in my ear. My stomach plummeted, an elevator with a broken cable.

"In Alabama. Where are you?"

"In Atlanta where we live."

"Oh, Rusty. Why did you hang up on me yesterday? I hate that so much."

"I'm sorry. I was pissed. Listen, you need to come home. Your dad needs you, and there is mail everywhere, and—"

"No," I interrupted.

"Yes." He coughed. "You need to come home. There's a million things that need to be done. The exterminator couldn't get in while I was at work. The yard guy says he broke a sprinkler head. Anna Morehead says you missed the organizational meeting for your mother's charity. You can't stay there any longer."

He was right.

I'd walked a few yards away from Pappy, sitting on a bench at the edge of the sidewalk. "We have a family," Rusty said. "My God, your dad has called me ten times. My secretary is running errands for him; shouldn't you be there for him? For Lil?"

"What?"

"You just left everyone, Ellie. Everyone. Not just me."

Guilt prodded at the outside of my heart, but

I wouldn't let it in. "Lil is at school, happy. I've talked to her every day. Dad is a grown man; you should not have your secretary running errands for him. I've also talked to him . . . he's fine. I've been gone for a few days. That's all."

"Shit, this is ridiculous." His voice changed: softer, gentler. "Baby, I'm just so hurt that you'd leave when I wanted you to stay."

"Rusty, please stop it."

"But I miss you."

"I miss you, too. You'd like it here. You would."

"I'm sure I would, but I have to work," he said. The hissing noise of emptiness pervaded the phone lines. "Come home," he finally said.

"That sounds like an order."

"See? See how you do that? I was trying to tell you I want to see you, and you act like I'm ordering you around."

"I have to go."

"You have to go?"

"I do. I'm out running errands. I'll call you later." I hung up as I felt my stomach lurch. There is static of the mind that comes with emotional confusion, like a loud rock band with discordant notes thrashing against one another, and this confusion wouldn't allow me to define what I have always ignored. But there in Bayside I understood finally: *manipulation.* A serrated word I'd never allowed to cross my spirit or allowed myself to believe about anyone I love. But there it was, as if the word were emblazoned in capital letters across the Bayside horizon.

Rusty used his words and his extremes, sweetness and rage, to keep me doing and saying and being exactly what he wanted me to do, say, and be.

No more.

I walked back toward Pappy's and resumed my discussion.

"So," I asked Pappy, who was wiping sweat from his brow with a handkerchief, "how do they grow seedless watermelons? I mean, what seeds do they use?"

"I don't rightly know," he said. "I really don't. So much of anything these days is a mystery to me."

"Me too," I said as I paid for my produce and left the change on the counter.

"Now you have a good day, Ms. Ellie. Don't be letting other people go ruining it for you."

"I won't," I said as I walked off, and I realized he'd changed his farewell, not uttered his usual, "Now go do what you need to do."

The county commissioner's office was on the far end of the main street in a cement building, a cornerstone of the town and the block. The marble steps were chipped on the edges, veined and cracked like an old woman's legs that have stood too long at their job. The double-wood doors had iron handles as large as my arm. I entered the air-conditioned hallway and shivered. To the right, an older woman with a leaning tower of hair, her glasses perched on her nose, looked up at me, squinting. "May I help you?"

"Yes, I'd like to see Micah Reynolds."

"Do you have an appointment?"

"No," I said. "My mother and he were good friends in the sixties. She just passed and I wanted to say hello to him, meet him."

"Oh, darling, I am so, so sorry you lost your mama."

"Thank you," I said.

She stood up and waddled toward me in the most peculiar walk I'd ever seen. She hugged me and held me against her bosom for a moment. "It is just so hard losing a mama. Just so hard. I'll be right back, let me tell Micah you're here. Oh, and what was her name?"

"Lillian," I said. "He would have known her as Lilly Ashford."

When Micah walked out and into the foyer, I was struck by his beauty and then secondly, his smile. He held out his hand before he'd even reached my side. "Hello," he said in a voice as full of authority as if he were narrating a documentary. "I'm Micah Reynolds. And you," he said as he reached me, "you must be Lilly's daughter. Good God, you look just like her." He pumped my hand.

"Yes, I'm Ellie Calvin. A pleasure to meet you."

"Well, well, how can I help you?"

"I am hoping I can just talk to you for a moment or two. I promise I won't take up much of your time."

"Follow me." He pointed down the marble-floored back hallway, and I followed him into his office.

He shut the door and I sat in the leather chair on the opposite side of his desk, but he motioned me away to two wingback chairs facing each other across a mahogany coffee table. "Come on over here, let's talk."

In his office hung framed photos of Micah with dignitaries and with awards, degrees, and honors, so much so that I could hardly tell what color the dented plaster walls were painted. I sat across from him, and after the pleasantries, after the facts of Mother's death and the condolences were complete, he bent forward in his chair. "So, how can I help you?"

"The summer of 1961," I said. "I'm hoping you can tell me a little bit about that."

"There are books and books and articles and articles written about that time, Ms. Calvin. It was a turning point in Alabama history."

"I know. I meant, can you tell me about Mother during that time?"

He smiled at me and settled back into his chair as if he had a very long story to tell. "You know, she never came back here as far as I heard. Birdie begged her; I know that. But she never returned after that summer of 1961."

"She did—once, but only briefly," I said.

He looked up at the ceiling and then at me. "Yes, she did." Placing his hands on his knees, he bent toward me. "What would you like to know?"

"What was she like?"

"Those days were heady and full. We were changing the world, and we knew it. We lived and thrived on adrenaline, on passion and purpose. Your mother wasn't any different. If you're asking how I remember her—I remember her laughing, full of life and ideas. She was the organizer, always the organizer. Tireless in her plans and means to get us where we wanted to go. We would meet and the entire time she would be taking notes, making charts and graphs to make sure that we were at the right place at the right time."

I laughed. "Yes, that was Mother. The planner. The organizer."

"But she did it with this great heart and laughter."

"No"—I shook my head—"that's the part I didn't know of her. The planning, yes. The execution of the plans, yes. The organizing, definitely."

He pursed his lips. "I'm sorry for that, Ellie. I am."

"Why are you sorry?"

"I'm sorry for you that you didn't know her like that. She was a joy."

"What do you think changed her?" I asked, prying and pulling at the threads of the past from this man I'd just met.

"We all change. We must. I was angrier then. She was more passionate then." He shrugged.

"This group," I said. "There were how many of you?"

"There were six of us for the most part, but others came and went through the two summers."

"Did she date any of the boys?"

"Now how would I remember that?"

"It seems like something one would remember about those days."

"It does seem that way, doesn't it? But you have to remember—all I cared about was making sure that I didn't sit in the back of the bus, that I could walk into a café and not be asked to leave. Ellie . . ." He leaned forward again, reaching out his hands as if grabbing for something. "I do remember this: She helped take Otis to the emergency room after the Montgomery riot. That I remember—she was like an avenging angel, screaming at the emergency room doctors that if they didn't take him in, they'd all burn in an eternal hell. I think they believed her." He laughed this low, bellow-ing laugh like an instrument I've never heard, a mysterious musical instrument from God alone.

My body tingled with knowledge: He was there—this man was also there, and he knew the best friend, Otis, who was beaten and left for dead. "Who was she with? Who else went to the ER besides you and her?"

He stared at me as if he knew this was the only information I had come for and the only information he was unwilling to share.

"I don't remember," he said. "Listen, Ellie. The only thing I cared about was my future. That's all. I wanted my state and my kin to have a different life."

I nodded, and I was overcome with admiration for this man I'd just met, for this man who knew my mother when she was passionate and kind and full of hope. I stood and walked around the coffee table where he stood. I hugged him. "I forget," I said, "that the movement was not that long ago, not just something in a history book. Thanks for taking the time to talk to me. I'm sorry to bother you. I'll let you get back to work."

He held my hands. "You'd never be a bother. Come by anytime."

When I stepped into the sunlight, I pulled my sunglasses over my eyes, hiding the tears that had formed and were threatening to fall. I found a park bench facing the bay. The horizon shifted, moved, fading and coming into focus with every cloud's movement. Maybe Birdie was right, maybe it didn't matter whom Mother loved, only that she did. Maybe her love letters were never meant to be delivered. If she hadn't given that last love letter to him, why would I? Why had she kept it?

I am now Lillian Caulfield Ashford Eddington, wife of Redmond, mother of Lillian Caulfield Eddington. Ellie. Her name should translate "my heart" because that is what she is. My heart.

How could someone I didn't know I needed be more than I ever needed?

I thought I knew what love was, but I never did. Not really at all. Love is not wanting and needing; it is knowing you would give your life for the other in a way that is absolute. It is knowing that there is not a day that will ever go by—for the rest of your life—when that person will not be on your mind or in your heart. That is Ellie.

So here I am again where the best and worst part of my year are the same. I think I like it better when they are two different things—when they are opposites. But this is the funny thing I am seeing—sometimes the best and worst things are the same things.

So Mrs. Prinkle asked me this question about being pregnant and I laughed at her. But she was serious. She asked me the last time I had a period and I had to think and think about it. When I realized how long it had been, I had this dizziness come over me. Not the kind of dizzy when you stand up too fast, but the kind that makes your entire body tingle and your head feel like it is floating off your body into space.

I knew.

Right then, right there, staring at Mrs. Prinkle's black ribbon headband, I knew.

I've never known anything that fast.

Eighteen

Sunday morning when Hutch came to pick me up for the book festival, he stood backlit with the rising sun behind him in the guesthouse door frame. He smiled and I saw the man—the forty-something-year-old man—and I understood exactly who Hutch O'Brien was for me: the love I let go for safety.

The emotions I felt with Hutch might not have been about what could happen then, but for what I'd let go for something misnamed. Like Mother believing that what she'd done with Dad was revenge; it had been something else entirely or something else in addition—it was the beginning of a life. My life.

What Mother had called revenge was really the beginning of my life.

What I had called love was really safety.

It was all in the naming, in the believing that one thing was something it was not.

When Hutch reached my side, I had trouble finding words. When you abruptly realize something you should have known all along, you are a bit off balance, as though someone jumped off the other side of the seesaw and you rise too fast, staring down at the ground, confused.

"Hey," he said. "You ready?"

"Yep." I grabbed my purse and walked toward him. Skin has a magnetic quality; I know this because I couldn't have stopped my body from walking toward him, hugging him. He held me for a minute and then stepped back. Sadness filled the small space between us, like dust falling into the cracks of floorboards. I wanted to diffuse this, scatter the sorrow, but I didn't know how.

The restaurant jutted over Mobile Bay like a tongue sticking out of a pretty face. Hutch and I sat around a table facing the water. We'd driven the half hour into Mobile and parked walking distance from the book festival, which was in full gear, crowding the streets. We ate and sipped our iced teas in silence, staring out over the water.

Hutch threw a piece of bread to a seagull that caught it in midair.

"I met Micah yesterday," I said.

"Who?"

"Well, Uncle Cotton told me that Mother was friends with him that summer, and so I dropped by to say hello."

Hutch laughed. "Just say hello?"

I told Hutch the entire story as we finished off our lunch and then wandered toward the tents. "I would have liked to go with you," he said, picking up a newspaper that in block letters announced what authors were speaking at which tent on what subject.

"Really?"

"Yes, really."

"I'll remember that." We bent over the schedule and then decided to go hear Cotton speak. We were late; our conversation at lunch had made time run away as easily as a river.

We slipped into the tent where Uncle Cotton was in the middle of the question-and-answer session.

"You know," Cotton said in that baritone voice of his, "I wish I were an outliner. I really do. I've tried. I want to be one so I can say I'm one. Wouldn't that be nice?"

The crowd laughed, and he continued. "For me," he said, "outlining takes away a certain mystery. If I know what's going to happen next, I can't ask this: 'What is the next best thing to happen here?' I can't ask, 'What now?' and that is my favorite part about the writing, finding out what happens next." He shrugged. "Now I'm not saying this is the best way to be. I'd never say that one way or the other is the best way to be. But it's the best way to be for me."

An audience member argued in a high, whiny voice, "But how can you write an entire story without knowing where it's going?"

"The same way you live a life, I guess. Just keep asking what is the next best thing to do. Or just watch and see what comes along and then deal with it. Like I said, I'm not saying this is a great way to live or write, I'm just saying it's my way. It's a messy way to write and I think maybe a messy way to live, but all that planning and out-lining can really get a man knotted up thinking things aren't going his way." Uncle Cotton laughed and paused. "It might be that things aren't going as planned, but they're going as well as they can. Now I'm not saying not to plan at all. I mean, sometimes you have to plan certain events."

The man in the front row didn't let the subject go, pulling at it like a dog fighting for a chew toy. "But how can you ever know if you've reached your goal or finished the novel?"

Cotton clapped his hands together. "Well, I think when it's done, it's done. That's it. You know when things are done. You just do."

"I don't get it," the man said, and slapped shut a notebook. "That just doesn't make sense."

"I didn't promise it would." Cotton looked out to the audience now. "Any more questions?"

The moderator appeared from the side of the stage and announced that the time was up and Cotton would be signing at the book tent for thirty minutes. I stayed seated; Cotton passed me on the way out, and I lifted my hand. "Hey, there."

He looked down at me. "Ellie."

I stood for his hug.

"Thanks for coming," he said. "I have to head over to the signing tent, but how about I meet you when I'm done." He turned to Hutch, held out his hand. "Hey, I'm Cotton."

"Oh, I'm sorry," I said. "I thought maybe y'all met at the party last night."

"Nope." Cotton shook Hutch's hand.

"Hey, I'm Hutch." He nodded toward me. "Old friend of Ellie's from college."

A low voice called Cotton's name. We all turned to Micah Reynolds, who gave Cotton a bear hug, slapping him on the shoulder. "Good job, old friend. Well done."

"Thanks, buddy." Cotton placed his hand on my forearm. "I'd like you to meet my niece, Ellie Calvin, and her friend Hutch."

Micah turned to me with his wide smile, reaching out with one strong arm and pulling me to his side. He squeezed me around the shoulders. "We're already friends."

"Hello, Mr. Reynolds, it's good to see you again."

"Call me Micah. Lilly's daughter should call me Micah."

Cotton shook his head. "You both are way ahead of me."

Micah greeted Hutch as a young boy ran up, grabbing Micah's hand. "Pops, they're running out of hot dogs. Hurry."

Micah leaned over and picked up this small child as if he were a stuffed animal, throwing him in the air to catch him. The boy burst into laughter and buried his head in his grandfather's shoulder. Micah smiled at Cotton, Hutch, and me. "See y'all soon. It's hot dog time."

"You two are really good friends, aren't you?" I asked Cotton as Micah walked away.

"Yep, we don't see each other very often, but when you go through what we went through together, you're friends for good."

"But you made a difference. In the end y'all made a difference."

"Yes, we did. It didn't seem that way at the time." He slung his backpack over his shoulder and lifted his sunglasses from his eyes; he held them between his thumb and forefinger, looking directly into my eyes. "Usually when you're in the middle of something you can't see your way. You think you aren't making a difference or aren't making progress when you really are. And that's how it was for us. I thought we were doing more harm. When we saw our friends beaten and bloody, when they lost their jobs and scholarships, I thought we'd done more damage than good. But Micah—he knew it would make a difference and he didn't care what it cost him."

The escort coughed now. "Mr. Eddington, you have a line forming."

Cotton replaced his glasses over his eyes and

pulled a pen from his backpack. "Off to sign," he said. "I'll find you over there when I'm done." He pointed to the bench.

"Perfect." I paused before I asked, "What you said up there—about just knowing when something is done."

"Yeah?"

"Is that true? I mean, you just really know when something is done? Without planning on it being done?"

"Sure. Probably not something to teach in an M.F.A. program, though."

The man from the stage made a frantic motion for Cotton to move toward the signing tent, and then Cotton was gone.

Hutch and I wandered through the festival, eating the one thing you eat only at a festival: funnel cakes. With powdered sugar on our lips, we finally sat quiet and still, as if trying to capture and keep that exact moment that would surely disappear. I settled back into the haze of the afternoon and the sweet taste on my lips when Uncle Cotton found us on the bench and greeted Hutch also.

Hutch excused himself to check out the band stage, leaving Cotton and me alone. "So you'd already met Micah?" he asked.

"Yes, I went to his office."

"Isn't he great?" Cotton asked. "One of the most brilliant men I've ever met."

"He was very nice. Yes. He has fond memories of Mother."

"We all have good memories from those days. That's what we do to memories—make them fonder. It was a terrible and wonderful time, but I'm sure we've all romanticized much of it."

"He remembers her being sweet and fun."

"She was. I didn't know her well after she married my brother. You know, I see Red, but she always had an excuse to stay home. I don't think she liked this area. . . ."

"Yeah, because of him."

"What do you mean?"

"She never came here because of him—she didn't want to see him, run into him."

"Him? I think she just didn't like Alabama . . . the memories."

"No, it was him," I reiterated.

"Well, she must have really grown to hate him."

I held back my words—this was Dad's brother, and Dad was a man whom I would never want to cause pain. "Maybe."

"Well, I need to go visit Red. I bet he's in a bad way without your mother."

"I feel terrible that I left, but I've talked to him every day. You know, he has so many friends, and the 'casserole brigade' has descended on the house, bringing him dinners. Every single woman from Atlanta to Birmingham has stopped by to offer her condolences. I know he feels lost and lonely, though."

Uncle Cotton looked away and then at me. "It's hard to lose someone you love."

"Yes," I said, "it is. And it's not always to death. You know, I was listening to you talk about the way you write—without much planning and so forth—and I realize how different that is than the way Mother taught me, in the way Mother lived her life—she was such a planner."

"There's a fine balance, I'm sure. One I haven't found. I could be a better planner, but I always find that just when you least expect it, something comes along, something you didn't plan on at all."

"That," I said, "can be a good or bad thing."

He settled back into the park bench. "It's so good to see family. I'm really glad you're here, Ellie." He took my hand and squeezed it.

Hutch and I arrived home after dark, and he pulled up to the end of the driveway and parked the convertible next to the guesthouse. With the car top down, I rested my head back and gazed up to the sky, clouds like islands in a sea. "Thanks for coming with me," I whispered.

"You talking to the sky or me?" Hutch asked.

I looked to his smile. "You."

"My pleasure."

"Do you know the legend of this house?" I asked.

He turned in his seat. "Drew told me a little bit, but let me hear your version."

I twisted in my seat so I faced the Summer House. "Supposedly, there are all these stories of people who come to stay with Birdie, only to discover the truth about someone or something. It might be a betrayal or a love or even a talent they have they didn't know they had. The whispers are that staying here will change your life."

"For example?"

"You'll have to ask Birdie. She never told me any of the stories, just the rumor."

He was silent for a long while, staring at the house and then at me. "I want to hear some of the stories."

"Well . . . there's this writer coming to interview Birdie. *Coastal Living* is doing a piece on houses with legends and myths surrounding them. So maybe we can hear some good stories."

"You think it's changing you?"

"I don't know what's changing me, but yes, something is. I think it started long before I came here."

"Does your mother think it changed her?"

"I can only know what she wrote. Which is really sad. God, I wish she'd talked to me about it, but all she wrote about the Summer House was that she believed that staying here would make him love her; would bring him to her."

He opened the car door and then walked to my side. "It didn't work, did it?"

"Not really, or maybe it did, but she messed it up or he messed it up or . . . the timing was off. I have no idea." I climbed out of the car and stood at his side, my body opening, slowly needing him. "I have to go . . . ," I said.

"I know." He touched the side of my face and then drew me into his shoulder, held me there. "I know you have to go."

I rested into that place I'd once fit, into that space I still settled, and exhaled into his warm cotton shirt. Then, to the music of bay water splashing against the dock's pilings, we stood next to the Summer House, under the open sky, until I let go and walked inside alone.

And I loved her. The baby. I loved her that fast. I knew it was a girl. I knew I loved her. The other stuff wasn't so easy, but that was.

I don't remember leaving Mrs. Prinkle's office or driving to Mama's house. But I did. And I told Mama and Daddy before I told Redmond. Mama cried. Daddy stared out the dining room windows as if someone might walk up the front walkway and take me away so he wouldn't have to hear me tell him what he hoped I'd never tell him. Mama finished crying pretty quickly and called the Eddington family.

That was the most terrible part because I wanted to be the one to tell Redmond. Maybe I should have thought it out, planned it better. Maybe I should have gone to his house first, but with something like this—you want your Mama first. You just do.

When he came to the house he was the same color as the white painted pillars on the front porch, but the weird part was that he was smiling. He didn't say a word when I opened the door and neither did I. Our parents had done the talking. What needed to be known was already known. He hugged me and held me so tight I was afraid he was hurting the child I already loved. "I love you," he said. I felt him shaking all over, and then he added that he'd loved me since the moment he saw me and that we were going to be okay. Yes, we were.

There was of course a wonderful relief in this knowing that he loved me, that he wanted me, that this was not a life-ruining thing for him. But I wish I could say it was more than a relief, that it was a joy or love or something like that. But it was just a nice, calm relief for me. I would be okay. He loved me. He wanted this and us. And that was enough.

I hope it will always be enough.

We married quickly in the small

chapel behind St. Michael's Cathedral. It is amazing that Mama could do in four weeks what takes most mothers six months. There were whispers. I don't care. I don't.

Ellie is here. Safe. Beautiful. And it was enough.

But then the letters started coming —the letters from Him. They went to Mama's house and it took her two months to bring them to me because I think she knew what they were. And she was right—they were love letters from Africa. I read two of them and then while Redmond was at work, I sat on the back porch and burned the unread letters one by one, lighting them in a trash can and watching them turn to ash while Ellie slept. That life was done; over; burned thoroughly. I told Mama to never bring another letter to the house; my heart and my bones began to remember Him and this could not be.

Nineteen

That next morning, I walked over to the Summer House and sat at Birdie's breakfast table. "Do you remember your life when you were very young?" I asked.

"Dang, I hardly remember my life yesterday," she said, laughing and then sitting. "Do you?"

"No. I have this dress at home in the cedar closet from a father-daughter dance when I was seven years old. I took it out last year and looked at it, and then went and found a photo from that same dance. I think I remember it—but maybe I just remember the picture: Dad and I stand in the middle of a ballroom at the Cherokee Town and Country Club, a buffet table with an ice sculpture of a princess behind us. So do I remember that or do I just remember the photo? It's all so weird that there's these things that happen to us that make us who we are, and then we don't remember them. I know more about Lil's days than she does, and still, and still . . . I can't know her completely."

Birdie took my hand. "Is it nice to see yourself from your mother's eyes?"

"Yes," I said. "Yes, it is." I took a deep breath

before I finally asked the question I'd held beneath all the other discussions we'd had. "Birdie, were you here when Mother came back for him? I'm not asking who it is or anything. I just want to know if you remember that day."

She nodded. "I do. It was the last time she ever came here. Of course I wasn't here—I still lived in Atlanta—but I knew she'd driven here to see him." Birdie turned so I wouldn't see the pain on her face, but I did see it and I cringed.

"So, I'm right. She didn't come here after that because of him."

"Yes, you're right about that." She paused. "We all have our own reasons for why we do and don't do things; for why we go and don't go places."

"I know," I said. "The saddest part isn't how he never wanted her, but how with each passing year she became more and more concerned with 'things' in her life. She wrote about houses and jobs and promotions and country clubs and trips to Europe; she wrote of decorating and local fame; of fund-raisers and haircuts and clothing. She wanted things just so. She stopped talking about stories or books and fun. Sometimes even I sound like an appendage. She believed—really believed—that if she wrote down everything she planned and wanted and needed that it would happen for her. And often it did."

Birdie filled my coffee cup again but didn't speak.

"Except for him. Every year she wrote her goals, and every year she said this: 'This is the year He will know He loves me.' It was the one thing that never happened. It's like she wrote her life story, but couldn't fix the love-story. He'd once told her he loved her and then reneged, took back his own words, and she wanted him to love her again and again and again. She wanted him to *know*. She tried to write that into her story."

"Writing our own story," Birdie said. "Yes, she believed that."

"Can we really do that?"

Birdie smiled. "In many, many ways, yes, we can. Not just in your mother's way. But no matter how many times you write it or wish it, you can't make someone love you."

"I know," I said. "And speaking of finding my way—I think I'll head down to the waterfront stores and galleries. You want to come?"

"No. You go on. I have a . . . date."

I broke into laughter and then slammed my hand over my mouth. "Really? With who?"

"None of your business," she said with laughter so intertwined in the words that I couldn't even think about being offended.

"Have fun," I said, waving good-bye.

The afternoon heat mixed with promising rain as I stood outside the folk art gallery, waiting on

Hutch. A table outside displayed jewelry, and I was holding a pair of silver earrings up to the sun when I saw Birdie walking toward me. She didn't see me, and she looked up to a man's face, laughing. Then they were both standing in front of me: Birdie and Cotton.

My out-loud laughter made them both look at me. "Oh, Ellie," Birdie said. "Hello there."

"Well, hello to you two," I said. "I thought you said you had a . . ." And then I grinned. "Ah," I said.

"You like those earrings?" a voice behind me asked, and I turned to a smiling woman with spiky black hair.

"I do. How much?"

"Twelve fifty," she said.

I dug through my purse for cash as I spoke to Birdie. "What are y'all doing?"

"Just wandering the bay front." Uncle Cotton picked up a necklace with a large blue stone dangling from a silver chain. He held it up to Birdie's neck. "You like this?"

"It's lovely." Birdie looked at me, and I smiled.

"I think I'll go look around. You two enjoy your day," I said.

"Bye," they called in unison.

I glanced around for Hutch—he would enjoy knowing these two were on a date. Nothing, I thought, seems nearly as funny alone.

I went inside the store, where my attention

was caught by a canvas painted with a field of abstract wildflowers, the colors blending together. It was like a piece of art I wish I could paint, and yet I was always snagged by the intricate beauty of a single flower. A young girl stopped, standing in front of the painting. "Mama," she said, "look. Those are like the flowers on Papa's sand dune."

The mama was distracted, talking on her cell phone, digging for something in her purse.

"Wildflowers," I said. *Gaillardia pulchella*, I heard Mother's voice inside my spirit. "Those are called *Gaillardia pulchellas*."

"Huh?" The little girl tilted her head.

"Those are pretty wildflowers that grow in the sand dunes. They're called firewheels."

"That's it," she said with a wide smile, her lips blue from the remainder of the Icee she held in her hand. "I knew I knew it; I just couldn't think of the name." She screwed up her mouth and eyes, as if the question she was about to ask formed itself in the sun-kissed skin of her face. "Did you paint that?"

"No, but I like to paint."

"Wow." She exhaled and twirled a strand of her hair in her sticky blue fingers. "I paint."

"You're an artist," I said.

"I draw, too. And I make sculpture things out of sticks and shells. And I can even paint on rocks."

The woman tuned in, smiling at me but grabbing her child's hand to leave the store. "Mama, look at those flowers."

"Those are pretty, sweetie. They really are. Just like you." The mama kissed her child on top of the head and they were gone and Hutch stood in front of me, smiling.

I smiled at him and held up my earrings. "Like?"

"Love," he said, and gave me a hug.

We wandered through the store, commenting on art and sculpture.

"Are you working on anything now?" Hutch asked, pointing to a painting of an alligator.

I laughed. "Nothing like that. Nothing that would sell."

"Meaning?"

"It's silly."

"Tell me anyway."

"I'm working on a timeline of '60 to '62, trying to fit the events of Mother's life into some semblance of order from the summer of 1960 to my birth. I'm sketching and drawing, but it's nothing . . . really."

"I want to see it," he said, stopping in midstep.

I stood without an answer when a flash of lightning lit the store like a thousand suns. We startled, laughing.

"I knew there was a storm coming," Hutch said.

"I really wanted to go to all the stores on the waterfront," I said. "I guess . . . another time."

"It's a sign," he said, grinning.

"A sign?"

"Take me to the guesthouse. Show me your work."

I stared at him until the rain began to splash against the windows like a fire hose pointed at the building. "Okay," I said. "I will."

Uselessly shielding ourselves from the rain with our hands held above our heads, Hutch and I ran into the guesthouse, laughing and soaked. I grabbed towels and threw one at Hutch. "I'm gonna change," I said, and shut the bedroom door.

I came out in jeans and a linen shirt, my hair wet and dripping onto my shoulders. "I'm sorry I don't have anything that would fit you," I said, sitting next to him at the dining table.

"I'm fine." He ran the towel through his hair and then draped it over a chair. "Ellie, this is beautiful." He pointed to the timeline. "Your sketches, your rendition of how things connect together. The house, the school, the man. Your black timeline is almost like a highway connecting one place to the other, taking what seems like random events and tying them together with some sort of meaning."

"Thanks, Hutch."

He placed his finger over the yellow star. "And this?"

"My birth. . . ."

He looked up at me. "September fourteenth."

"You remember."

"I remember everything of you." He turned away from me as he continued to scan the time-line.

I reached across the table and grabbed the set of colored pencils and charcoals. "You want to help?"

"How?"

"Tell me what you see; tell me what you think happened here and here—" I pointed to the empty space between the bus burning and my birth. "You read her journal and you know the 1961 history better than I do. Talk to me while I draw."

He settled back into the chair as I took the charcoal in my hand. "After the bus burning, she returned to Bayside and her job as a lifeguard at the country club."

I drew a rectangle, making small squares of tile around the pool, a lifeguard stand. Hutch stood and walked to the kitchen. "You have anything to drink around here?"

"Wine in the fridge, glasses in the cabinet on the left." I didn't look up from my sketch, now filling in the pool with blue water. The sounds of an opening refrigerator, clinking glasses, rain

251

running with the sound of a whispered waterfall outside the window. Then music: Hutch had found my iPod in the speakers and turned it on. Melody Gardot sang "Love Me Like a River Does." And Hutch came to sit next to me.

"You know her work?" he asked.

"No." I turned to him and smiled. "I just have it on my iPod."

"Smart-ass." He handed me a glass of wine. "She's one of my very favorites, but most people haven't heard of her, and when they do hear her music, they always assume—"

"That she's Norah Jones."

"Exactly," he said, then took a sip of his wine and watched me sketch the pool.

We were silent for a long while, listening to Melody sing of love and pain, and when I finished the pool, Hutch said, "and then during the nights they went to meetings and bars."

"It's almost impossible to imagine."

He placed his hand on top of mine. "Full of righteous anger, I think maybe one of the first things they would have done after the bus was spend time all together planning. I see them sitting in smoky honky-tonks, listening to jazz or bluegrass music, drinking warm bourbon . . ."

I lifted the charcoal again, and my hand moved across the paper. A booth appeared and then the people, both colored and white, leaning toward one another, faceless and nameless.

Our wine was finished and the rain now mixed with wind, clamoring against the windows with force. I stopped drawing for a moment, listening. Hutch's finger trailed down my arm until he reached my hand, taking the pencil, winding his fingers through mine as if he were slowly sewing us together again and then again.

He stood and pulled me up also. The afternoon sun was obliterated by a dusk created of rain and cloud. Together we sat on the long couch, my head resting on his shoulder. Without words spoken or excuses made, we stretched out, our legs winding together as roots of one. My flip-flops fell to the floor and I looked down at him, my hair falling, brushing against his face. His hand came up and wrapped around my neck, pulling me down, and then farther down to what I thought would be his mouth, his lips, his warmth; but instead he settled my head onto his shoulder, where he ran his hand through my hair.

"Sleep," he said. "I know it's been a long time since you've done that well. Sleep now."

"I didn't tell you that," I murmured into his neck.

"You didn't have to."

I exhaled and couldn't discern where my body and skin began and his ended.

The shaking and pounding were the sounds of thunder, and I awoke from the deepest sleep I'd known in years; the kind of sleep that I don't come out of easily. I gripped Hutch's shirt, orienting myself, and then looked at him, smiling.

"What time is it?"

"Midnight . . . ," he whispered.

"Wow. I've been asleep for hours . . . I'm so sorry. I probably would've slept a hundred years except for the thunder."

"Ellie, that's not thunder. Someone is at the door."

I jumped up, stumbling, falling, and then righting myself. Hutch sat up and glanced around the room as if looking for escape.

Then the door opened. I'd never locked it—why would I?

And my husband stood on the threshold, holding an umbrella, staring into the room as if his eyes were drinking in every detail, getting drunk on rage.

"Rusty," I said, walking toward him.

"Well, looks like I surprised you." He shook his umbrella and threw it into the house, where it landed on the hardwood floors, scattering rain like tears.

I turned and Hutch was standing at the dining room table. "Hello, Rusty," he said, walking toward us now, grabbing his car keys from the side table on the way to the door. He reached out to shake Rusty's hand, but Rusty loped past him to me.

"What the hell is going on?" Rusty asked.

"We were working," I said, pointing to the timeline.

"At midnight? You were working?" He glanced at the timeline. "Yep, that's it. Working."

Hutch stepped forward to Rusty. "Yes, working. Ellie has been a huge help to me with this history center exhibit." He turned to me. "Bye now. We'll talk soon." And he was gone.

Rusty stared at me and then started to laugh, a hysterical sound that made my stomach lurch. "Work?"

"Yes," I said. "Wow, what are you doing here?"

"Is that the first thing you'd say to someone who came to surprise you? Someone who needs to see you?"

"I'm sorry," I said. "I don't know the right thing to say. I'm . . . surprised. Yes." My legs were weak.

"You want to know why I'm here? I'll tell you." He threw a small blue box onto the table; it landed on top of the Summer House sketch. "I had something to tell you. You wanna hear it?"

"Of course."

"Here is what I was going to say." He stretched out his hands. "I don't know a lot of things, like how to be the perfect husband or how to be the perfect dad. I don't always know the right thing to say. Or the right thing to do. But this I do know: I've never wanted to live my life with anyone but you."

I gripped the edge of the table behind me. "Oh, Rusty."

"But that is what I was going to say. I practiced it the entire drive here, sick and missing you. But now I think I have something else to say."

"What's that?"

"What in the hell are you doing?"

"I don't know what to tell you that I haven't already told you."

Rusty walked to the window and stared outside. "This place is beautiful, Ellie. I can see why you wouldn't come home. I can't give you something like this. . . ." His voice had the sound of the "other" Rusty.

"That's not it." I was defensive, feeling like a child who had been accused of being selfish yet wasn't. "I am so sorry this is hard for you. I am. I know you're trying to say and do the right thing. I just can't find it in me to believe you. That's all. It's not that you don't give me enough. And it's not that my life doesn't look perfect; it does."

"So what do you want? Really, I think it is perfectly evident what I want. I want you to come home. What do you want?"

"I want the tender pieces of me to survive."

"What do you want *me* to do?" he asked.

"I don't know."

Three words that fell into the room like dyna-mite.

His hands moved before the lecture began. "Ellie, for God's sake. You've left all of us at home. Your dad. Me. Your friends." His fist made bullet points in the air as if he were giving a presentation. "You've left your responsibilities. I understand you're grieving about your mother and you miss Lil. But this is called running away. You're here in the middle of nowhere without any friends."

"I have friends," I whispered.

"Who? Your mother's best friend and an old boyfriend?"

"Stop," I said.

"Okay, this isn't going the way I planned." He rubbed his face and eyes. "I just don't under-stand at all. One minute we're fine and the next you're weeping over a bird and packing a suit-case and off to Alabama alone in a guesthouse with your old boyfriend. Seriously. What the hell is going on? I want you to come home. I want our life. We've worked so hard and made it so far. I understand if you need some time to yourself, but this is long enough. Really, long enough." He backed away and plopped onto the lounge chair, dropping his head into his hands. "I've never seen you like this, and I can't stand it."

I walked toward him, slowly.

"You've become obsessed with these things of

your mother." He motioned toward the table. "What is this, some kind of midlife crisis—you need to find yourself? Do you know how trite that sounds?"

"I never, ever said, 'I need to find myself.' That is not what I said. I said I wanted to know my mother in a new way. And maybe, just maybe, I'd know myself better because of it."

"Same thing," he said.

"No, it is not the same thing. Can't you hear me? Please. I don't just want you to say all the right stuff and give me things—I want you to *hear* me."

"I can hear you perfectly well. You just aren't making any sense at all."

"Maybe I'm just not making the sense you want me to make." Some kind of strength—a type I hadn't known I possessed until now—wrought itself like steel into those words. I wasn't shaking. My throat wasn't closing, and the fist inside my middle let go, wiggling fingers free.

He jumped up and then took three huge steps toward me and then slammed his hand onto the dining room table. A set of charcoals fell to the floor; a pencil skittered across the wooden top.

A new breed of rage formed inside my chest. I would not and could not allow him to use my emotions to appease his desperate need for control. If I relinquished my own strength here, it would be the final time: I'd never again be able to stand up and say what I believed was true; I would again choose to calm him. My vehement surety was also slight and fragile, a small green shoot above the clods of Alabama soil that could be easily torn, stomped, or ripped. I protected this new growth. "Please leave," I said.

"Anything you want, Ellie. Anything you want. That's what I thought I'd been giving you all these years—anything you want. You're telling me that everything I've given you isn't enough."

"I didn't say it wasn't enough." I held up my hand. "I won't do this. I won't defend myself against things I didn't say. Please, please leave."

"You're losing your real life, Ellie. Me. You're losing me. You're losing your life and your friends while you hang out with these people you call friends who you don't even know. Is that what you want?"

"I know I want you to leave," I said.

"Shit, Ellie, at least you know something."

His footsteps were concrete blocks thumping against the hardwood floors. He reached the front door and turned, staring at me for the longest moment, and then slammed the door as he left. The framed nautical sketch to the left of the front door fell, shattering. I stood still, listening to his car start, and then there was the crunch of gravel as he drove away.

I shook, from my hair to my feet. I allowed

this earthquake of a shifting life to pass through me, and then I grabbed the broom from the kitchen and cleaned up the glass, placed the picture on the kitchen counter, and sipped the last of the wine.

What else, really, was there to do?

There is this one thing about having a baby—

I don't get any sleep, so I am very tired right now. I want to write more. Tell you (whoever You are) more about the year and the birth and the wedding. But I have a feeling you already know. And I am so tired I feel like my bones are made of water and that my eyelids are made of concrete.

I need to say that I hate Vietnam. Lulu's brother was killed over there. If only I could wish for it to stop. Everything seems to be going crazy—race riots, Martin Luther King, Vietnam, the 10th street hippies and flower girls— and then I look at Ellie and I am overwhelmed with how lucky I am.

Oh, and Redmond had a portrait painted of Ellie and me by the Grande Dame of southern portraits, Miss Kate

Edwards. My friends are so jealous. Like I said, I am so lucky.

Maybe my lesson is nothing what I thought it was and I need to learn this: to be happy with what I already have. To be content with what I have and stop yearning and weeping and gnashing my teeth for something I don't have. Isn't what I have enough? DO I really think I deserve more???

But this is what loss is—the constant realization that what you thought was possible is not.

So this is the year . . .

I will learn to be the most perfect mother ever. That's all I want right now. It is just all I want. I will do every-thing just right. Exactly right. This I will not mess up.

Twenty

That next morning after Rusty left, I stood in the kitchen, Melody Gardot again playing from my iPod, and I saw the gift Rusty had left. I'd forgotten about it. I picked up the small, baby blue box—the Tiffany signature known by every woman, wrapped in a white satin ribbon. I shook it lightly and heard something shimmy inside. I undid the ribbon and allowed it to fall to the table as I lifted the lid. Inside, staring up at me with one accusing, sad eye, was a single, at least three-carat diamond atop a platinum band.

I still wore the engagement ring Rusty gave me—it was a simple one-carat diamond set onto a gold band. He'd asked me many times, as had my friends, if I wanted an "upgrade." I'd always said I did not, that I liked my ring: a promise made. There was no note or letter with this new diamond, and I could only believe that he'd had a speech about recommitment and promises.

I sat on the ladder-back chair and lifted the ring from the velvet. *He loves me,* I thought. *I am so mean and cold, and he loves me.*

Then I said it out loud: "He loves me."

But the words fell flat, untrue. "He does," I

said out loud. Why else would he have bought this ring?

Because, another, quieter voice inside said, *he can't stand to lose you.*

There was a difference between not wanting to lose someone and loving someone.

I took the ring from the box and stared at it, then placed it back into the box. I didn't know which voice to listen to, and I wanted to scream. Instead, I sat at the dining room table and tore a fresh sheet of cotton watercolor paper from the pad. With colored pencils in my hand, I began to draw. This time—yes, this time—I wanted to draw and paint an entire field of flowers, a plethora of flowers, so many of them that I wouldn't be able to count them. I began; sometimes that is the best I can do: begin.

My cell phone rang, startling me. I glanced at the screen, having already decided I wouldn't answer it if it was Rusty.

Hutch.

"Hey." My voice came out with a crack in the middle of the word.

"You okay?"

"Yep, and you?"

"Can you come meet me at the library?"

"Sure . . . why?"

"I want to show you something."

"On my way," I said.

I looked at the clock and realized I'd drawn

my way into the midmorning with flowers blooming in vivid color on cream paper.

Before I left for the library, I walked over to the Summer House, finding Birdie on the back porch.

"Good morning," I said, the screen door slamming behind me. "Good *late* morning." I sat across from her, and she put down the novel she was reading.

"You okay this morning?" She placed her book on the side table and leaned forward to gaze at me in that way that unsettles and soothes simultaneously.

"I'm better than I was. I'm sorry I didn't come over for breakfast, I got carried away with a drawing and . . ."

She held up her hand. "Oh, honey, I understand. No worries."

"Did you have fun on your . . . date yesterday?" I tried not to smile through the words, but of course I did.

She made a shooing motion with her hands, as if a swarm of nonsense words had flown into the porch.

"How long have y'all been going out? I thought it was such a coincidence he was here and really it wasn't, was it?"

"We've tried to date before and it hasn't worked, but we're older now." She laughed.

"Much older, and we've been dear friends for what seems a hundred years, so maybe . . . this time."

I nodded. "It's really nice."

"Yes," she said, pausing. "It is. Love really is a surprise sometimes."

"A surprise. Yes." I settled back into the chair. "Well, right now I'm on my way to the library. I'll see you this afternoon, okay?"

She nodded. "This afternoon it is."

The library's air-conditioning chilled me. I shivered and glanced around the room, where children sat at the far end in a semi-circle, listening to the librarian read a story while someone dressed as Clifford the Big Red Dog sat in the middle of the circle with a child in its red-dog lap. To my right a door was cracked open. A sign read MICROFILM, and I opened the door, peeking in to see Hutch bent over a machine, his face pressed against the eyepiece.

I walked up behind him to watch for a moment before I tapped him on the shoulder. "Don't they have the Internet for such things as this?"

He startled, yet when he looked up at me his smile was warm. "Hey, you." He stood and faced me. "Are you okay? I am so sorry about last night. I hope . . ."

I held up my hand. "I'm fine." I sat on the chair next to his. "You find anything?"

"I get it. You don't want to talk about it. But don't tell me you're fine if you're not."

I patted the chair. "Sit, I promise I'm okay. Show me what you found."

He also sat and shook his head. "Well, when you told me your mother was in on some planning meetings and maybe even a sit-in or two, I decided to just look through all the Bayside newspapers from those two summers. I have the details, but this exhibit and timeline are visual and I wanted some pictures. . . ."

"I get it," I said, leaning closer.

"So, I have the one we found from the Freedom Ride, but you can barely see her face. But check this out." He glanced back into the machine. "Hold on, let me find the photo again." Turning knobs, Hutch quietly fine-tuned the machine.

I waited and held my hands together to keep from running my finger along his hairline, tracing the line from ear to ear at the back of his neck.

He reached his hand behind the chair while still staring into the machine. "Don't go. Wait." His hand found mine without even glancing backward, and I allowed him to hold me there until he said, "Got it. Look."

The view into the machine took me to a place and time I had never known existed. There was my mother sitting at a lunch counter next to a black man on one side and a white man on the other. They were eating sandwiches, Coca-Cola glasses at the counter. Mother was glancing over her shoulder at the camera with a closed and resolved smile. I couldn't see the two men's faces because they were faced away from the camera. The caption below read, "Desegregation laws tested at Murphy's Cafe."

I glanced up at Hutch. "Wow."

"I know. It's amazing. I read the article. Your mother was quoted saying it was peaceful. They ate and left, but the owner asked both your mother and the men to please never return. They had made their point and to please leave him alone so the KKK wouldn't target him."

"Who are the two men?" My heart sped up and I squinted back into the view, attempting to make them turn around in my mind, to see their faces.

"It doesn't say." He paused and stood up so fast that his chair fell backward, slamming onto the floor. He reached behind and picked it up while he spoke. "I have the best idea. Come with me." He pushed "print" on the machine, and while two copies of the article printed out, he gathered his things. "You're coming with me."

"Okay . . . where are we going?"

He handed me the photocopied article. "Here." He pointed to the café. "That's where."

Murphy's Café could still be on a postcard from the 1960s with the blinking neon sign and the vinyl red-checkered table coverings and booths set up against the window. The long bar faced the kitchen with salt and pepper shakers in metal holders, rice inside the salt to prevent clumping. The plastic place mats on the counter had an Alabama State map and the words *Sweet Home Alabama* scrawled across the bottom. The logo on my place mat was scarred with a coffee stain, changing the "e" in Sweet to an "a."

"Look," I said to Hutch as we sat. "Sweat Home Alabama."

He laughed. "In late June, I think that's the only proper thing to call it."

The waitress came over to us, wearing a white apron with ruffles. I felt as if I were in a black-and-white TV set. "What can I get ya?" she asked.

I glanced at the laminated menu, which had pictures. "Patty melt looks good," I said. "With fries and a Coca-Cola."

Hutch ordered a cheeseburger and excused himself to the men's room. I settled into the stool, reading the ancient but local sports news in clippings framed around the room. There were stories of touchdowns and home runs and state championships.

"Ellie . . ." Hutch called my name, and I glanced over my shoulder.

A flash went off. I blinked and a confetti of light was tossed through the air. "Hey," I hollered. "No paparazzi."

He sat next to me, shouldering his camera. "Couldn't help it."

Our food showed up, and I pulled out the newspaper clipping about the sit-in. "Okay, so they sat right here. I wonder who these two guys are."

"They wouldn't talk to the paper, but my God, Ellie, your mother would. She gave her name and the reason for being here. She wasn't scared of anyone or anything . . . it seems."

"And"—I laughed through my words—"she was obviously totally inappropriate."

"Huh?"

"My whole life, Hutch, my entire freaking life, this woman was worried about what was and what was not appropriate. And look at her." I took a juicy bite of my melt and wiped at the grease on my lips.

We turned to face each other, our knees touching. "What do you think changed?"

"Her heart broke, and then she was a wife and mother. The End. I think . . . I think this experience—whatever happened between this man and her—broke her heart permanently, and she decided that being appropriate was a much easier path. And she wanted an easier path for me. . . ."

"I'm not sure I understand."

"I'm not sure I do, either. But whatever broke her that summer made her want to protect me from any such pain. I don't blame her. I mean, I don't ever want Lil to hurt or be broken. But . . ."

"But your mother wanted to make sure you weren't a wildflower in her botanical garden."

I looked away from him, digging my fingers into the corners of my eyes as if I could absorb the unbidden tears.

"Oh, Ellie. I'm sorry . . ." He took my hands and removed them from my face. "Look at me. I'm sorry."

"I don't think I ever, once, thought of it that way."

"I was out of place there. I shouldn't have said that. I'm sorry."

I lifted my napkin and wiped my eyes. "You shouldn't be sorry for telling the truth. Now, tell me about some of the other women in the exhibit."

He took a french fry from my plate. "None of them are near as interesting as your mother. I can tell you that much."

"Even after the things she said to you, you can talk nicely about her? After . . ."

"She just was who she was, Ellie." He pointed to my purse. "You need to get that?"

"Huh?"

"Your phone—it's ringing."

"Oh." I glanced down and then looked at him. "You know how sometimes you're with someone and you're talking and thinking about something or someone else . . . how you're preoccupied and wish you were . . . elsewhere?"

He laughed. "Of course. Was your mind somewhere else?"

"No, that's the thing. When I'm with you, I don't want to be anywhere else."

He settled back into his chair and smiled at me, taking one slow swallow of his Coke before he said, "I don't think I have to tell you I feel the same."

We talked our way through our sandwiches and two more refills of Coca-Cola.

"I should go," I said.

"Yes."

He dropped cash on the counter and we walked outside, where Hutch took a few more photos of the café from the outside. "Before and after photos . . . ," he said.

"Nice idea."

We walked to our separate cars and hugged good-bye. "Thanks for helping me. I'm sure I would have found some of this, but you make it more meaningful."

I nodded. "You're welcome."

In the bright sun, he held my hand. "You wildflower." He laughed and kissed my cheek, then left without saying good-bye.

"Bye, you," I said to the empty sidewalk.

Wildflower.

It was a story I'd told Hutch, and I hadn't thought he remembered. But he had.

Mother's garden was a flurry of color and wild splendor. As a child, I'd thought it was the purest expression of beauty. Even I understood Mother's love for flowers, for their beauty, for their fragrance and extravagant fragility.

I also understood her frustration with their unpredictability and wildness—a flower's ability to become what she didn't expect or intend. When she planted a pink Lady Banksia and a red bloom emerged, she blamed the soil or the grower or the humidity.

Limestone rocks, flat and raw-edged, lined the paths between the flower beds. Moss grew in between the stepping-stones: sphagnum—even moss has a "real" name. Mother believed all living things had an ordinary name and then a cultured name.

Ellie, she'd once told me. *Yes, we call you Ellie, but your name is Lillian. Never forget that. We might call you by your ordinary name, but your real name is innocence and beauty. And this— no matter what you are called—this is who you are—Lillian.*

There was one day—a day of very young and unspecified age in my memory—when the weather was frigid and clear. I'd walked with Mother as she gently placed blankets and fleece over the rosebushes to protect them from the frost that would come that night. She mumbled their botanical names while covering the bushes, as if she were tucking precious children into bed, murmuring bedtime prayers. I was jealous in the way a child can be when the world isn't centered.

I shivered as I followed Mother. She didn't notice me or my coldness, only the flowers. Oh, how she adored them and called them by their full and real names. I ran off—I don't remember where I thought I was going, but I know what I sought: warmth, compassion, and someone who spoke my name "that" way.

I'd ended up at Sadie's house with her mom, Birdie, bundling me in blankets. "Child, what is wrong with you?"

"I want to be beautiful like those flowers. Not ordinary." What I'd really meant was that I wanted Mother to treat me the way she treated those flowers.

"Nothing living is ordinary," Birdie said while rubbing my back. "There is no ordinary beauty."

I nodded at her. "Oh, yes, there is." I wiggled closer to Birdie's warm body. "I am."

"No, precious child, you are no ordinary beauty. You are extraordinary."

Birdie had then called my parents. Mother and Daddy took me home and sat me in front of the fireplace with hot chocolate warm against my lips. I heard their voices as all children do when parents believe they can't be heard. I deciphered their words in jigsaw puzzle pieces that I put together as I pleased.

"Weren't you watching her?" My dad's voice.

"Of course I was. She was right behind me, and then she was gone." Mother was crying. "Oh, Red, she is such a wildflower."

Months later, the frost passed and the warm earth opened, allowing flowers and grass to pass through the once frozen soil. When Mother went to the nursery to buy more bulbs, I snuck a packet of wildflower seeds into the pocket of my red sundress. I figured I would be forgiven for stealing if I was doing it for a good purpose—to make Mother happy. This packet was a secret surprise for her, one that would make her smile and laugh and look me in the eyes and say my name with warm sweetness. Surely, oh, surely, she loved wildflowers.

In the middle of a moonless night, I snuck out and scattered the seeds throughout her cultured garden. Then I waited with the expectant breath-holding pleasure of any child waiting for a birthday party or a trip to Disney World. I lay in bed at night and envisioned the seeds below the deep soil, opening and thrusting upward with green stalks and wild colors like fireworks bursting into the sky.

I was coloring in my *Brady Bunch* coloring book at the kitchen counter when I saw her: Mother weeding the garden. Her straw hat covered her platinum hair, and the strings dangled below her chin, flowing in the wind. Her pink-flowered gardening gloves were yanking green stems from the ground and tossing them into a wicker basket she carried in the crook of her elbow.

I dropped the crayons to the floor and ran, slipping and running out the back door. "Stop!" I screamed.

Mother looked up from the ground. "Ellie, what is it?"

Tears were warm on my face and in my mouth —I tasted them. Mother dropped her basket and the new green shoots and brown crumbling roots landed on the ground.

"The flowers. Stop," I whispered.

"I'm picking weeds, darling. What is wrong with you?"

"Those aren't weeds. They are me. They are wildflowers. Me." I took a long breath in. "My wildflowers." I pulled the crumpled packet from the pocket of my culottes and held it out to Mother. "These."

Mother looked at the packet. "Oh no, Ellie. You planted these?"

I nodded.

"These are just ordinary wildflowers."

"There is no ordinary. All flowers are extraordinary." I tripped over the words I didn't fully understand, repeating what Birdie had told me.

"I don't understand."

I dug small holes with my fingers, trying to shove the disconnected roots back into the ground. "But you love wildflowers. . . ."

"Not in my garden, Ellie. Not here."

I froze, the heat and wetness of the day felt only as a cold ice settling over my body. I ran inside and up to my room. Mother found me under the bed. She sprawled down next to me. "Ellie, what is wrong with you?"

"I thought you wanted wildflowers. I was surprising you."

She held out her hand where dirt sat under her fingernails, the dirt from my flowers. I took that hand and crawled out. We sat on the edge of my white chenille bedspread.

"You wanted to surprise me? That is so sweet and wonderful. Thank you so much," Mother said in a singsong voice.

"But you don't love them."

"I just didn't know. That's all. I just didn't know. I thought weeds were taking over my garden. You see, wildflowers aren't a specific kind of flower. They are a mix that grow wild. . . ." Mother paused and then pointed out the window. "That garden is for botanical and cultured flowers."

"Oh," I said.

"There are thousands of wildflowers, and they grow where and when they want. But that garden is a botanical garden—one where I document and cultivate specific plants for ornamental purposes."

"Huh?"

She laughed. "Let me try new words. It is a

garden where I grow very specific flowers for their prettiness and cultured pedigree. Okay? So no wildflowers in my botanical garden. And you see, wildflowers usually aren't planted on purpose."

"Okay."

"Thanks for trying to do something sweet, Ellie. Would you like to plant a wildflower garden on the other side of the yard?"

"No, thank you, ma'am," I said.

She kissed me on the forehead. "You okay?"

"Yes."

She left me alone in my room. I stood and walked to the window overlooking her botanical garden.

Her garden: Cultivated for ornamental purposes.

Me: Not planted on purpose.

I'd told that story only once, and it was to Hutch.

I was stunned that Hutch remembered this story, yet I was filled with warmth, like the concrete sidewalk absorbing the sunlight. I walked until I reached the courthouse. I hadn't told Hutch, but I was determined to find out who else sat at Murphy's counter.

The marble steps were warm and I sat on them for a few moments, folding and unfolding the newspaper article. Happiness opened inside of me, spreading its wings. Being near Hutch always opened my heart in all the good places. I was smiling when Micah appeared in front of me.

"Well, well, little lady, what are you doing?"

I jumped up. "Micah, hello." I stumbled and righted myself on the banister. "I was about to come in to visit you when I sat down for a moment."

He sat on the steps and motioned for me to sit again. "Now, this is a lovely place to sit and watch the park, isn't it? All these years I've worked here and I've never done this."

We sat in silence for a moment, watching two boys kick a soccer ball around the grassy area across the street. "So," Micah asked, "to what do I owe the pleasure of another visit?"

I handed him the folded article. "My friend found this article and I was hoping you could tell me who the two men are in the photo."

Micah stared at the photo and his lips moved soundlessly as he read the words below. He then folded it along the same lines and handed it back to me, shaking his head. "That's me and Cotton."

"Really?" I shook my head. "This is amazing. I still can't figure out why she didn't tell me about this."

He twisted on the stairs to face me. "Don't be sad, Ms. Ellie. It only matters what your mother did and how she helped change our town and our lives. Okay?"

Micah, I understood, was not a man to argue with. He patted my knee, and then we stood to face each other. "That was an amazing day," he said. "Mr. Murphy didn't ask us to leave. He was so damn nervous I thought he might have a heart attack, and when we left, he begged us not to return. And because he didn't make us leave that day, we didn't return another. And now . . ." He paused, staring up to the sky and shaking his head in wonder as if he could see something I couldn't. And maybe he did. "Now my son's and grandson's pictures are on the walls in sports clippings. My daughter worked there her junior year in high school. We changed things. You understand?"

I nodded. "You did change things."

"Anyone can," he said, and hugged me goodbye. "Anyone at any time can change things if they care enough to do so."

When the courthouse doors swished shut, I dialed Hutch's cell phone. I wanted to tell him every word of that conversation with Micah. By the third ring, I realized that over the past few weeks, Hutch had been the first person I thought about calling or needing to talk to about anything and everything. Fear of heartbreak crawled over my chest—it had taken me years to stop making him the first person I reached for, and there I was, slipping so easily into it again.

But I didn't hang up; I waited for his voice and then told him everything Micah had told me.

I'd thought I was doing so well; that I'd shut Him out of my heart and bones, and then it happened: I awoke one morning and the pain came again and again like waves rolling on top of waves. I did the most awful of all things and lied to Redmond; the only man who has ever loved me. I told him that I must go visit Birdie because she was heading toward an awful depression and needed my help. Mama came to watch Ellie for two days and I drove to Bayside—alone and with only one obsession—to see Him.

I needed to know what He thought and felt and understood. When I arrived at His apartment, He wasn't there, but the door was unlocked. I waited and hours later when He arrived I still sat in the same chair, my hands folded, my body waiting.

He knelt in front of me to tell me the words I can barely stand to write, but that I must write because they are true and truer than truth. I must be able to read these words and remember them. He said this: "I do not love you anymore, Lilly. Go have a happy life."

I knew He was angry about the marriage and the baby, but there is no way to know what these words (I don't love you), just words, really, feel like. They must—in that order—be more than words. They are knives.

I drove straight home and crawled into my safe, wide king-size bed. It took days, but I talked myself into getting out of that bed, into living my happy life just as He had told me to do. Just as I am doing now pretending to live this happy life. . . .

But here is still and always what I wish: This is the year that He will know He loves me. This is the year He will love me as much as I love Him and He will know how it feels.

Twenty-one

After I'd left Micah, I sat on the back porch with Birdie, telling her what Hutch and I had found. My cell phone rang twice, with Dad's number flashing on the screen. "Sorry," I said to her. "I must get this."

I took the cell phone out onto the porch and returned Dad's call. We went through our formal greetings and talked of weather and Lil, and then he got to the reason for his call.

"Ellie, darling, I don't think your mother would appreciate or approve of what you're doing right now."

"You don't think she'd approve of me sitting on a back porch drinking wine with Ms. Birdie, her best friend?"

"You damn well know that's not what I mean."

"Dad, please."

"No, I've kept my mouth shut long enough. I would've let your mother deal with this, as I always let her deal with anything that had to do with you, but she's not here, is she?"

"No, she's not. And can I remind you that I'm closer to fifty than forty and I'm really not something to deal with? Not a child?"

"Then stop acting like one." His voice shook and he mustered all his emotional strength to say these things to me.

"How so?" I asked.

"Running away. You're running away like a child."

"Oh, Dad. Has Rusty been over there?"

"Of course he has. We only have each other now. This insanity must stop. I see how miserable he is without you."

"Oh, Dad."

There was silence on the line and I thought Dad had hung up, but then he spoke. "I talked to my brother yesterday. He said he's seen you a couple times."

"Yes. It was great to see him."

"Well, it sure would be nice if *we* could see you."

"Soon," I said, and walked off the porch onto the lawn, wiggling my toes in the grass. "Not today."

"Not today," he said. "Nice."

"I've got to go. Thanks so much for checking on me. I love you, Dad."

"I love you, too, Ladybug. I just want . . . you to come home."

"I know," I said.

He hung up without saying good-bye, and I stared at the phone to make sure service hadn't been dropped, that my dad really had hung up on me.

"Ellie," Birdie called me from the porch.

"Yes?" I returned to her.

"*Coastal Living* just called, and that writer is coming over to interview me. Cotton and I are gonna take her out on the boat. You want to come?"

"Absolutely," I said, and walked onto the porch. "Can I invite Hutch? He wants to hear these stories about the house."

Birdie smiled at me. "Of course. Leaving in an hour, okay?"

I settled back into the guesthouse. I'd never thought of myself as someone who ignored reality or didn't face the truth of circumstances, yet here I was pretending that my husband hadn't walked out in the middle of the night. I dropped to the couch in the guesthouse and first dialed Rusty's cell phone number. I closed my eyes as I waited for him to answer.

"What do you want?" he asked without a hello.

"I want to talk about all this awfulness. Please can we just talk?"

"Ellie, on that hell drive home all night, I decided that I will not talk about any of this to you or with you until you come home. I will not put up with this shit."

"I'm sorry, Rusty. I'm sorry you drove all night. You didn't have to leave; you could've stayed."

"There?"

"Yes, here."

"No, I couldn't have, Ellie. You come home or there is nothing to talk about."

He hung up and I curled into a ball on the couch, my heart's doors closing one by one, locks clicking shut.

And even as I knew the wrongness of it, I called Hutch and asked if he wanted to come on the boat trip and hear the Summer House stories. Of course he did.

The forty-foot Boston Whaler was named *Blind Faith*. It was tied to the edge of Birdie's dock, and Uncle Cotton was pulling the covers off the seats, tossing the fishing poles into the storage bin, and checking the engine. Birdie handed a cooler to Hutch, and he loaded it into the bow of the boat.

"Who is going to drive this thing?" I asked, stepping into the hull.

"I am." Birdie threw a pile of towels into the backseat. "It's mine. No one else touches it."

Uncle Cotton laughed and wiped down the dashboard. "Yep, until it's time to dock at dark with an outgoing tide."

Birdie threw a cleaning cloth at him. "Don't go telling all my secrets. I like everyone to think I know how to do it all."

Hutch jumped up onto the dock and unwound the front ropes. "I still believe, Ms. Birdie."

A voice then called out from the yard, "Hello."

We all looked up to see a woman walking toward us wearing white pants, a pink button-down, and a pink headband, as if she were in a Lilly Pulitzer commercial for "a day on the boat." I looked to Birdie and we both smiled.

Uncle Cotton walked toward her and offered to take her bag. He then helped her onto the boat. She smiled a pink-lipstick smile. "Hello, I'm Babs Friedman, writer for *Coastal Living*." She held out her hand to Hutch, and introductions were made all around.

Birdie drove slowly and narrated the history of Bayside. When she had finished, she turned off the motor, and with the water caressing the hull like silver hands, she allowed us to float while she opened the cooler and handed out lemonade and cucumber sandwiches. "So, Ms. Friedman," she said, and swiveled around in her captain's chair, "tell me what you'd like to know."

"Well . . ." Babs smoothed her hair back into her headband, blotted her lips. "As you know, this is a story about legends connected to homes. I've heard—through the grapevine—that when people stay with you, their wishes come true."

"Well, well . . ." Ms. Birdie shook her head. "You've heard wrongly, then. That is not the legend at all. At all."

"Oh," Babs said, switching her sandwich from one hand to the other. "Then what is it?"

"That when people stay at the house, they

discover a truth. There is a big, big difference between coming here for wish fulfillment and discovering the truth."

"And how so?" Babs took the tiniest bite of her sandwich.

"You can ask for what you want or you can ask for the truth. They are not always the same thing at all."

"Well, tell me, then, how this rumor about your home started."

Birdie settled back into her seat and glanced at Cotton and then back to Babs. "It wasn't always my house, so really the legend has absolutely nothing to do with me and everything to do with the house and the bay. My great-grandmother owned the home. And here is how the story goes . . ." Birdie paused and then took a deep breath.

Babs pulled out a pad of paper. "Do you mind if I take notes?"

"Yes." Birdie held up her hand. "I want you to really hear the story, not the facts. If you want the facts, we'll go over them later. Right now, listen to the story."

Babs tucked her notebook back into her bag. "Got it," she said.

"In a time before I knew time, people came to this house for rest and parties, for socializing and respite. My great-grandmother, it is told, had a best friend from Atlanta who came to stay with her for a month. Her name was Mitzi Burroughs. During this time, Mitzi's very well-sewn life fell apart at the seams. She met a woman here whom she became friends with, who she then discovered had been her husband's mistress for years and years. During this time, she also found a talent for pottery, and while taking a class at the studio, she met a man with her maiden name and soon discovered that her well-bred aunt, royalty in the Atlanta environs, had once had a child she left with relatives in Alabama."

"Wow," Babs said, her feet now tucked under her bottom.

I settled back into the seat. "Then what happened?"

Birdie laughed. "She panicked. What else? She went back to Atlanta and told everyone she knew to never, ever come to the Summer House unless they wanted to have their life come undone. Every time she drank at a party, she talked of the Summer House until the stories began to grow as stories grow, turning into something mystical and dreamy."

"What did she do with all that knowledge? Did she leave her husband? Confront her aunt? Start a pottery business?" Babs asked.

"No, those are all the things she could have done, but didn't. Nothing. She did nothing. She went back to her life. And that's the choice everyone has. They can wish for what they want in their life or they can face the truth, but sometimes you can't have both."

"Well, only one woman? How did this legend start with only one woman?" Babs asked.

"Ah, see, that's the thing," Birdie said. "All rumors start with one person, don't they? What happened after that was all about curiosity. What Mitzi meant as a warning became for many a challenge. Some people really did want to know about their life, to search and find. And many did."

"So what do you think it is about this house . . . your house, that . . . does this for people?"

"I can't answer that part. I just know that if you are really searching for the truth, you'll often find it in the quiet here. It might not be what you want to hear, but if you listen, you will hear. You'll discover synchronistic events all around you."

Babs leaned closer, pushing with her words. "But why this house? Why here?"

Birdie sipped her lemonade and smiled without an answer.

"Why here?" Babs asked again.

Birdie started the boat. "I don't know. I hope you didn't think I could answer the *why* part of the story for you."

Hutch leaned over then, whispered in my ear, his breath warm, "Did you know any of this?"

I shook my head. "Only the story that if you came here, your life could change."

"Let's go to the beach for a little while. You all okay with that?" Birdie asked.

"Perfect," I said, leaning back into the seat.

As we flew over the water in *Blind Faith*, I lifted my face to the wind until Birdie anchored the boat and we jumped into knee-high water to walk toward the beach. Babs stared out over the edge of the boat, biting her bottom lip. "Um, maybe I'll wait here."

Uncle Cotton held out his hand. "Come on. You'll enjoy it. Roll up your pants and get in."

Babs smiled at him and allowed him to guide her over the edge, laughing.

We walked through water until we reached the beach, where a ribbon strand of wet sand told of a retreating tide. Small shells like scattered stars sprinkled the beach. The waves were diminutive but insistent in their steady presence and sound.

I smiled at Hutch. "So do you believe all that about a single place changing a life?"

He pointed to Birdie and Babs walking away down the shoreline, still talking. "Sounds true to me."

I trailed my toe through the sand. "You know, the only time I've ever been to the Gulf Coast beaches were when we would go with the sorority in college. Remember when you and I went for that long weekend in February? We sat on the beach in sweaters and didn't even care."

"Yep, how could I forget?"

"Otherwise, my family has always gone to the Georgia coast."

"Same here. When I hear the word *beach* I think of the Georgia coast. The beaches we love end up being the ones we went to as a child."

I sat on the sand. "So," I said, leaning back and soaking in the warmth from the earth. "Remember when Cotton gave that lecture?" I pointed to Uncle Cotton walking with Birdie and Babs.

"We heard only the end."

"He talked about not really knowing the ending."

"I think there's more to it than what we heard. It was called 'Life as a Story'—I'm sure we only caught the question session."

"You think life is a story in a way?"

"Yes, I do. Don't you?" he asked.

"Sometimes . . . yes. I mean, if I saw my life as *my own* story. Really, if I saw my life as my story and not a player in someone else's story, if I wasn't *just* 'the wife' in the story. Or *just* 'the mother' in the story. Or *just* 'the daughter' in the story . . ."

"How can you not be, though? You are also all those things. I think we can be both. Living our story and in someone else's story."

"And you really can't make someone else live yours."

"You can try. If you really want to spend your entire life controlling others, I guess you can try."

Life slowed and I understood, in the certain way the tide knew when to ebb, that it was time for me to go home and write my own next chapter. Or at least the next page.

"I think," I mumbled, quiet and with my eyes closed, "all you can do is write the next page."

"Yes," he said. "Sometimes that is all you can do. Or just the next sentence, even." He brushed my hair off my forehead. "Do you think the Summer House is changing your story?"

"Yes." I drew a circle in the sand, twirling my finger in a spiral toward its center. "Maybe the rumors are true."

Babs, Uncle Cotton, and Birdie were so far down the beach that they appeared as children against the coastal backdrop. Hutch stared at me and then stood, reaching his hand to pull me up.

"Sit down," I said.. "Where are you going?"

"I can't do this. I can't get lost again."

"What do you mean?"

"You always did that. Said 'What do you mean?' when you didn't want to respond." His voice was changing, but I couldn't yet say how.

"Because I don't know what you want me to say. I don't know what you . . . really mean." I sat up, brushing the hair out of my face, the dizziness out of my head.

"I mean this—us—is too easy. I could get lost

in *us* in a bad way. And I want to, but I won't."

"Oh. That's not what I was . . . trying to do. That's not what—"

"I know that's not what you're trying to do. It doesn't matter what we were trying and *not* trying to do, really. It matters what happens. I can't ever let myself get lost in this again."

"I'm sorry, Hutch. I wasn't trying to start anything . . . I just like being around you. The feeling I have when I'm with you." I sank into myself, frustrated.

"I know."

"When you left Birdie's party that night, I thought about how you're this mirror to me, this person who shows me who I was—the me I really liked. You're more than that, of course. But that, too."

"There are just some people that can only be who they are in your life. No one else can be that person. That's you. But I just needed to say how easy it would be to ruin everything. And I want to be careful about that. You understand, right?"

"Me too. I don't want to destroy anything." I paused. "Yes, I do understand."

Hutch sat down next to me again, and my heart ached with an old bruise.

When we returned home, good-byes were said as Birdie took Babs inside the house for a tour. Hutch walked me to the door and we stood facing each other for a long moment before he spoke.

"Thank you so much for helping me with this exhibit."

"You could have done this without me."

He smiled and dropped his forehead onto mine, whispering words that tickled my skin. "But I didn't want to do it without you."

"I'm going home tomorrow," I said with my eyes closed, as if this could hide me from the truth.

"Well, I hope you come to the exhibit opening in the spring."

"Of course." I opened my eyes to look into his.

"Okay. Bye, you."

"Bye, you."

He then kissed me, softly. We rested there, our skin finding its familiar place. He stepped back and released me, but I wasn't ready to let go. I pulled him forward, placing my head on his chest. We swayed back and forth as if cicadas were an orchestra, as if water were music in the background. Then he moved away, placing his hand on the side of my face.

"Ellie . . ." His voice was warmer than the air, more humid than leftover rain. "That was a nice kiss good-bye, but it was good-bye."

And he was gone.

Yes, I understood—when you ruin a friendship, when you destroy a heart, you can't walk back into it as if the damage were never done. I'd said "sorry," but even that word wasn't enough.

Sometimes there aren't *any* words that are enough to heal what's been broken.

As I prepared for bed, exhausted more in spirit than in bone, I knew it was time to go home. To Rusty.

The first time Rusty had told me that he loved me we'd been in his car, driving to his parents' house for a dinner party, when we were at a stoplight and I'd garnered the nerve to ask him about his old girlfriend. "So, really," I'd asked, "what's the difference between Olivia and me?"

He'd turned to me, his hand resting lightly and casually on the steering wheel. "The difference is that I didn't love her." Then he'd smiled that charming smile and turned his gaze away from me to the road, the road that took us to his parents and a future together.

I knew it wasn't exactly the same as saying "I love you," but it was enough for me then.

And slowly through our dating he'd shown me his feelings.

I'd lived in a one-bedroom apartment in Buckhead. It was an ancient building, drafty and tiny, but it was all I could afford on my salary working in the High Museum absorbing art history while shuffling papers and memberships. My passion for my job was more important than my passion for a higher paycheck, which Rusty hadn't understood.

I painted the plaster walls a creamy vanilla and hung framed reproduction posters and postcards of famous artwork. I scoured flea markets and antique marts for beautiful quilts and sheer curtains. I found mismatched plates and cups and refused Mother's offer of unused family china. When I splurged on anything, it was pillows. I loved the purest down pillows piled all over my bed.

One February, I succumbed to something I'd always bragged that I'd never had: the flu. My body felt invaded and not-mine, as if I'd somehow given permission for something else to take residence in me while I shivered and ached. Time took on an odd dimension, sometimes moving too slowly, and then I'd lose hours to some fogged memory of sleep and vivid dreams of water and ice and fire.

Rusty had come to me in the middle of this disorientation. He'd entered my room and I'd rolled over to see him, grateful for his presence in a way I'd never been before. He sat on the side of the bed and placed his cold hand on top of my forehead, pressed lightly. His voice was soft. "Oh, you poor thing. You're burning up. I'm gonna get you some Advil, and make you eat some soup your mother sent with me."

I attempted to sit up, but the room spun as if I were on a hyperspeed merry-go-round. I slumped back into the pillows. "Oh, Rusty, you're so sweet. Look, that painting is moving." The Matisse *Flowers in a Pitcher* poster across the room blurred into a mass of colors and kaleidoscope confusion.

He laughed. "Someday I'll buy you real paintings, not posters." He brushed my hair back, kissed my cheek. "And I brought your favorite cookies—those meringue things."

I laughed, and it felt good. "Silly," I said. "It's madeleines I like, not meringues."

"Can't blame a guy for at least trying, right?"

"I love you," I said, and rolled over to place my head on his lap. "I'll have the soup in a few. I just need to sleep."

He placed my head back on the pillow. I moaned, "Don't go."

"I'm not," he said.

Moments later, he returned with a glass of ice water and two Advil. I took the pills and drank the coldest water, a blessed cold. I sank back onto the pillows and he crawled in bed next to me, placed my head on his shoulder.

When I awoke, my fever had broken and I had settled into the crook of Rusty's shoulder. He was asleep, and I stared at him for the longest time, taking inventory of my body and its healing while looking at his face and wondering how I was lucky enough to have this man love me.

Just me. And me alone.

Twenty-two

The aroma of my home was familiar and native: mine. It was as if I'd been gone for thirty seconds. Nothing had changed, yet I knew that everything had been irretrievably altered. I stood in my bathroom, dropped my clothes to the floor, and walked to the shower, turning on the water and holding my palm under the flow until it was hot. I closed my eyes and allowed the water to beat on my back, my thighs. Then I went to my sanctuary—my attic studio—where instead of painting I searched for words, any words, to tell Rusty that I didn't know how to love him. It was just gone. All of it seemed gone.

His footsteps came up the back stairs and I turned to watch him walk into my studio.

He smiled. "You're really home, aren't you?"

"Yes, I am."

"Do you want to talk?"

I leaned against the old desk and folded my arms across my chest. "I do. I do want to talk."

He walked toward me and then took my right hand, lifted it to his lips. "Did you ever open the gift I bought you?"

I nodded.

"And?"

"It's beautiful, Rusty. It's amazing."

"Where is it?"

"Downstairs. In our bedroom."

His face crumpled in the same minute that my heart did the same. This was my husband. He continued. "This is just . . . not a home without you. Please tell me you're here to stay. Please." Tears filled his eyes and he sat on a threadbare chair, his head slumped into his palms.

"Oh, Rusty. I don't think . . ."

He looked up, and for the first time ever I saw my husband cry. "I'm begging you to give us just one more chance. You can't make this kind of decision after your mother's death and our daughter going off to college. You can't. Just promise me you'll give us one more chance. I know I'm not perfect, but we'll go talk to someone—you can choose. We'll go on vacation somewhere alone. Please don't walk out."

The fairy tale returned. My prince was here on his white horse. Or so it seemed. "I don't know what to do next," I said.

He looked up. "Let's start simple, okay? Dinner. Let's go out to dinner and talk. Just us. Okay?"

"Yes, that would be nice."

He smiled his cutest grin, but it had the same effect as blindfolding me in a locked labyrinth —panic.

"Oh, good. Really great." He took me in his arms and I allowed him to do this, to hold me.

∙ ∙ ∙

Rusty held my hand in the car as if we were on a date, as if he were courting me. He had a huge smile on his face, and when I asked where we were headed he said, "It's a surprise."

We drove toward midtown, and before we turned left on Piedmont, I knew where we were going. "The botanical gardens," I said.

The XM radio played Melody Gardot and my heart squeezed with pain. He turned the music up. "Great Norah Jones song." And then he turned to me at the stoplight. "Yes. There's a jazz concert tonight. I wanted to surprise you. I have a picnic from Henri's packed in the trunk. I thought this would make for a nice evening."

"This is an amazing idea," I said, wondering how he didn't hear the jagged edges of fear in my every spoken word. How could he not feel the quiver of my skin as I withdrew from his touch? Not see the tightening of my throat? Had I become that good at faking satisfaction, so expert at feigning contentment, that he couldn't read a single emotion?

While he spread the picnic onto a blanket, I became an observer, floating above myself and watching the crowd filter into the gardens. How could I ever be in a place like this and not think of Mother? The crowning achievement of her life was being president of the Atlanta Botanical Society. If they'd given her a crown and banner, she'd have worn it every day. "God, Mother worshipped this place," I said.

Rusty stuck a corkscrew into a wine bottle and laughed. "More than she loved most people, I think."

"Me too."

And see, that's the thing with marriage—after years and years, you don't have to explain what you're talking about, you just know. You speak in code and there is an understanding, as if you are two parts of one whole and one thing could not be understood without the other.

My thoughts were as murky as muddy water, shifting, changing, clearing, and then darkening again.

The night was muggy, but a breeze blew in from the south almost as if the bay wind had followed me to Atlanta. We sipped our wine, listening to music. Friends stopped by and said hello. My heart slowed, and understanding flooded over me: I'd been in a rough place, but everyone can be, and surely we could overcome. What is anything worth if we give up on it just when it gets difficult? All my surety about telling him how I felt fled like a flock of egrets startled on the waterway.

When we returned home, Rusty turned on ESPN and I wandered back to the bedroom to read. Rusty entered the room. "Ellie, what can I do to help us go back to normal?"

"I don't want it to go back to normal."

We sat on the edge of the bed. "I don't know what you want to change."

"Maybe we just figure that out as we go along. I just know I want it . . . better."

"That's a little vague. Name one thing you want better," he said.

I closed my eyes. "I want you to speak kindly to me. Even when you're mad—be kind. Your meanness has taken something out of me."

He took my hands. "I've never, ever, meant to be unkind. Anything you want to change about you? Or is this only about me changing?"

I stared at him without an answer.

"Ellie, I love our life. I just do. This empty house was the worst thing I've ever experienced."

"But can't you see—that loving our life is not the same as loving me."

"What the hell are you talking about?" He jumped up to pace the room like an animal looking for an escape. "Love isn't a feeling, Ellie. It's commitment to stay. It's that. If love were a feeling, we'd all be in trouble. Feelings come and feelings go."

"Then mine are gone."

His face shifted into ten faces—moving, raging, calming . . .

I held my breath for as long as I could. "I'm sorry, Rusty. That was mean."

"Something is wrong with you."

"Maybe there is, Rusty." I stood, facing him. "Maybe there is something wrong with me. But how the hell would you know when you don't care about what I care about or want or need or . . ." I took in a long breath, taking advantage of his shock. "You only care that I'm doing all the things you need me to do to make your life . . . easy."

"That's not true." His face shook with the words. "I love you. I don't ever want to be without you. I don't need to understand your insides or anything crazy like that."

"What if I want to know you that way?"

"There is nothing you don't know about me."

"There's so much I don't know."

He sat on the edge of the bed, pulling me toward him. "You're just upset, darling. This has all been awful. You don't mean all these things you're saying. You don't." He gently pushed me back, sliding his hands underneath my silk blouse; I pulled away. He leaned back. "I know these have been hard days, but Ellie, please love me."

I looked at my husband and knew that if I couldn't love him then, I couldn't at all. I placed my hand on the side of his face. He leaned in and kissed me harder now, lifting off my shirt and unbuttoning my linen pants. He stood over me and smiled, then removed his shirt and khakis before climbing into bed. The motions were familiar—I'd known them for over twenty years—and my body slipped into the movements with ease.

Clothes were scattered on the floor and our bodies came together until Rusty was finished. He rolled to his side and stretched out next to me, placing his hand on top of my breast. "You are all I have ever wanted or needed, Ellie Calvin."

I turned toward him so his hand fell to the mattress. I lifted the covers over our bodies. "I'm so tired." My eyes closed.

He kissed each of my eyelids, and then he left the bed. "You sleep, darling. I'm gonna go catch the Braves game on TV."

" 'Kay," I said, and dropped back onto the pillow.

He turned off the light and shut the door. My house surrounded me with its warmth, with all I'd invested in its rooms and spaces. This, I thought, was where I had spent my married life. *Spent. Invested.* I knew the words and what they meant.

I was wrapped in a bedsheet, and I had a thought as vivid and particular as any flower petal I had ever painted: *I don't want to live this story.*

Maybe Rusty was right: Something was wrong with me, deeply and terribly wrong with me, if I couldn't love him. I thought of Mother and the ways she loved; of Dad and how he loved; of Rusty. And Hutch. And Birdie. I saw this landscape of different loves: mountains and valleys and rivers and lakes; beaches and deserts and seas. And then I heard Hutch say, *When I hear the word* beach *I think of the Georgia coast. The beaches we love end up being the ones we went to as a child.*

I had married the landscape of my childhood —a distinct geography where Mother pointed out the appropriate landmarks.

"Oh, Hutch," I whispered.

But I refused to be that woman—the one who spent her life loving a man she could not have, loving the distant past more than the present or future.

Did, I wondered, my parents' choices come down to me through unspoken DNA, whispered choices that my soul heard?

Choose safety, Ellie. Choose safety.

It's the same as love. Or close enough.

Close enough.

The dream that came that night was vivid, seeming not a dream at all, so that when I awoke, startled and shaking, I was stunned to be in bed.

I am in my backyard, under the largest of our magnolia trees. The cardinal, the one with the injured wing, is above me looking down, staring at me with her dark eyes. I admire the beauty of the day, the clearest of blue skies, the greenest grass, and the oversize leaves on the ground. I am filled with joy. I attempt to step toward the largest leaf I've ever seen, fascinated with its size and shadows, when I realize my feet won't move; I am fastened to the ground. I look down to see the roots of the magnolia tree wrapped around my feet, around my legs, the knobby bark twisted and knotted tight and high to my thighs. I try to scream, but no sound comes. The branches stretch into the sky until they become part of the clouds. The magnolia blossoms are as large as human heads, and the bird has disappeared. I am stuck; the roots climb higher, toward my hips, higher. I bend over to grab at these roots, but my hands are useless against the solid bark. I claw at my legs, at the air, screaming in a voiceless terror.

When I awoke I was covered in the coldest sweat, scratches on my legs and thighs. I wrapped my arms around my knees, wiggled my feet below me, and then turned to the empty side of the bed, relieved that Rusty wasn't there, that he'd probably fallen asleep watching the Braves game.

Relief was not the emotion I wanted or needed, but there it was, squatting on my heart to remind me of my inability to love. I curled into a tight knot and shut my eyes.

This was an incredible year of financial success. Atlanta is growing in reputation and size just as Redmond is in his job and I am in my volunteer duties. I think I have finally made Ellie realize that marrying Rusty is a logical choice. All her life I have tried to make her understand that her heart cannot go making willy-nilly decisions about life, as I know better than anyone those are the decisions that cause the problems.

There are certain things we have control over in our lives—and love CAN be one of them. She can choose whom to love and spend the rest of her life with. If my hard-earned lessons can do anybody some good, it should be Ellie, and this is what I know: the heart is deceitful and therefore choices must be made with logic and care, not emotion. Of course it would have been silly and irresponsible for her to stay with that Hutchinson person from Alabama who obviously has no family prospects for a decent life. Now, Rusty with his Atlanta family close to ours, with his money and his reputation, is a much, much better fit for Ellie, and I believe I have helped make her understand this truth.

If only I had understood these things when I was her age—if only I had known that love is fickle and foolish. It is commitment and logic that make a home, a solid and beautiful home. How I could have ever thought otherwise is amazing to me. I look back at the girl who loved Him like that and I am embarrassed for her. Of course those were just hormones, just feelings. Nothing more. Nothing less.

Twenty-three

The morning arrived along with the pattern sewn over years of marriage. I rose and began "the list" of what must be done that day, avoiding the thorough comprehension that the house felt carceral and tight. I sorted the mail and waded through the voice messages and urgent requests until Sadie arrived. We'd planned on lunch and a visit to Mother's grave. Each time Hutch entered my mind (about every five seconds), I shoved the thought away, which was akin to shoving a boulder up a hill. But I was determined. I was.

Sadie and I had just left Mother's grave, where fresh dirt still surrounded the outside rim of the rectangle where she was buried. I couldn't seem to add facts—she was dead plus she was in a coffin plus she was buried here—to equal anything I fully understood. I'd left a fresh lily at the side of her gravestone. Sadie stood with me in silence.

Together we walked toward the lake, where swans floated like plastic ornaments. We sat on a bench and I pointed to a dark wood chapel a few hundred yards away. "I've always noticed how beautiful that church is, but I've never been."

"Let's go in," Sadie said. "I've always wondered what it looks like inside."

A gravel walkway led toward the all-stone structure, where I hoped there would be air-conditioning. Sweat gathered on every surface of my body; the oppressive August heat made me dizzy. We approached the chapel and realized there was a ceremony of some sort. "Come on, let's see what's going on," Sadie said.

We entered and found there were no electric lights or candles; the nave was lit with only the afternoon sun flowing into the room. There was a crowd around a rope, staring into the center where I couldn't see. A bald, smiling monk wore a yellow robe and walked through the crowd; he wore a name tag.

"Monks?" I asked Sadie.

"A monk with a name tag," she said. "I wouldn't think a monk would wear such a thing." She placed her hand over her mouth to stifle her laugh. "Let me figure out what's going on. I'll be right back."

A hole opened in the crowd and I moved forward: My breath caught in between an inhale and an exhale. There on a table surrounded by black rope was a round design, artwork of the most elaborate and intricate pattern I'd ever seen—a mosaic or tiny tiles set into the glass table. I leaned over, looked closer, and saw the design was made of sand. The circle was completed with symbols and patterns I knew must have sacred meaning. I turned to the woman on my right; her hand was over her heart. "What is this?" I asked.

She lifted her eyebrows. "It's a Tibetan sand mandala."

"Huh?" I scooted closer. The beauty of the art, a pattern I could never paint with any brush or pencil, struck my heart like an ancient bell. The pattern wove in and out of itself, the beginning and the end unclear; the design began anywhere the gaze landed and yet never really ended.

The woman continued, "They—the monks— spend days making it. Hours every day in some kind of meditative way."

I glanced between the sand and this woman. "Anyone here could just blow on it and it would be gone. Why isn't anyone watching it or something? It would take only one big wind. One breath."

"Exactly."

Sadie came up next to me. "They're about to have some kind of ceremony. You want to get out of here?"

"No." I pointed to the design. "Look at this. I mean, really look at it. If you do, you won't be able to stop. There's no way to see it all. And these monks made it out of sand granules over the past couple days."

Sadie turned and we stared at this mandala

until a woman asked for everyone at the front to please make room for others to see. We stepped back and found chairs at the side of the chapel. Windows stretched from the top to the bottom of this sacred space; light spilled into the room as if magnetically drawn by the mandala at its center.

"I bet every single thing on it means something," I said.

"Yeah." She pointed toward a group of monks coming in the front door. "I don't think they'd spend all day making something that didn't matter."

The monks entered the space in a procession. They wore yellow robes and yellow hats with large plumes that reminded me of the fake Roman soldiers in front of the Colosseum hawking their photos. "What's going on?"

She shrugged.

The monk with the name tag took the front microphone and in broken but calm English explained the mandala, how it was made in meditative silence over the past four days; how the sand was dropped through the end of a metal funnel; how this design had an outer, inner, and secret meaning; how its destruction symbolized the impermanence of all that exists; how the sand would be swept up and poured into the river for healing.

"Destroyed?" I whispered to Sadie.

"Maybe they allow it to blow away slowly over time or something."

Upon reaching the front door of the chapel, the monks walked down the aisle onto the altar, where they each took an instrument. They were lined up in front of the mandala, and the monk in the middle began this low, thrumming noise in his throat, a sound that vibrated through the chapel and into my chest. Tingling began at the edges of my heart and moved outward. The other monks joined, and for the ten minutes they hummed and chanted, my heart slowed. I closed my eyes in that place where monks chanted some sacred promise or blessing, in that place where I was quiet and serene.

A loud gong sounded; crashing cymbals; a bell. I startled and my eyes flew open. My chest seemed to expand. Something that sounded like a bagpipe, but wasn't, began its haunting melody, and the low, deep voices changed into a sweet chanting that was more like a lullaby.

A monk broke away from the group. He carried a bell and he strolled around the mandala, filling the room with the sweet tenderness of a single bell rung—perfect patience extending across time and space.

I was smiling when the monk lifted his finger, and I knew what he was going to do; I jumped up. Sadie grabbed my arm. "Ellie," she whispered.

I looked at her. "No," I said, and moved in a half step to stop this monk from obliterating what had taken days and meditation and practice and skill to create. Something visceral and broken in me wanted to stop this monk from sweeping away the sand, the art, the sacred beauty they'd created. I didn't want him to destroy what I hadn't known existed an hour ago.

Faces turned toward me, and I was back in my body, back in that chapel. I sat, knowing I couldn't stop or change what was about to occur. The monk took his forefinger and ran it across the sand from the far left corner toward the center. He divided the mandala into six pie-shaped pieces and then used a small handheld broom to sweep the entire structure into a miniature pile in the middle of the table. The other monks joined him and swept the sand into small bags to then distribute to the audience "for healing."

"Why do they do that?" I asked.

The woman next to me turned to me and smiled. "It represents the impermanence of life; of everything. Letting go. It's a healing ceremony."

"How can destroying their art be healing?"

She smiled and stood, looking down at me. "This is my favorite mandala design. The Mother."

"Excuse me?" I stood to face her.

She explained the mandala's meaning and symbols from the center to the outside, the vessels, how it was meant to engender compassion, healing, and purification. But I couldn't hear her words because the only word that reverberated through me was "mother." I turned to Sadie, but she was gone.

I searched the crowd and then went outside to gulp fresh air.

Mother.

The dissolution. The dissolving. The destroying. The letting go and healing.

I found a stone wall and sat, stared out across the wide lawn. Sadie found me, and she sat, handing me a plastic bag with a teaspoon of sand in it. "I got you one," she said.

"What am I supposed to do with this?"

"Whatever you want, I guess."

I walked alone to Mother's grave and spread a few granules onto the dirt in silence. But inside I knew: I was letting go of expectations and demands—not only the ones I had placed on her, but the ones she had placed on me. I tucked the bag into my purse and knelt before her grave and whispered, "I love you."

By dinner, I'd made some kind of order from household chaos. Rusty and I stood in the kitchen sipping white wine while he grilled steaks and I roasted asparagus and rice simmered. He told me about his clients and the assistant who lost the documents he needed for a meeting; how

Sinclair Morris had been busted for embezzlement. He talked of gossip and conquest and common friends.

I dropped into the armchair in the sitting room, staring from the fireplace with the fake logs and the gas starter, to the oil painting of some hunting scene in England—a sport my husband does not do in a place we've never been —hanging over my mantel.

"I want to talk to you," I said.

He sat next to me, turning on the TV and sipping his tumbler of whiskey. "Hmmm. Yes, darling?" But his eyes didn't move from the TV, where he switched channels until he found the baseball game.

"How can you do this? How can you pretend we didn't have a huge fight last night?"

He stared at me as if I were speaking another language. "Why drag last night's fight into today like a dead animal?"

"It's not a dead animal. You didn't hear a word I said."

"Yes, I did, Ellie. Why can't you just let things go?"

"I don't want to live this story," I said.

He clicked a button on the channel changer so the TV was mute, although the game continued on the screen. "Live a story? What do you mean?" he asked, but his eyes wandered to the TV.

"I want to live a life with a heart and a soul and choices and characters and beautiful scenes. I don't want to live in a pile of facts. Perfect, nicely lined-up facts—like my lists."

"I don't . . . get it."

I took his hand. God, I wanted him to understand this. "Mother." I took in a breath. "When she first started writing in her journal, she told stories. And then things didn't go her way and she started giving the facts, started talking about only specific circumstances. That's it. I think when we start telling the facts instead of the story . . . when we start living for the stuff and how it looks, we close our hearts."

Rusty screwed up his face in confusion.

"She battled her heart and then she lost it. I do *not* want to do that." I shook my head.

Rusty looked at the screen; saw that the Braves were losing. "Shit," he said, and clicked the "off" button. Then he looked at me. "Okay, so you feel like you've come to some . . . understanding?"

"Yes."

"I'm relieved you've found some peace with it. Happy. I just want us to be okay. To get past all this," he said, and I heard the slightest slur to his words, which meant he'd refilled his whiskey a few times.

"Rusty, did you hear what I said? I don't want to live this story."

"You mean your mother's, right? Not this

318

one," he said, and waved his hand around the room.

"Both."

I so wanted him to lean forward with something that resembled a real emotion, something that rang of soul. I wanted him to tell me he wanted to be part of my story and I'd be part of his. With expectant breath, I waited.

Here, this was his choice.

"I have no idea what in the living hell you're talking about. Seriously, Ellie. Story? Are you crazy? Has your mother's journal made you insane? You want a new story? This one isn't good enough?"

I whispered, "I didn't say it wasn't good enough."

"Can't you just be happy with what you have and why you have it? Can't you look around you and see that you live a great story or whatever the hell you want to call it? What do you want? A fairy tale? Looks to me like you've already got one."

"No, see, that's the thing. That's the exact thing—I don't want a fairy tale."

His face softened and he leaned forward. "You're my fairy tale."

"See?" I stood now. "That's the thing that makes me crazy. The thing that doesn't let me find your heart."

"What's *the thing?*"

"The way you can go back and forth like that. Mean, then soft. Angry, then sweet. All in a single breath. You have two ways of controlling the conversation, of managing our life and me: super-sweet or rage. You go between them until you find the one that will rule the situation."

"I have no idea what you're saying. You don't make any sense anymore, Ellie. I'm worried."

"You really don't have any idea, do you?"

"This is what I have no idea about—Ellie . . . do you love me?"

When silence was my answer, he stared at me for the longest time, the world stretching itself out in waiting. Could I say it? I knew if I did, I'd be lying. Would I lie to save a marriage? To save a lifestyle?

Rusty stood and threw back his whiskey. "Don't fucking bother to answer. I already know." He grabbed his car keys and was out the door before I inhaled.

I ran out to the garage, but he was already backing out, his car just making it under the rising garage door. The headlights were off and his car appeared as a black hole in the air, something dark and ominous that would suck the rest of our world into this furious place. The car careened toward the street in reverse, and then there was the squeal of tires as he turned sharply to be parallel to the street, driving forward. There was the quick thump-thump sound of something beneath his wheels and then the night filled with those sounds of darkness—crickets, a siren far off, the hum of the air-conditioning system—and then my voice calling his name. I sat on the driveway, the dew seeping through my skirt.

I saw then the source of the thumping noise— a chipmunk lay flattened and bloody at the end of our driveway. Sneaking through the yards in the middle of the night, this small animal could not have known the car would be backing up. How was he to know the danger in his usual safe darkness? How were any of us to know the danger in our safe darkness?

The next noise was the resonant but farraginous sound of twisted metal; a nightmare squeal followed by eerie silence, as if the night held its breath with me.

I ran while dialing 911 on my cell phone. I needed only to go a block before I saw Rusty's car splattered like paint onto a tree. He climbed out of the driver's seat and I stumbled to him; I didn't feel the branches that scraped my face or the broken glass that sliced my feet. His car was embedded in a pine tree, as if it had grown from the trunk like an appendage.

He screamed into the night, "Shit. Shit." His right arm dangled at an odd angle that made me dizzy. Together we stood in the middle of the suburban street with the sirens approaching and blood dripping from a cut in Rusty's cheek.

"You called the police?" Rusty attempted to lift his hand and groaned, pulling it to his chest.

"Of course. God, you need an ambulance."

He glanced down the street, where red lights flashed against trees like children playing ghost in the graveyard. He grabbed my hand. "You have to say you were driving. I've been drinking. You have to say you were driving."

"Huh?"

"Ellie, listen to me. Carefully. I'm not drunk, but they'll give me a breath test and I probably won't pass. Just say you were driving." He glanced at the police car now rounding the corner. "Please say you understand me."

"Of course I understand you, Rusty. Of course I do."

The cot in the emergency room was thrust against the far wall. Rusty's eyes were closed, his hair matted and moist against his skull. The pale blue gown was gathered and tucked under his left leg. I reached over and freed the fabric, then pulled it over his bare leg. Vulnerable and bruised, Rusty seemed a sudden-child, not a man to fear. I placed my hand on his forehead over the bandage; he groaned. As a body heals, maybe we could also.

There was relief that nothing was wrong but a broken arm and some bruises. The discharge nurse entered the room when Rusty opened his eyes. "This is what happens. You know that, right?" He spoke in a harsh voice through closed lips.

"What?" I was cut loose in a rapid and dizzying motion from the world I'd just built: the healing world.

"It's what I told you from the beginning— breaking up a family destroys things, Ellie. You know that. I know that."

"Wow, and I thought this was all because you drove drunk. But this is my fault?"

"Of course it is." Rusty closed his eyes. "Could you please leave so I can get dressed and get the hell out of this place?"

I walked out of the room as the last and most fragile bones of our marriage broke inside me.

Excerpt from Unsent Letter Found in Lillian Ashford Eddington's Journal
THE LAST LOVE LETTER

I can no longer bear the missing of you; it is like a weight in my bones holding me down, keeping me from living the life I am sure I was meant to live. The desire and the missing are sewn into my soul with a dull needle, stitches of need that ache in my innermost parts. How does a girl live with this? How does she go on with this pain?

I was completely prepared to hurt, but not like this. No, definitely not like this. . . .

Twenty-four

The deep voices coming from the kitchen confused me; there was the aroma of coffee and a cramp in my neck. Then I was fully awake—I'd slept on the chair in the sunroom. My cell phone rang on the side table and I fumbled, dropping it to the slate floor.

"Hello—" My voice cracked.

"Ellie."

His voice. Hutch's voice.

"Oh, you," I said, sitting up and rubbing my eyes. My heart flipped over in delight, reminding me once again of the treasure of him.

"I shouldn't have called. I know."

"I am so glad you did." I glanced at the clock, orienting myself to time and day and space. Ten A.M. My sunroom.

"I just wanted to see how you are; make sure you're okay."

"Where are you?"

The clang of metal against metal. "My kitchen."

"I can't talk now, Hutch. I . . . can't."

"I understand."

"Can I see you?" I asked.

"No."

I dropped my head into my hands, my heart tipping over. "Okay. Then why did you call?"

"I'm not sure." He paused, and the sound of a microwave or coffeemaker beeped in the background. "I felt like you were in trouble or . . . I'm not sure. But now that I hear your voice . . ."

"Trouble."

"You're not, right?"

"I guess that depends on your definition." I looked up then, and there was Dad staring into the sunroom, watching me as if I were twelve years old and had broken my arm; sympathy on his face like a veil. "I have to go." I hung up the phone and stood to Dad.

"Ladybug, are you okay?"

"I think."

Rusty came from behind Dad. "She's fine."

Dad took my hand. "Rusty called this morning to tell me about the accident. My brother is on the way, too. He wanted to visit anyway and—"

"Uncle Cotton is coming?" I walked out of the sunroom.

Rusty grabbed my arm. "Where are you going?"

"Coffee." I pointed to the kitchen.

Dad followed me. "Seriously, are you okay?"

"Of course." In the kitchen, I opened the cupboard and took out a mug that said, "World's Best Mom." It was a Mother's Day gift years ago, one that Lil had made in art class. I filled it with hot coffee.

"It's so weird how you weren't hurt at all. Thank God." Dad's voice tripped on the word *hurt* as if it were a broken stepping-stone.

Rusty coughed. "Listen, the tow truck already got the car. I took care of that."

"I'm not hurt," I said to Dad, "because I wasn't driving."

"What? I'm confused." He looked between Rusty and me as if he were playing a ping-pong game of eye contact.

"I told the police I was driving because Rusty had been drinking."

"This is absurd," Dad said.

Rusty made a noise that somehow resembled a laugh but was not one at all. "Absurd? So would you rather be bailing me out for a DUI or standing here in the kitchen drinking coffee?"

"I'd rather you not have driven," Dad said.

Rusty glanced around the room and, finding no ally, said, "I'm going to the office to get some files. I don't need to explain myself. This is my home. I'll be home in thirty minutes."

Rusty placed his coffee mug on the counter and left without speaking again, yet his words had filled the kitchen, leaving no room for air.

Dad and I stood quietly until I said, "Let's go outside and sit on the patio."

Dad placed his arm over my shoulder. "I brought that box of stories you asked me about. I found them in the attic next to the Christmas decorations. I looked everywhere for them." He tapped a blue plastic bin I hadn't noticed sitting on my counter. "Your mother kept everything you ever wrote. Did you know that?"

I nodded. "I did. I just couldn't find it."

"This one is labeled 'Ellie's Stories.' You know your mother; she labeled and organized everything from her clothes to her photos. I'm surprised she didn't box and label my underwear." He laughed and shook his head. "Anyway, it's right here for you. I'm gonna head over to the hardware store and pick up some tools I need to fix your back fence. I see it separating in the far right corner. I'll be back in a few."

I hugged him. "Thanks, Dad."

I wandered out to the back patio and sifted through the box of stories and drawings from my childhood and then lifted my face to the sun, knowing that this was the day I would leave Rusty Calvin. If fear and calm can live together in harmony, they did for that moment.

The screen door slammed and I spun around, expecting Rusty and finding Uncle Cotton. I jumped up, hugging him. "What are you doing here?"

"Well, I was planning on visiting your dad anyway, and when he called last night and told me about your accident, I figured now was as good a time as any."

I took his hand and squeezed it. "Thank you

so much, but really . . . it wasn't my accident."

He nodded. "I know. Your dad just called me."

"Sit," I said, pointing to the other chair. We faced the yard and the morning. "Rough night?" he asked.

"The worst."

Uncle Cotton pointed to the box. "What's this?"

"Childhood drawings and writings." I lifted the top and leafed through the stories, laughing at my crooked handwriting and awful sketches. I held one up to Cotton. "My masterpiece. It's called 'My Life.' I wrote it when I was ten years old. I guess I thought my life was worthy of a full story by that time."

He took it from me. "So sweet."

I then found "The New Cinderella" and unfolded the page. "This one had a sketch, too, and Mother kept the picture in her journal. I have no idea why—but this is the story that went with it."

"Read it," he said.

"No way. I'm not reading my nine-year-old handwritten story to a novelist."

"Please," he said. "I'm always the one reading and never being read to." He smiled at me and I couldn't resist.

"A New Cinderella," I said in a too-loud voice, and then softened to a whisper. "Written by Ellie Eddington, nine years old. 'Once upon a time in a beautiful castle lived a princess. The castle was made of stone. Ivy crawled up the walls so you couldn't see the cracks. The princess lived in a room overlooking the gardens and fountains. She loved her mother, the queen, who loved her in return. Then one very dreadful day the queen died and the princess was alone. There was a king, and he was nice and kind, but he was always off fighting wars and taking over kingdoms.

" 'The princess was sad and lonely and thought her heart would break into ten million pieces. She walked through the gardens and nodded hello to the court attendants and jesters, but she forgot how to smile and would return to her room to stare out the window and remember her good and beautiful mother.

" 'Then one magical day the king brought home a new mother. The princess's heart leapt with hope. But then something terrible happened— the queen looked up at the window to the princess and the princess saw the queen's mean eyes.

" 'The king returned to war and the queen took over the castle. Having this mother was worse than having no mother at all.

" 'The princess found many places in the castle to escape; one day she hid in the library and read the story of Cinderella, of the princess who swept the ashes and slept in the cellar. This Cinderella princess waited and waited for the prince to come with the glass slipper and take her away because she was beautiful. He put her on his white horse and carried her away to live in a better castle away from the cruel queen.

" 'For a long while the princess wasted days waiting for her prince. The princess did all the princess things she was supposed to do, like going to balls and eating dinner at the long dining room table and hugging peasants. She did everything she was supposed to do, including being nice to the cruel queen and pretending to be happy. The princess was pretty, quiet, and very good, but the prince still didn't come.

" 'Then one day the princess woke up, packed her fancy golden suitcase, and ran away to a far-away land where there were no kings, queens, or princes. Just really nice people. And she lived happily ever after.

" 'The End.' "

"Wow," he said.

"Yeah. Brilliant literary talent at such a young age." I placed the story back into the box, then settled into my chair.

"It was brilliant, Ellie. It was. You saw something at that age that others rarely see as adults."

"And what is that?"

"That we can save ourselves."

I nodded. "I guess I believed that then. I would have never believed I could say this, but in saving myself, you know what's the biggest temptation?"

"What?"

"To just not love at all." I leaned forward on my knees and looked to the grass where I'd found the flightless bird. "To just not fly again."

"Sometimes when damage is done to our souls, we stop loving to protect our hearts. Everyone has their own way, but that is not your way."

I nodded and closed my eyes, leaning my head back on the chair. Then his words filtered through the morning air and into my open soul with a simple whisper of truth.

My eyes flashed open and I jumped to stand. "Don't move. I have something for you."

"Huh?"

I ran into the house and grabbed Mother's journal. Returning to the patio, I tripped over a broken slate tile and almost landed in Uncle Cotton's lap. I held a piece of paper, extending my hand to him.

"What is that?" he asked.

"A letter," I said. "A letter I believe was meant for you." I held Mother's last love letter in my hand, offering it to Cotton as I imagined she once offered him the last piece of her heart.

"How did you know, Ellie?" His voice came from another decade, a time before I existed, a time when he could have read this letter and maybe, just maybe, neither one of us would be standing here because another world would exist.

"I didn't know until right this minute. When you said that sometimes you choose to stop loving to protect your own heart, I knew. That's what you did. That's what Mother did, and only you could know why."

He looked up. "I never stopped loving, Ellie. Not once."

My hand was still out, the letter wavering in the breeze. "Take it," I said.

He did.

"I want you to tell me about you and Mother." I paused while a wind of emotions passed across his face. "Please," I said.

He fiddled with an empty bud vase in the middle of the table and then met my gaze again. "I never want to hurt my brother. Ever. I want to keep this from him. He can't find out."

"Is this why you were never around? Why we never came to see you?"

"Partly, I'm sure. Our separate lives were another part. We just lived such different lives, Ellie. And your mother refused to see me; she avoided me at all costs. I think she hated me more than she could tolerate."

"Are you kidding? You told her that you never really loved her at all." I stopped, placing my elbows on the table and leaning forward to whisper, "You tell me first."

Pain passed across his face in an expression I can only call pinched, his features drawing in on themselves and then pulling apart. "I told her that so she could have a happy life with my brother. I told her those lies so she could get on with her life and be with my brother. I never stopped loving her. Not once." He took in a breath and exhaled the next words. "Do you really want to hear this?"

"More than you can imagine."

"I did everything I could to convince her that I truly loved her; I begged her to wait for me. But she didn't. She slept with my brother."

"I know," I said.

"So you can imagine how I'd have trouble believing in her broken heart, right?"

"This is the saddest part, though," I said. "You hate her."

"No, I loved her. Listen, waiting is hard. I know that. The waiting time is the time when anxiety destroys anything you believe. Waiting is the time when you lose faith, when you give in to fear and feel like you have to do something, anything, to fix the pain. If she just would have waited . . . but maybe it was too much to ask of her. Knowing her, it was too much to ask of her to wait on me while I was out of the country."

"But if you trust enough . . ."

He stared off and then returned my gaze, returned to the story. "When I came back from Africa, she came to see me. I'd written her letters from Africa until I got the telegram that my brother had married her and they were having a baby. I'd given up hope for us, and then she sat there, her hands folded in her lap, tears staining her face. She told me she wanted me. But of course I knew about the baby. . . ." He stopped and stared at me. "About you. I knew about you and about my brother."

"Yes, me." I paused. "You know she only read your first couple letters, right?"

He nodded. "Yes, she told me. I asked her and she said that in the beginning—when I first left—she hadn't believed in me, and by the time she did believe—it was too late. Too late."

"Too late to believe. My God."

"Yes," he said. "So whose heart do you break? Your brother's or your lover's? Those were my two choices."

"Impossible choices," I said.

"I chose to save my brother. I still, to this day, don't know what was right and what was wrong. Or even if there is a right or wrong. I just chose. And then I lied. She needed to go home to my brother. And she did."

"All these choices," I said. "All these choices we make when we're broken."

He looked up at me now. "Exactly. That we're broken isn't new, but we all get to choose what we do with that."

"You lied."

"To protect her. To protect my brother. I wanted to free her heart to go to him."

"Her whole life she tried to talk herself out of loving you."

"I don't think that's possible," he said. "I don't think you can talk yourself out of or into loving someone."

"Yes," I said. "I know."

"Ellie, I love you and your family, but I never want to talk about this again, okay? I want us to continue to have this beautiful relationship we've started this summer . . . but I never want to talk about this again. Okay?"

"Okay."

"And your dad can never know."

"I agree."

"It was a long, long time ago."

"It never was for her. It was never a long time ago for her—it was always with her."

"Why was this so important to you? You were relentless in finding out . . . why?"

"I don't think I knew why until right this moment." I took his hand. "I think in my mother I saw that heartbreak can come to define your whole life. It can become who you are instead of something that happened to you. And I don't want that. I want to figure out how to get past the brokenness or at least live with it in a loving, creative way. And knowing her entire story, knowing the full truth, seemed the only way to figure that out."

"Sometimes the whole truth is more hurtful than the lie," he said.

"I know," I said, and hugged him. "Thank you, Uncle Cotton. Thank you for sharing this with me. I'm sorry, so sorry, if any of this has caused you pain."

"You are a wonder," he said, and kissed my cheek.

That was the last time we'd speak of this—my uncle and I. He left to help Dad fix the fence, and I sat alone at that table, thinking of what is common to man—a broken heart. And thinking of what is uncommon—how each soul deals with a broken heart. For Mother—it was shutting down her heart. For Cotton—creativity and a life of writing.

That was where Rusty found me—on the back porch still, my cold coffee at my side, "The New Cinderella" folded on my lap. He looked down at me. "What are you doing?"

"I was talking to Cotton," I said, fingering the edges of the story.

"No, I mean what are you doing just sitting here now?" His voice was torn and mingy, as if he didn't want to waste one more syllable.

I pointed to the yard, the magnolia tree to my right. "You remember that bird, Rusty? The cardinal that slammed into the window the day Mother died?"

"Of course," he said.

"You have no idea how badly I wanted her to fly away."

"Yes, I think I do have an idea." He slammed his cast on the iron chair, an ineffective move of anger that merely caused him to flinch. "I think I do. But I will not leave, Ellie. If that is what you want me to do—I. Will. Not. Leave."

"I know," I said.

So for all the speeches I planned, for all the words I wanted to wrap around my reasons for leaving, there was now nothing left to say.

Excerpt from
Lillian Ashford Eddington's Journal
New Year's Eve 2010
Seventy Years Old

I am tired this year and the angel above me does not seem to be any longer listening.

It is the year I feel older; I don't know why or how, I just do. A settled fatigue that makes me want to skip writing this year. But there is so much more I want to do and see, and I have come to know that if I weary of wanting, it will all stop.

The best thing about this past year was the month I spent with Lil and Ellie in St. Simons. They took a month this summer before Lil went off to college and we spent it at the beach. There must be things to say about why this was so wonderful, but I don't know the way to say it. The wonderfulness didn't come from anything we did or didn't do, or anything we did or didn't see. It was . . . the best part of my year. My charity did win an Atlanta Constitution Philanthropy award.

The worst thing about this past year was the flood. Record rainfall flooded our backyard and basement, ruining years and years of our life's photos. I should have known to keep them in the attic or in those special archive-safe boxes I see they have now, but I waited too long and they are ruined. So many memories in those boxes of photos and they're gone— not the memories but the pictures of them. And sometimes I think that is all the next generation can have. They can't have my memories. Lil and Ellie can't know what I know. But they could have at least had the photos. Some are saved—only the ones in books upstairs. This broke my heart.

I think I will end this early tonight.

This will be the year I will again get to spend a month with Lil and Ellie at the beach; that Redmond will win the club golf championship. I have decided I finally want to take a trip on the QE2 to England.

This is the year He will know He loves me.

Twenty-five

Within an hour after Rusty told me he would never leave, I'd packed my car and driven the four hours to Bayside. The gate to Birdie's driveway was closed. I punched in the code and drove down the gravel way to the front of the guesthouse. I'd called her to tell her I was coming; she'd told me to just let myself in. Surely I still had the key. Yes, I did.

Summer heat had finally begun to take its toll on the foliage, which was wilting. I parked next to the guesthouse with evening light settling over the lawn and the bay. My suitcase was light as I carried it through the front door.

Birdie's house lights came on one by one: the kitchen, the living room, her upstairs bedroom. I stood on the front porch of the guesthouse and watched and I waited. And then when the back porch light turned on and a candle flickered, I made my way across the lawn. I found her sitting on the rocking chair waiting for me, as I knew she would be.

Her hug filled my heart, and we sat facing each other. "Are you okay, my dear?" she asked.

"I think so, yes."

"I'm sorry for all you've been through. I know this has been an incredibly difficult summer for you in many ways."

"Miss Birdie," I said, "I know about Cotton."

Birdie closed her eyes.

I continued, "He didn't tell me. I figured it out and then we talked."

She opened her eyes and nodded. "It wasn't my place to tell you."

"I know," I said.

"It was an awful time, Ellie, and it was before you. Your mother loved you greatly."

"I left Rusty." I flinched.

"I'm sorry." She reached out and took my hand.

"I don't understand all of it yet, but I know I had to go."

"As if anyone can understand anything in the middle of living it."

"Maybe I won't understand at all, but at least I'll have given it my best shot."

"Yes, you do that. You give it your best shot and maybe you'll end up living it while you're spending all this time trying to understand it."

"Speaking of giving it my best shot—I want to ask you if I can stay here for a while. I'll pay rent. I just can't go home. I know leaving him is awful, so please . . . no lectures."

"Lecture you? My God, Ellie. I was going to say how strong you are. How doing the awful thing is sometimes the only thing we can do to save our souls."

"Oh . . . this was not my dream when I stood at the altar in a white dress."

"Dream?"

"Plans . . . divorce was not in my plans."

She leaned forward and took my hands. "Don't you know by now that most things in our life were not in our plans?"

I looked up at her. "Maybe that's when things get the most screwy—when we try to make things go according to our plan when it's better for it not to go."

She smiled without answering. "But, yes, of course you can stay as long as you need. And no, you can't pay rent. You'll get through this. Here. Right here at my Summer House."

"Thank you. More gratitude than I can possibly express."

We sat in nature's quiet. A breeze blew out the candle, and the buck moon was lucent. "Birdie," I said, "Cotton and I were talking about how we're all broken. All of us in different ways." I leaned forward. "When your husband died or when anything didn't turn out the way you wanted—what did you do with that brokenness? What *do* you do?"

"Look where I live, Ellie. I told you things happen at this Summer House. Hearts open; truth is revealed. I don't know why. I think it's because we're on the Bay of the Holy Spirit. But I don't need to know why . . . I just know."

"How?"

"Instead of closing the cracked space tight, I allow grace to fill those places."

I lifted my face to the breeze coming off the bay. "Thank you for letting me stay. What a gorgeous night."

"The air feels like silk tonight. Smooth."

Silky air. I'd heard this before, like a voice from childhood that could not be named. The wind whistled around the corner of the house, a loose shingle banged against the cedar shakes.

Jubilee.

Those were the notes and lyrics to a jubilee.

I jumped up from the chair. "A jubilee is coming, isn't it?"

"Probably. You can never ever be sure; you can only feel the signs. You don't know until it's really here and the whistles blow and the little ones come hollering. First you feel. Then you know."

"Sometimes," I said, feeling the breeze and a deep shift inside my body, "you feel before you know."

"Of course."

The feeling first, and then the knowing. And sometimes also—the waiting.

I kissed her on the cheek. "Thank you, Ms. Birdie." I walked out the door and back to the guesthouse to prepare. A jubilee: when all debts are forgiven and we are offered a new beginning.

I waited on the jubilee and spread out the poster board, which was still on the dining table, and I finished what I'd started—her timeline, filling in the blanks I now understood. Then I read Mother's last entry one more time. I would never read the journal again after that. I let go of the need to know any more.

She hadn't written her death. Who would? She did have goals for the next year, but the only place her true heart-wants were known was there in the life she wrote.

My life would pass not in written wishes, but in days lived fully.

WITH THAT MOON LANGUAGE
By Hafiz

Admit something:

Everyone you see, you say to them,
   "Love me."
Of course you do not do this out loud;
   otherwise someone would call the
   cops.
Still, though, think about this,
   this great pull in us to connect.
Why not become the one who lives with
   a full moon in each eye that is
   always saying,
with that sweet moon language,
   what every other eye in this world
   is dying to hear?

Twenty-six

NINE MONTHS LATER

The hum of conversation is punctuated with laughter and the occasional louder voice. The crowd in the Atlanta History Center moves as a single mass down the line of photos and panels of information about each woman who had been the Woman of the Year from 1960 to 1969.

Hutch stands at the far back of the room, greeting patrons, shaking hands, and smiling that damn soul-opening smile. His longtime girlfriend, Hillary, stands next to him with her hand on the small of his back; she wears a long pale blue silk sheath dress and a smile that seems born of red lipstick and satisfaction. She is at least a decade younger than me, and I find one hand covering my stomach and the other my cheek, as if I can conceal my years with my hands.

I miss him. With a singular and desperate ache, I miss Hutch O'Brien.

I also know that there are some things that cannot be fixed or healed. Forgiven: yes. Healed: no. I see my need for him as the heart-scar I bear for once choosing safety over love; for choosing a legacy of perfection over my own heart's knowing.

It's been nine months since I left Rusty and moved part-time to Bayside, Alabama. I drove to Atlanta today for the history center opening of the new "Woman of the Year from 1960 to 1969" exhibit. There is a special cocktail party for patrons of the history center and the families of the honored women. Dad and I have come here together. The road between Bayside and Atlanta has become as familiar a landscape as my childhood backyard or anything one stops noticing because what was once new has become ordinary.

I didn't take back my maiden name; for over half my life I've been Ellie Calvin, and it's also my daughter's name. In these months since I've walked out of our family home, the anger, hurt, and insanity that rose from the depths of our marriage during the divorce were so horrible that many times I almost gave up or gave in for the sheer pain leaving involved. I often reminded myself—and Lil—that the things Rusty said about and to me were from anger, not real hate. She didn't believe me. I wasn't sure I believed myself.

I live half the time now in Birdie's cottage and the other half in my childhood home with Dad. I've started teaching kids' art classes at the studio in Bayside and have added adult classes, forming friendships. I believe it's a miracle in life when you find people who care about and desire the same things you do, and creativity does that —brings those people together in one place.

In the beginning of those dark days right before the divorce, I'd gone to Hutch, and although he'd been kind, he'd also told me that he wouldn't and couldn't be used as a consolation prize. I'd kissed him good-bye and understood that this was my payment and my redemption— learning to live without his love.

The Summer House was the cover story for the "House Legends" article, and I sent a copy to Hutch with a note inside that read only, "Now that was a great day. xo, Ellie."

Two days later I received the same torn article in the mail with a note that read "Nice Memory. Hutch." I smiled and knew that we had torn and sent the article on the same day, and he would be opening his envelope even as I had just opened mine.

Lil often comes to Bayside to see me, and when I go home to see Dad, she stays with Rusty in her childhood bedroom, which is where she should be. The first few times I went home to Atlanta I was constantly reminded about the wrongness of what I'd done: "Women," I was told, "do not leave a marriage for no good reason." When Rusty began to date Sara Matthews, the chastisement died down. "Oh," they began so say, "maybe there was more to the story." For me, that part doesn't matter. Maybe there was more to Sara and Rusty that I knew but didn't know—but my reasons for leaving had nothing to do with a possible affair, and everything to do with not closing my heart off for good and all.

I had seen only two ways to live: stay and begin the slow, agonizing process of closing my heart, or leave.

It's not like I don't understand the consequences of broken vows. I do understand.

But only one person was going to save me.

Me.

We all make our choices.

And then we live with them.

All of us.

Dad walks through the crowd with me and I greet familiar friends who move in and out of our space.

"Ellie." I turn to see Belinda's smiling face; she holds a glass of wine. "You look so fabulous." She steps back and shakes her head. "Seriously, I don't think you've ever looked more beautiful. Like Diane Lane in that Tuscany movie I think."

"Thanks," I say, laughing. "But I think you just haven't seen me in a while."

"No, I'd know." She smiles shyly and lowers her voice. "I am so sorry that I was rude when you and Rusty . . . well, I'm sorry. It's really good to see you."

I hug Belinda. "It's okay. Go enjoy the evening."

Dad stands behind me and I hear him take in a breath. We've reached 1968 and Mother's timeline. "Ellie," he says. "Look at that."

I spin around and there are two Plexiglas panels six feet tall and attached with iron hinges so the panels are swung at a ninety-degree angle, almost facing one another. On one panel is the newspaper article with Mother at the luncheon counter, glancing over her shoulder staring as if she is daring the camera to take her on. On the opposite panel is a photo of me on the day Hutch and I had gone to the café. I am staring over my shoulder at the camera; my smile is not daring or belligerent, but content. Above each photo are the dates and an explanation of how Mother's actions changed life for the next generation—her daughter's generation.

"Oh," I say. "Oh my gosh." I take Dad's hand and he is silent as he reads the information board about Mother and her charity work, and then about a life he knew nothing about. People move past us and around us as a river would a rock or boulder, silently and swiftly, not bothering father and daughter holding hands. Finally Dad turns to me. "You told me, but . . ."

"It's amazing, isn't it?"

"Yes." He looks at me, almost as though he would look through me if he could. "She was a treasure. I know maybe not for you or to you all the time, but she was amazing. I love her greatly."

"I know, Dad. I know."

We stand for long moments staring at her photos until I hear his voice—Hutch's voice—across the room.

Of course I've imagined a hundred scenarios—how to approach him, what to say, how to say it. But now my breath is gathered at the bottom of my throat and I've forgotten every well-designed sentence. He catches my eye and waves over the white bob of a woman's head. I wave back when Sadie comes up next to me.

"Hey." I hug my friend and step back. "That is a gorgeous dress." She wears a red Tibi halter dress and her hair is down, curling and free around her face.

She sweeps her hand around the room. "Everyone is talking about your Mother's exhibit more than any other. I feel sorry for the other women's families." She laughs. "It's that photo of you two facing each other. It's eerie and fantastic. So poignant."

"Thanks," I say, glancing at Dad, who has engaged in a conversation with the man next to him. "I think Dad is a bit overwhelmed."

Sadie nods toward Hutch. "And you?"

"I'm fine."

She rolls her eyes. "I am sure you are."

A microphone squeals and the president of the

History Center begins to speak about the exhibit. Slowly the evening fades and the crowd thins. Finally, when I feel I can no longer breathe, I walk outside into the cooler spring air and sit on a bench. I feel Hutch next to me before I see him.

"Hey, you," I say without turning around.

He sits next to me. "You look beautiful tonight."

I blush, but he can't see me in the starless, moonless night. A single lantern is lit along the pathway to the right, and Hutch is more a shadow than a man. "You can't even see me," I say.

"Oh, trust me, I saw you."

"Hutch, this is your best work yet. It's spectacular. Really, it is."

"Thank you so much."

We are silent for a few moments and I twist to face him. "Are you hiding out here?"

"No." He pauses and then speaks in an almost whisper. "I saw you leave and I wanted to say good-bye."

"I just needed some fresh air. It's a bit much in there."

"Yes, it is."

"So . . . how are you, Hutch? I know you've probably been buried under this show, but how are you?"

"I'm well, or at least I think I am. You're right —I've been consumed with this show and am just now getting my head above water." He laughs. "God, how cliché is that?"

I decide to say the one truth. "I miss you, Hutch."

"Of course I miss you, too. Are you okay, Ellie? Are you doing all right?"

"Yes."

"Good." He turns to stare at me as if he can read my face. He knows I'm not lying, but I'm not telling the truth.

"So . . . how's Hillary? I'd love to meet her . . ."

"She's fine." He pauses before he says, "I'm so sorry . . . about your divorce."

"Thanks."

"Thanks?"

"I never know what to say when someone says they're sorry. You didn't do anything to be sorry about."

A wind of unspoken words washes over us, unsettling as we fidget in our seats.

Finally, I speak. "Well, I guess in a way you did do something."

"What?"

"You showed me, or reminded me about unconditional love."

"Oh . . . you didn't do this because . . ."

"I didn't get divorced for you, or for anyone."

"Okay."

"But here's the thing: once I remembered, felt, and saw unconditional love—anything else was dark and awful." My words are rushed, quick, as if someone had turned on the faucet of withheld words full blast. "This wasn't about you, Hutch. And it wasn't for you. But it was about your love. And I guess that's all I wanted to say. It was about your love. That *kind* of love. And I miss you terribly. And I'm sorry for any pain I ever caused . . . and . . ."

"Shhh." He places a single finger over my lips. "Stop. I don't want you to be sorry anymore." He pulls me against him for a brief moment. We don't speak because there really is nothing left to say. "We should get back in to the show." He releases me abruptly and stands.

"You go ahead," I say. "I'll be a minute."

"Okay. . . ." He touches my cheek and then is gone, shadow blending into shadow.

When I enter the room, I see Dad is looking for me and I wave to him. He walks toward me. "Where have you been, Ladybug?"

"I needed some fresh air. You ready to go?"

"Very," he says. "I can't even find any more words for small talk."

"Me neither."

Dad and I drive home in silence until he pulls into the driveway and presses the garage door button at the top of his dashboard. "Ellie, why would anyone delete an entire year of their life?" He doesn't turn to me as he watches the garage door lift, grinding into the night.

This is the first time Dad has asked me anything about Mother, and the weight of it squats my chest. I look to him and tell the truth. "We all have our own way, Dad."

"Own way?" He turns to me now, the garage door open and waiting for us to enter.

"To live our broken lives."

"Yes," he says, his foot still on the brake. "Yes, you're right." And then he presses on the gas and parks as the garage door closes behind us.

The restlessness born of unanswered questions kept me awake most of the night, but this morning I find fragments of peace in Mother's garden. The flowers in the early sun are a brilliant array of colors, almost too vivid to be real. I am clipping marigolds for the breakfast table. Wrapped in a long cardigan and wearing jeans, I pick a weed from the rose bed, the only weed I can see. Dad has hired a full-time gardener to keep Mother's garden pristine. It is his monument to her. I often see him walking through the lanes and pathways when I know he never entered this sacred ground when she was alive.

I place the bundle of flowers in a basket, and then I hear Dad's voice. "There," he says.

Hutch walks toward me, lifting a hand to his eyebrows to shield his eyes from the glaring morning sun. He's at my side before we speak.

"Good morning," I say. "What are you doing

here? You should be sleeping for the next month."

"I brought your dad a copy of all the photos from the exhibit. He asked me last night."

"That's really nice of you. Thanks."

"God, it's been twenty-something years since I've been here, but this garden is exactly as I remember it."

"Yes, it is."

He glances around, bending over to pick a rose.

"Hey," I say. "I read the article in the paper this morning. They gave you rave reviews. I laughed when I read that your facial scar was from a fishing hook."

He smiles. "Well, if the reporter was going to be rude enough to ask, he deserved a b.s. answer." He takes the basket from my hand and places it on a serrated rock. "I'm not here to talk about the exhibit or the article or to give your dad the photos I could've mailed. I want to ask you something."

"Sure," I say, the blood leaving my head and rushing to my heart as if it needs to protect itself, as if it needs to prepare for his question.

"Last night you said your leaving was about my kind of love."

I nod.

"What about yours?"

"My what?"

"Love."

"Oh, Hutch. The words don't seem to be enough anymore."

"What words?"

"I love you."

"You know I can't do this again, Ellie. I can't believe in something that isn't real."

I step toward him, touching his arm, and then taking his hand. "Why don't you believe this? Why don't you think it's real? I love you, Hutch. I never stopped for even a single moment."

"Why now, Ellie?"

"When you know you love someone, when you know it's finally the right time, you don't just wait around for the right words, you just say the sentences even if they're all mixed up and imperfect."

"And what are those imperfect words?" His voice is now inside my body, moving.

"I want to be near you every moment. When something awful or wonderful happens, you are the first person I want to see or hear or touch. You're the one I reach for first. I loved you first and I'll love you last. Isn't that enough?"

He steps back and looks me directly in the eyes. "It's enough," he says.

When he kisses me, his lips are soft, the inside of an extraordinary flower.

Center Point Publishing
600 Brooks Road ● PO Box 1
Thorndike ME 04986-0001 USA

(207) 568-3717

US & Canada:
1 800 929-9108
www.centerpointlargeprint.com